STAYING
UNDER

OTHER BOOKS BY CAROL ALMA MCPHEE, WITH ANN FITZGERALD

*Feminist Quotations: Voices of Rebels, Reformers,
and Visionaries*

*The Non-Violent Militant: Selected Writings of
Teresa Billington-Greig*

CAROL ALMA MCPHEE

STAYING
UNDER

PAPIER-MACHE PRESS

WATSONVILLE, CA

02 01 00 99 98   5 4 3 2 1

ISBN: 1-57601-056-2 Hardcover

Cover art by Charlotte Lambrechts, Melissa Passehl Design
Design and composition by Melissa Passehl Design
Author photo by Karen McLain
Copyediting by Sangeet Duchane
Proofreading by Kimberly McGinty
Manufactured by Malloy Lithographing, Inc.

This novel is a work of fiction. The characters are not intended to resemble anyone the author has known, and the events take place only in the fictional world that evolved as the story was told.

Library of Congress Cataloging-in-Publication Data

McPhee, Carol.
     Staying under / Carol Alma McPhee.
     p. cm.
     ISBN 1-57601-056-2 (alk. paper)
     I. Title.
     PS3563.C38869S73 1998
     813'.54—dc21   97-43626
                         CIP

FOR ANN FITZGERALD

ACKNOWLEDGMENTS

I owe much to the many women who have provided encouragement and emotional support as I worked on the book, including Linna Thomas, my sisters, and my daughter Beth Norton. To several other women I owe special thanks. Betty Kitzman and Ruth Zank read the manuscript in an early version. My daughters Noelle and Claire Norton have been sensitive and helpful critics. Diane Wild lent me her remarkable insights and perceptive and careful editing skills for the final manuscript. Ann FitzGerald read and commented on the several versions of this work, as she has everything else I've written for the last twenty years.

STAYING UNDER

1

"Remember" always begins Maureen's imaginary conversations with Joann, who was her friend a long time ago. "Remember" is part of her plan every time she thinks, Why don't I just sit down and write Joann a letter?

Once she even had a letter started: "Dear Joann, The other day I was watching a television program on the California missions. Of course they showed the Refugio Mission and the new plaza they've put up blocking off Valencia Street. A few years ago my sister told me you still live there, and I wondered...," she hesitated, wrote, "if you remember...," and stopped, staring out the window and biting the end of her pen.

Twice in the last three years she has driven the coast route from San Francisco to Los Angeles, passing through Refugio on the way, and once she climbed out of her car in a Refugio gas station, went to the public telephone, checked Joann's name in the book—and didn't call.

But on this mid-August evening a year or two ago, with the sun flickering across the Pacific Ocean, almost blinding her and several other drivers in a pack racing north on Highway 101, she remembers, decides. Remembers, decides. In a few minutes she'll swerve northeast through a gap in the hills, then follow a shallow canyon into Refugio. On the other side of the town she'll climb over a steep pass through the Santa Lucia Mountains. If she doesn't stop.

M A U R E E N

I *am* decisive, I know I am. I intended driving this way when I left San Diego. Besides, I told Sheila I was stopping off on my way north so I wouldn't have to travel into the night.

But when she asked, "Where is it you're spending the night, Mom?" I couldn't give her a straight answer. Because I really didn't know.

Don't know now. There's Refugio Mountain straight ahead. I'll stay in the left lane, speed, keep my eyes on the highway: there's Tolosa Street, Corcoran Boulevard, Osos, Santa Helena, California Avenue. Del Norte, the last off-ramp before the pass, and I'm shaking my head, putting my turn signal on, and swooping across the right-hand lane at the last possible moment. The young woman in the car behind me gestures at my grey locks. Too bad. Decisive, intrepid, fast-acting Maureen will sign into a motel, pick up the telephone, and talk to Joann. If she's home. If her number's listed. If she's still married to Gil Henderson. If that's really his last name. If I remember. Correctly.

I pick the first motel on Valencia Street with a vacancy sign, grumbling to myself at its design, brand-new lacy Victorian, a post-Disneyland style. But I approve of the woman at the desk, who has a middle-aged face, wears a sensible cotton blouse, and puts a cigarette into an ash tray before she comes to help me. This homely gesture soothes me, distracting me from the uneasiness I'm feeling about not going on, farther north, to Encina or King City where it wouldn't bother me to be an anonymous stranger.

Above the woman's head the office wall displays a set of old photographs of the town, to go with the frills and oak wood decor, I suppose. One picture catches my attention, a building called The Pavilion, where I took music lessons when I was six. One year, probably in the early 1940s, it was torn down. For me it just disappeared, I was never sure when. I remember one day in my early teens passing by the corner where I thought it should be and wondering whether I was wrong, whether there had been such a building, or whether it was still standing some other place. I asked my mother about it, but she couldn't even remember my taking lessons when I was six. I am fascinated, fifty years later, to see it almost as I had remembered it: there are the stairs I climbed, that pillar was where I used to lean waiting to be picked up in the black Buick, inside the door you turned to the left and went up another set of stairs.

The woman at the desk, observing my fixed stare, tells me the picture comes from the collection of the owners of the house that used to stand where the motel is now.

"Who were they?" I ask.

She is filing my registration card, but stops with one bright red fingernail resting on the edge of an index tag to peer at me as if I'd asked her the name of a glacier in Switzerland. "I don't know," she says, and pushes my room key across the shiny oak surface of the desk.

My uneasiness is already refining itself into regret, and the stiff mattress where I sit staring at a red telephone doesn't help. The trouble is, I have to admit to myself, to call Joann might not be fair, not to say ungenerous and irresponsible. Maybe I'm only curious about her life, trying to see into it the way I like to look into lighted windows on my evening walks. Maybe the urge is only another symptom of approaching age, a fear of forgetting, like the way I started to keep newspaper clippings or began a year ago to make card catalogues of the books I've read. I've also recently noticed in myself a strange nostalgia for landscapes—the line of a once-barren hillside depicted on a postcard, a wooded former picnic ground from a family snapshot, an elderly building preserved in a history book. My all-time favorite, given me by my mother after my father died, is a watercolor of the Golden Gate before the bridge was built. Though I can't be certain, especially since I've been looking at the painting all my life, I believe I saw that view myself once.

Joann as landscape, I'm thinking. Hello, Joann? I'm calling you because you remind me of my picture of the Golden Gate before the bridge. Hah! But she will have changed, like everything else: the hillside filled with houses, the picnic ground a mall, the wooden building replaced with cream-colored stucco and lots of tile, Joann's long chestnut hair faded to grey, her face—will she be overweight like me? And when things change it's damned hard to recall what I used to see or know. The new blots the old: I can barely remember Chet now when we were young, or even, to tell the truth, how he was before he got sick.

Her memory as landscape then. Hello, Joann, the reason I telephoned is that I've been in the habit of calling my life to a halt and waiting for lost hills and valleys to come into focus and you're one of my lost vistas. Smile.

That's worse. I arise, wash my face and hands, brush my hair, pick up my key, and I'm on my way down the street to eat my dinner at the San Luis Inn, the only structure remaining on this end of Valencia Street that was standing when I left Refugio. I'm seated at a table before the deep reason—I say deep, not real, because all the reasons are real—I've wanted to talk to Joann bursts through the clutter of apology and self-analysis. Sure, I'm curious about what's happened to her. Sure, I get a certain satisfaction from recapturing the past—a satisfaction I'm not sure she'll share.

Hello, Joann. What I really want to say is this: What made you decide not to be friends any more after that trip to San Francisco, the summer of 1948? I must have done something wrong, but what exactly was it?

That's a good beginning, but I'll have to phrase it carefully.

Hello, Joann, this is your old friend Maureen Lewis, and I've called to apologize. For what? I'm not sure. I thought you might have regretted getting rid of the baby, and blamed me. Or...For god's sake don't call it a baby, Maureen.

I'd do better to start with the landscape.

I have two glasses of wine with dinner, and I read ten pages of my book. The wine doesn't help the ache in my back and shoulders. Not only the long drive, but sleeping on Sheila's sofa for three nights has got to me.

Back in my room, I lean against two pillows folded at the head of the bed, but this doesn't help much either. Next time I'll tell Sheila the sofa bed won't do. She's old enough to stop treating her mother like a forty-year-old. By the time I have constructed an imaginary conversation with Sheila to my satisfaction, I have decided. The telephone book is opened to the page where I've found the name of the man Joann married. The telephone squats on the bed beside me, and all I'm undecided about now is what time I'll pick it up.

Joann, I'd always thought I was a responsible person, until that trip to San Francisco when we were trying to find some way to get rid of your pregnancy. Not someone who could desert you or force you into something you didn't want. I thought we'd done this together, just like when we were little kids.

Better, but I haven't said it all. Joann, and this is hard for me to say, after all these years, but was it, could it have been, the last night before we came home? When I held you that night, and you were crying, did I frighten you? It doesn't make sense, but then I was so intense.

No, never say to Joann that you knew anything frightened her.

Hello, Joann. The last time we were together, forty years ago or so, we were on the train returning from San Francisco. All right, forty-five. I still think about...No. One moment returns...No. Try again.

Remember how the train shrieked and shuddered on its way

downhill? I thought you were nervous about it. I couldn't see your face. The early afternoon sun is suddenly glaring on the orange upholstery as we come out of the tunnel. You, in a blue blouse and your grey suit skirt, mussed from sitting, are reaching to the overhead rack for our jackets, yours grey, mine yellow. I watch you, silent, worried about you. A little sad we had to come home so soon. You haven't spoken either, and I'm certain it's because you don't feel well. I'm afraid to ask.

I'm still afraid to ask. That afternoon, you remember that afternoon on the train? Was that our last day? It must have been, but I really can't remember anymore. You called me—didn't you tell me not to call you?—the next day, or was it the day after?—and told me you didn't want to see me again. I can't remember the reason you gave, or whether I asked, or whether you even gave a reason. And now, I think we're old enough for reasons.

I'm calling you now because I've always been bothered about whatever happened. Don't worry, I'm pleased with my life, and I've always been, well, at least satisfied. But every once in a while, about three times a year, I think, What happened to Joann? Not necessarily what happened then, forty, no, forty-five, years ago. But is she pleased with her life now, and (I've got it now) if she isn't, am I the one responsible? Did the way I felt about you then—and believe me, I didn't understand it myself—did it harm you in any way? Or was there something else? I thought from the way you cried that night that you were going to need me forever, to get over it. But you didn't. I guess.

So here I am, Joann, a plump-cheeked, blue-eyed specter from the past. And still too intense, no matter how hard I try. What was it Sheila said a year ago? "Mom, don't you think we can all see through that casual pose you like to put on?" And I said, "It's not a pose. It's the way I wish I could be." And she said, "Why?" And I said, "Because it makes it easier for other people."

So try again. Be natural. Hello, Joann. This is Maureen Lewis. Got to remember to use that name. I'm just passing through town, on my way back to San Rafael, and I thought maybe, if you have time, we could get together tomorrow.

Yes. Then when I have her in front of me across the lunch table, I'll ask her how she likes the changes in Refugio. If she doesn't tell me about herself, I'll talk about me. I'll say I teach at Sonoma State. Since Chet died, that was five years ago, I've been doing odds and ends, a little politics, a few articles, a little community work, the usual. Planned Parenthood, shall I bring up Planned Parenthood?

What I wish I could remember—I'll say this when she's sitting across from me—is what happened between us after the trip to San Francisco, in 1948, the summer we were eighteen. When we were trying to find someone who would do an abortion. I won't lower my voice—it's not a reckless question, it's really quite ordinary. Then, if she can't or won't tell me, I can make my own confessions.

Just so. If Joann will see me. Not at the beginning, of course, but later when we're comfortable with each other.

Remember the suits we bought for that trip? Yes, not for the trip exactly, but for wearing in the fall when we were supposed to start college. For months I'd been trying to deny having to start dressing up a lot of the time, that is, wear heels and stockings, the kind of clothes my older sisters wore. Then one day when I was waiting at the library for you to finish work you showed me the college issues of women's magazines. It was suddenly like the games we'd played when we were kids, like finding the right costume. I could see myself in a sporty looking suit arriving at a train station in some eastern college town, camel's hair coat over my arm. Neither of us was going East, but that didn't matter.

I catch sight of myself in the mirror opposite the bed, grimace at the grey-haired busybody there, and shake my head. So much for tact. The next sentence, logically, would be, I was going to Berkeley and you had a scholarship to Mount St. Mary's, wasn't it? Tact? I might as well say, but then you didn't go, did you?

If I could say just what I remember, it would go like this: We bought the suits at the dress shop on Dana, I can't remember the name, where your mother knew the owner. (Then she'd fill in the name and I'd go on.) On the trip to San Francisco you were wearing your suit with a blue blouse your mother made for you—she made almost all your clothes, I remember. Mine was a yellow beige gabardine, with a somewhat longer skirt than yours and a split in the back that didn't work. I had to sew it up a couple of times over the next few years. I never could learn to pull in my long stride for that skirt. My hair was yellow, too, and so long it flopped down over my shoulders; I must have looked like a cream-colored cocker spaniel. (We'd laugh.) I admired you that day because you'd controlled your hair with a twist and a pin, a puffy front above your forehead and behind your temples. Usually you let it hang down like mine, and I thought it made you look very adult to change it that way.

Neither of us had been on the streamliner before. My parents stuck to their cars even when they went out of state, and yours rarely traveled out of the county. You recalled for me once that the only time you remember traveling was before the war, when you were little, and your parents took you camping in Yosemite.

Our mothers came to see us off. My dad had his Rotary Club lunch that day, and I had gone to his room the night before to say good-bye. I think he'd forgotten I was leaving and had to be reminded by Mom. Your mother had taken pains to go home after the morning rush at the cafe to help you pack and to remove her uniform and replace it with a dress. It was the one she wore to graduation; I remembered it because it was a frantic combination of blue and green, a little too big for her, as if she'd lost weight. You and she were already standing beside the tracks when Mom and I drove up with my sister's kids in the backseat, Debby shrieking about the choo-choo train. I was embarrassed because Mom was wearing flats without stockings, and there were some freshly washed spots from Jackie's lunch drying on the sides of her skirt, so I sat in the car for a moment, half-heartedly hoping that Mom would decide it was just easier for all of them to stay in it and let me manage to find my place with only your mother to help.

Your dark blue eyes, I remember those eyes when I walked over to you. You were frightened and I felt as if I were watching you slide away from me down a cliff into the ocean. Your mother had an old box camera she had already taken your picture with, and she wanted some more poses, with me beside you, and one with you beside her, and one of my mother beside me, and in the flurry, with my mother saying no, she wasn't dressed right, and Debby demanding that I pick her up, and Jackie running up and down, and a man calling out to us to watch out, the porter said it was time to get aboard.

What's strange about my memory of the train trip to San Francisco is that I'd wiped it out for years. I knew we'd been to San Francisco, but we could have gone by car or even by bus. Then one day driving through Refugio on 101, Chet at the wheel, the two girls in the back, I saw the orange-and-silver passenger train crossing an overpass and I remembered. "Once I went to San Francisco on the train when I was quite young," I told the children.

"What for?" Nancy, my older daughter, asked.

"Just for fun," I lied. Another year when that train trip came to mind, I found I had begun to taint my recollection with a lie about feeling pleased and excited. I began to wonder then if Joann really had told me how I'd failed her, and I hadn't listened. Or maybe I pretended to myself I didn't understand.

2

Joann, watching a nature program on television the night Maureen wavers on the edge of calling her, almost never thinks of trains at all, though she has not forgotten the details of the journey to San Francisco. She has never traveled on a train since, or an airplane, or a boat, confining the few trips she has made to her own car and the highway. She stays within Refugio County as much as possible, explaining to her husband and children and their friends that she just isn't interested in strange places. She has always known this explanation isn't true, but only recently has the falsehood made any difference to her.

She rarely thinks of Maureen, either, these days. When she does, it's disconnected from her present life, as if her childhood were something she had read in a book or seen on television. Driving homeward between the apartment houses and tiny tract homes on Foothill Boulevard, once a country road where Maureen's parents had lived on a fenced three acres, she can't help but say to herself occasionally, Maureen used to live here. Or now and then, passing the site where Murray Elementary School once stood, she recalls her first day at kindergarten and the sunburned, skinny blond child sitting cross-legged beside her. But she refuses to focus her thoughts on what she remembers, dismissing such stray images as quickly as she can. She prefers thinking she has no connection with that past.

For several years after the summer of 1948, ghosts from a conversation she'd had with Maureen that July had haunted her. What she remembered humiliated her so much she couldn't bear to think why she felt humiliated. The scene sliding through her memory had taken place on a hike across some sand dunes eight miles northwest of Refugio. This was three weeks before she and Maureen left for San Francisco in August.

"Aren't you bored with just lying around on the beach?" Joann had asked Maureen, and Maureen, driving her mother's car that afternoon, had nodded and turned off the highway. They moved north on a two-lane road splitting a narrow valley in half, dairy farms set back against the hills every mile or so. At the end of the valley, the road curved up and over the base of the hills, between small truck farms, and then after a slight decline through scrub oak and eucalyptus, slanted upward again, within sight of the ocean and Pecho Rock, an immense

granite dome set at the entrance to a small bay. This was the way to
Ladrone Canyon and an easy path between sand dunes down to a
strand. No one they knew had ever called this place a beach because
no one went there to swim or tan. They had each been there with
biology classes, however, scrambling about among tide pools and
layers of sandstone reefs.

All the way down the valley Joann sat silent. At first she felt an
enormous relief, a sense of freedom—almost—to be away for the
afternoon from Silveira Beach, where she would have to take her place
among girls tanning themselves, fixing their nails or their hair, chattering. Often at Silveira she felt like a spiky rock among the waves, a
piece of glass in the sand.

Now that she and Maureen had decided to be friends again, the
girls in Maureen's old group were trying as hard as they could to be
kind and draw her in, but they didn't know how. They admired her
tan—she thought there wasn't much to admire, just a mild beige
under the freckles on her arms—and they wished they could get their
hair to grow as long as hers and Maureen's. They would have allowed
her to be quiet and listen to their reports on the movies they'd been
seeing, but she had to tell them she didn't like what they liked. None
of them even mentioned their boyfriends, though that didn't stop
them from gabbing about how cute some of the strange boys they saw
at the beach were. Not one of them ever mentioned Bobby, though
she would have liked them to. She would have liked an excuse to tell
them she really didn't care he was dating someone else.

Then as the car turned up into the hills, her relief gave way to
uneasiness, and she had to talk. "I don't know what was the matter
with the mouse story," she said.

"What mouse story?"

Joann didn't answer, but stared out into a bean field where three
men were walking. One day about a week before, she had told the
girls at the beach one of her stories. This was about a mouse's body
she found in an old tree house she was taking down. It had been
caught by a leg, and couldn't get out. The circle of girls had listened
soberly to her describe the spray of pyracantha berries just within the
mouse's reach, several of the berries nibbled upon, obviously a source
of food for the poor trapped thing. When she wondered whether the
mouse had forgotten what it was to run around, and maybe had just

lived there and died of old age, thinking, "Well this is all there is," and so ended her story, no one said anything for a while. Then Wanda had suggested a game of hearts and they had all spread themselves belly down for the game.

Maureen remembered. "I think they thought it was cruel. No one wanted to ruin a day at the beach talking about it."

"They made it cruel by not talking about it. I wanted to discuss whether a mouse like that, surrounded by berries, forgets about trying to move its leg. Maybe somewhere there's a small universe filled with great red globes, all of them deliciously nourishing."

Maureen smiled to show her agreement. Joann's uneasiness increased. She would have liked a discussion, an argument, anything to keep her mind off the calendar she had been poring over every night—frightening herself, reassuring herself, frightening herself—until she thought she might as well go out and pick a daisy and count, I am, I'm not, I am, I'm not. She had not had a period for eight weeks.

"Let's stop up here," she said at the top of the hill, before the road took its steep descent into the canyon, and when Maureen pulled the car to the side of the road, she climbed out. Far off there was Point Buchon, its edges slightly blurred in a faint mist, then Pecho Rock, grey, bronze, and green, then the strand, a string of sand dunes like a mountain range, golden in the afternoon sun, and beyond it the line of ocean surf. She thought she could hear its faint roar underneath the sharp tit-tit of a brown bird rustling in the bushes at the side of the road. "Let's hike down through here," she said. This is what it would be like to be a free adult, to drive where you want to, stop the car where you want to, hike where you had never been before, follow impulses down through every imaginable possibility. She wondered whether Maureen felt as she did. "Do you want to?" she asked, but Maureen had already decided and was climbing out, zipping the car keys into her pocket.

Joann began to run, down a trail through the sage and scrub oak, toward the dunes, and Maureen, following, yelled, "Watch out, watch out," until, a better athlete than Joann, she had passed her and was finding the leaps, the slides, the turns of the path first. When they came upon a sign advising them the area had been used for army maneuvers during the war, they stopped and read its warning about unexploded ammunition. Without speaking they ran on.

At the base of the hill the trail led up into the dunes through a small steep sand canyon bordered by ice plant. They were out of breath and trudged up the canyon to the first ridge of the sand hills, continuing on toward the ocean across a span of miniature dells and peaks. At the crest of one dune, Joann spotted a log and underneath it a darkness. A hole, a burrow, she thought, and her heart pumping with the effort, she crawled up and peered inside.

"It's a den," she called down to Maureen.

"You mean a bunker?"

"I don't know. What did they call lookout posts? Maybe they sat up here and watched for Japanese submarines." With a swift push of her arms she slid down the sand, face first into the dark of the hole. She turned around, crawling back up to the light. "Come on, there's room for two."

She was pushing sand back from the opening to make a space for Maureen when she found it, at first something hard, not giving, then, as she pushed harder, smooth, cold with the coldness of metal. "Just a minute."

Scrabbling with two hands like a dog with its front paws, Joann uncovered what at first felt like a metallic rock, all uneven, grooves, pits, and bumps, its shape rounded off at one end.

"I can't see, get out of the way." Lying atop the bunker, Maureen leaned her head, neck, and shoulders down past the log, over the hole Joann was digging, so close that a strand of her yellow hair brushed Joann's cheek.

Joann pushed the fingers of both hands through the sand, down under, around, and tugged. It moved, less than an inch, and abruptly she drew her hands back, yelping as if she'd been burned. "I think it's a grenade," she said.

On newsreels during the war they had both seen soldiers throwing grenades. In the movies and in comic books soldiers bit or pulled at the ends of dark, potato-shaped balls and then threw and ducked while the loudspeakers in the theater growled and roared. Maureen put one hand, fingers outstretched, down to touch. "If we pull the sand out this way, make a kind of trench to the side of the dune, we can look at it without having to touch it," she suggested.

They worked together, lying on their bellies in the sand, clawing and pushing it aside for several minutes until at last, the dark, dimpled metal casing appeared close to their eyes, grains of sand tumbling down over its ridges. Joann, remembering pictures in *National Geographic* of alligators' eggs discovered in the sand, gently brushed the grit from one of its indentations. What if, like an alligator's egg, it was ready to break open, releasing—what?—its destructive power into the world. All this time, waiting under the warm sand, expecting them to come. "Have you ever done something really wrong?" she asked.

They lay side by side on the sloping sand, the grenade in its hollow just visible at eye level beneath the log marking the entrance to the bunker. Joann's breath made little stirrings in the sand as she waited for Maureen's answer. She blew gently, making small empty cones.

"I've done lots of things against the rules. You know that."

Joann waited, blowing lines between the cones. They looked like nests.

"But on purpose, to hurt something or wreck something, I don't think I have. What about you?" Maureen asked.

One last tiny dimple-like nest. "I'm not sure."

"I knew someone once who threw a rock down from Refugio Mountain, where the path is steepest. One of Marilyn's old boyfriends. He said he did it on purpose, just to see if it hit anything; then he laughed and said—or anyone."

"What if you broke one of the rules and later found out there was a good reason for the rules because something was going to get hurt or wrecked?" Joann's heart began to pound; she was slightly nauseated. The fine sand, blown from the hollows by her heavy breaths, covered her lips and stuck. She tried to wipe it away, her hand moist with perspiration. "Had to get hurt or wrecked, one way or the other. And you had to choose." Once she had broken the rules, when they were thirteen, and Maureen had stopped being her friend.

Idly, stilling all thought, she reached up to the grenade, her finger pressing lightly. It moved, and she put her hand around it, then slowly lifted it, holding it finally in her palm. Its weight surprised her. She had been expecting a hollow object, like cap pistols she had once played with. It filled her palm and covered her fingers; right at the tip of her fingers, the operating levers projected, squared off, long.

"I don't see any pin, you know the thing that's supposed to be pulled out," she said. "It must have been thrown and then landed up here without exploding." She hefted its weight, wondering how far she might throw it.

Maureen sat up, fished in her pocket for a pack of cigarettes, lit one, cupping her fingers around the match the way she had been taught by her brother, and buried the match under a piece of ice plant. She blew out smoke, staring at the grenade in Joann's hand. "We should probably carry it back and turn it in to the police or something."

Joann rose, sliding down the dune on her feet to the path below, the heavy grenade braced against her breast with one hand, the other out to her side, for balance. She did not yet know what she was going to do. She tested the bright feel of it against the sickness in her stomach, thinking, shall I start back up the trail to the car? She was imagining herself carrying the grenade up the path to the top of the hill when she turned to face the ocean, ran several steps, and with a mighty heave, threw the grenade. It rolled awkwardly upward, against the sky, Maureen shouting, "Hey," and it came down slowly, slowly, and dropped, out of sight on the other side of a dune. She stood still, waiting for an explosion, and when none came, strove to run in the direction she had thrown it, her feet sinking in soft sand. "Hey," Maureen was yelling, again. Following the course of the grenade, Joann came to the last ridge before the dunes plummeted to the beach, and stopping short at the top, she looked down to where the grenade bounced against a rock, rolled, rested, while dislodged sand trickled in its wake. Nothing else. Her mouth was filling with saliva. Trying to swallow, she began to vomit. She could not stop vomiting.

One conversation from an earlier visit to another beach appears among the shadows that haunted Joann during her early twenties. She sometimes had the sense that it had taken place on this day, adding to her humiliation.

Whatever day it was, one time that summer they had strolled down Silveira Beach, now and then running in and out of the sharply cold tide. They had been playing hearts and gossiping with Maureen's friends, and Joann felt overcome by a weariness she was trying to ignore.

"Did you ever hear what happened to Jackie?" Maureen asked, continuing the conversation they'd just been having with her friends.

"Just that she got in trouble and was mixed up in some kind of court trial."

"I heard the gossip. Someone who was a court reporter at the trial said they got her drunk and then three of them did it to her. The reason she dropped out of school was, she was pregnant." Maureen had been skipping flat stones after the outgoing tide. She shouted, "Hey, pregnant!"

"Is there something the matter with that?"

"No, I just wanted to yell. Notice how we can say things here at the top of our voices. Pregnaaaant."

Joann splashed out until the water rushed past her calves. "Pregnant, pregnant, pregnant!" she yelled into the west. It made her feel better. Back at the tide line, she asked, "What was the trial for—to make one of them marry her?"

"I don't think so. I wonder what happened to the baby. Maybe it died."

"She never came back to school."

"They wouldn't let her, I mean Mr. Manning wouldn't. I think. Anyway, she wouldn't have wanted to. I used to hear the boys make jokes about her," Maureen said.

"What about her mom and dad? That's what's really sad."

"Why?"

"I don't know, I don't really know." Joann began to run, as fast and hard as she could. Someone had heard her shout "pregnant" to the waves. Someone was watching, and she could not escape.

Maureen makes the incidents of the day on Pecho Strand indispensable to the complete story of her life. They take their place with other memorable experiences in the first circle of her consciousness, just outside the present. Waking up in her mother's arms one hot day, with her mother singing "My Bonnie Lies over the Ocean." Walking in on her big brother when he was urinating in the toilet. Lying in bed looking at the chicken pox on her stomach and wondering why that made her sick. Getting her first library card from the old lady at the top of the stairs whose hair looked like a great turban of white silk. Hearing the news of Pearl Harbor at the dinner table the day the Japanese attacked. Deciding one Friday, walking past a procession of children and nuns on their way to Refugio Mission, that she didn't believe in God after all. Watching people dance in the street the day the war ended. Making love with Chet in the backseat of his car on the road around Twin Peaks in San Francisco and having her first orgasm there. Breaking her ankle skiing at Yosemite, shivering in a cold wind, wondering how long before anyone would come to help her. Realizing she was pregnant the day she and Chet arrived in Alabama with the Freedom Riders. Hearing her mother's voice on the telephone quavering with the news of her father's fatal heart attack. Waking up just before dawn with the first wrenching pain of labor. Staring into the eyes of the police officer arresting her at the draft board demonstrations in 1968. Hearing a woman in her consciousness-raising group describe her feelings for another woman—then remembering suddenly her own totally irrelevant joy at being allowed to hold Joann in her arms the night after the abortion. Reading the expression on Chet's face when the doctor telephoned with the biopsy report.

She knows the stories of these unforgettable moments change when she tells them, depending on her audience and the point she is trying to illustrate, even in those moments when the audience is only herself. But what she saw and sometimes what she heard remains intact, though often she is permitted no more than an instant's flash of the scene.

She is almost sure the unaltered part of what she remembers of this day is running as best she can across the sand separating her and Joann, confused about what has happened. Something is the matter. Has the grenade gone off, inexplicably without sound, and has a piece of it struck her friend? Is Joann merely frightened, waiting for it to explode, bending down, her head between her arms, her hips up, waiting for the explosion? Will the whole pile of sand come tumbling, like a great castle of sand hit by a rock? Still she runs—it takes a long time—and then slumping to her knees beside Joann's head, she sees the sandy rolls of moisture and is puzzled, and then sees more coming from Joann's mouth and knows it is vomit.

She does not remember waiting beside Joann for the heaving to end, handing her first a crumpled tissue, and then tidily covering up the vomit like a cat in a litter box, her hands moving slowly so that Joann will not know she is keeping herself from gagging. "It must be something you ate for lunch," she says helpfully while Joann rubs a sticky part of her long hair into the sand to clean it.

She does remember Joann rolling over onto her back at last and saying, eyes closed, softly, as if just going to sleep, "I'm, I'm...in trouble."

"Trouble?" she remembers saying, and if she is telling the story to a group of friends, Joann reduced to anonymity as "this girl I knew in high school," she makes fun of herself for not understanding. "Everyone knew what 'in trouble' meant in those days," she would say, and if her audience was over fifty, the women would grin and nod, thinking, as she wanted them to: hopeless, naive Maureen, probably thought the grenade had killed someone. If she was talking to the young, one or another of the women would say, "Well it's the same thing nowadays," and she would become embroiled in an argument about social attitudes, family attitudes, and ways in which the problem could or could not be solved.

She also remembers but never speaks of the numb silence within her when she realized what Joann meant. She has felt it since, maybe four times: the day of Chet's operation, another when she found her mother lying on the floor after a slight stroke, a third when her daughter Nancy said her husband had thrown her against a wall, and a fourth when she thought she felt a lump in her breast. Each of these other times has been followed by a pause for reinforcements, and she has come out of it with an array of defenses ready for herself and for whoever else might need her strength. Call the doctor, an ambulance, check financial resources, make peace with the universe, take your chances, accept the consequences, find out the truth. For Joann, she had as yet developed no resources.

When Maureen began to feel again, fear and anger clawed at her stomach. She also felt a throbbing, tightening of her genitals. It must have been Bobby Moss, she thought, someone she herself had gone steady with the year before and pushed away a hundred times. Joann had been going with him before graduation. How could she let him? Was it in the convertible? He's repulsive, we'd talked about how repulsive he was.

She stared down into Joann's face, the thin mouth now deliberately composed, her eyes closed, squeezed against the sun. A thin sprinkling of fine sand remained stuck to her chin. Her hands dug into the dune, fingers trying to grip the sand. Gusts of wind sucked and popped in the hollow, spraying more sand over her tangled brown hair.

Joann remembers precisely, when she cares to think about it, the feeling of being contagious, as she opened her eyes to watch the expression on Maureen's face change from incomprehension to fear, to—at last—acceptance of the leaden reality Joann had cast them into.

"I don't even love him," Joann said.
Maureen's first words to her were, "What are we going to do?"

3

The images are ordinary, reflections I'm familiar with. They arrange themselves like a deck of playing cards in rows: the first row to be bent, wrinkled, my face and hands no longer recognizable to anyone; to remain snared by this house for all the time I have left; to be frail, maybe dying in the bedroom with yellow curtains where I have slept for twenty years, the sunlight in summer just the same triangular patch on the left side of my bed, all of my life at once cupped in these hills, these walls. A second row, some face cards, winners, now: to roll through a town on the freeway, any town, just so I don't recognize it; to enter a room high up in a city, one I've never seen before, but where my children, even Michael, poor Michael, greet me, "Mom, you've been a long time, but at last you're here"; to wave, slowly and just once, from the deck of a ship to a shore where the people I've known all my life stand—there's a mountain and a cave behind them, and I set my eyes on it, not on them. And the next row, three, another suit: to strike all people and all houses from this valley, leaving just myself; to pretend I have lived here alone all these years, with no one to find my face either familiar or unfamiliar; to mark out the trails I have made—fewer than ten in almost sixty years—one broad, into the center of the valley where the mission church and the library are, three old, to the schools both I and my children attended, and four deep, within the boundaries of this house, from the bedroom to the bathroom, from the front door to the kitchen, from the kitchen to this room, from this room to the bedroom. Where now I slouch, back curved, legs extended, arms bent in on me, in the dark, my eyes closed against the flickering colors of the television in a corner of the room.

When the phone rings I am considering how customary and familiar these thoughts have become, these ruts within the crannies of my skull.

"Hello." I am standing now, across the room near the library table, staring at a shelf of old children's books—Robin Hood, hidden forest glades, flashes through my consciousness. The television behind me flickers light, dark, light, light, dark. "Hello." A familiar voice, a little nervous, hesitates. "This is…it's Maureen." Pauses. The barren land-scape of the valley gives way, I am having watery sensations—I can't describe them any other way—in my chest. The voice goes on, "This is Joann Ridley Henderson, isn't it?"

"Maureen, Maureen Lewis?" I say. I could be neck-deep in water at the bottom of a well, when suddenly a face appears over the edge, not far above my head, but far enough that though I cannot make out the features above me, she can see my face clearly.

"Yes, it's me," she answers. "You still answer the phone the same way, soprano and upbeat, remember? The way we practiced in seventh grade."

"Yes," I say, but I do not remember. I can think of nothing else to add, though I scan my repertoire for the usual polite phrases. She too is silent. I could ask, Why have you called? but that would not be cordial or courteous, and I always try to be cordial and courteous to whoever calls. So, in the still seconds, the faint telephone buzz in my ear, I consider responses. They roll through my head while she takes over.

"It's great to hear your voice. It's been a long time," she says.

"Forty-five years," I say.

"Or thereabouts." The words are faint, a definite preliminary. She must be going to add some other words, and so again I wait, but nothing comes. Are you comfortable down there? whispers through the well, ripples the water. Of course I am, why shouldn't I be?

She must be in Refugio. She must want to see me. Why else would she telephone? "Are you in town?" She is. I do not want to see her, even speaking to her right now is painful, but I say as I'm expected to say, "What a surprise!" "What brings you here?" "Where are you staying?" "Just overnight?" until she asks the question I have begun to realize is inevitable, "Can we get together tomorrow?" My answer too is unavoidable. If not tomorrow, I must talk with her tonight. Yes, I say, suggesting a time and place for lunch, away from my house. Then comes the Maureen question, nothing so direct as, can I throw you a rope ladder, but "How are you?"

Why can't I think it the other way? That it's my face at the edge of the well, Maureen who wishes me to bring her up out of the water.

"I've often thought of you," she goes on. "I really want to hear all about you; it's going to be so wonderful to see you again." Pause. "So exciting."

"So exciting" is what my mother used to say all the time, clasping her hands as if to keep them from trembling when Maureen was coming over to sleep out in the tree house with me or when my team had won a volleyball match at school or when I announced a school honor like making the class speech for graduation. "So exciting," Maureen says on the telephone, and I am silenced, cordiality and politeness impossible.

"At noon tomorrow then." My words rise to the surface, skim away.

She's disappointed that I have no response for her emotions and takes her turn at silence. At last she promises, "We'll talk tomorrow then."

She puts down her phone, I hear the click, and then no more voices. She is no more, after all, than a shape outlined by the past. With no face. No present or real presence. Less actual, therefore, than the crouching wolf, the running caribou, the mountains of snow that assail my senses from the television. And therefore, without the power—I must insist on this—to make my heart beat faster or my chest tighten the way it does now, as this shape, this set of attitudes and recollections that calls herself Maureen drifts into my life.

I would like to turn the television off and just sit in the dark, but when Gil comes home from the study session or whatever is going on tonight, he will ask, "What are you doing?" In the morning, if he's around, his guilt will overwhelm him and he'll fuss at me about depression or not having enough to keep me busy these days. I've heard him on the phone explain my solitary peculiarities to Brenda thus, "She's on one of those religious kicks again, just like your grampa." He seriously believes I've inherited something from my dad, varieties of religious experience. When I told him I stopped believing in God two years ago, he thought it was only one more attack on the patience he imagines he has. I made a joke, suggesting I was looking for nirvana.

Maybe I am. I rise, take my sweater from a chair, pick up my flashlight in the kitchen, and walk out of the house, not locking the door. Behind the house is a fence, over the fence is a steep grassy slope leading up the hill to a small grove of oak trees and my rocks. I dismiss my family thus.

Within the grove I pause, preferring for a while the utter blackness. What will I say to Maureen—if I must see her? That I'm ashamed of my life? No, I will tell her I have spent my life searching for the truth, trying to remember the rare moments when I've perceived it, so I can carry it with me. I will be taking a bite of chicken salad at the moment, and I will look demurely downward while she tries to find a response. She always did try to find something to reply, even if all she can think of is a nonsense question. Can you describe one of the rare moments you remember? she will ask.

No. Maureen will have become a practical woman of the world, like her mother, only less decisive. I wish I could imagine her face as it is now. I probe for an image of her face as it was and fail, though I have a sharp sense of her body as she was at seventeen, long, thin, fair-skinned, stretched out on a striped beach towel, her hair, shimmering yellow over her shoulders. Remembering her hair reminds me of the fat curls bounding down her back when we were little and of her tiny, knobby knees. What I should say to her—what she would most like to hear— is that I have spent my life doing good for others. If my mother always said "so exciting," her mother was always saying, "You should try to make the world you inhabit a little bit better."

But why must people who haven't seen each other for forty-odd years meet again? What self is present? Was I the self I now call myself when I knew Maureen? I have been myself so rarely—the search for me like the search for truth, rarely found—that the times I myself was present I can hardly even now remember. When I knew Maureen, the world outside Refugio was as blank as the sky over it, and all I knew was that I had to escape into the blankness or lose myself. All my life, even now, is a long wait, with imaginary flights, to enter that world.

What shall I tell Maureen? All about my children, is that safe? But Michael is dead. I must not sound bitter; I do not feel bitter. Yes I keep busy. Books, gardening. Religion, dare I bring up religion to Maureen?

"Have you thought what you're going to say to your mother?" Maureen had asked the morning after they first discussed the pregnancy. She was opening a bank of casement windows one after the other in the Ridley's breakfast alcove.

Joann stood at the sink in her pajamas, measuring orange juice into a cup. "Are you kidding?" She poured the whole cup down the sink and turned to the refrigerator to take out a bottle of milk. "Have you forgotten she's a Catholic, and I'm supposed to be one too?" She poured the milk into the same cup that had held the orange juice, gagging, grimacing. Then she cleared her throat and added almost inaudibly, "She tried to make me go to confession a couple of weeks ago, but I wouldn't."

"I didn't mean I thought it was a good idea."

"Can you imagine telling your mother?"

Maureen reflected on the day her sister Rosemary, recently married, gathered the courage to tell their mother she was pregnant. This was while her husband was overseas, fighting somewhere in Italy, and Rosemary was certain their mother would not approve. She had chosen the family dinner hour to make the public announcement, and their mother, without speaking, had risen to fetch her cigarettes and an ash tray and had smoked three cigarettes one right after the other, leaving her dinner unfinished on the plate. "How will you finish at Cal?" she kept asking. "What profession have you prepared yourself for if you're made a widow?" Later, after the dishes were done, Maureen heard her mother in Rosemary's room, asking whether she and Frank had ever heard of birth control. Rosemary's answer—that she'd been too embarrassed to ask the doctor about it—made her mother sigh in resignation.

"No I can't, I mean imagine telling her," Maureen replied to Joann, seating herself at the table. It occurred to her to ask whether Joann and Bobby had thought of birth control, but she didn't.

These days Maureen's daughters tell her more than she wants to know about them. Not long ago Nancy telephoned from Durham, North Carolina. "Can I ask you a question? Jack and I—you remember, he's one of the law partners—have lunch now and then, especially if we're both in court. Perfectly friendly and all that. Now that Dirk is out of town Jack wants to take me to dinner. What do you think? Do you think Dirk will be jealous?"

Maureen has never considered herself an arbiter of manners and morals for her daughters, and refuses to answer. Yet what are young women to do in this world of shifting traditions but ask their mothers, she often says to herself, recalling her mother's deep sigh over

Rosemary. She had always thought she knew quite definitely what her mother's opinions on manners and morals were until recently, when she has begun to ask her directly. Her mother's answers surprise her.

As Joann poured the cup of milk down the sink, she tried again to imagine telling her mother she was pregnant, but the scene would not stay still. She would wait until her father was out of the house, gone out for a walk maybe? But then she would never know when he would be back; it would take her too long to talk with her mother, she would have to explain, mention things she had never talked with her mother about before. So where could her father be when she talked to her mother? He could be at the cafe. Immediately her thoughts would shift to him at the cafe, sitting with his books and astrological charts in the back booth, talking about reincarnation, and at home her mother's hands would be restless on the table, tearing little pieces of newspaper and rolling them into balls while she talked of calling the priest for advice.

"I can imagine telling my mother, but I can't imagine what she would say," Joann confessed to Maureen. "But what she would say wouldn't be important, it would be how she would look. The only time she looks happy now is when she thinks about me and how my happiness is going to change her life. I'm going to have chances she never had, that's what she's always saying."

Maureen frowned and rubbed the tip of her tongue into the corner of her mouth, an expression she often took on when concentrating. She had seated herself and was rolling two pieces of bread and a handful of cereal up in a piece of paper so that Joann could throw them into the garbage can without her mother discovering that she had again failed to eat breakfast. After a moment she said, "You can't make this go away by magic. We have to do something about it."

"Don't you think I know that?"

"What about your scholarship?"

Joann shrugged. "All I know is I'm not going to marry Bobby Moss."

"He's not that bad."

Joann shook her head, no. "It was my fault anyway."

"It couldn't have been."

Joann stared at Maureen, her eyes as expressionless as a bird's.

"I didn't mean I thought you had to marry him. But if you wanted to, you could. I could help. I could talk to him." Joann had turned away and was looking down into the sink. "I'm just trying to say…" Maureen went on, "It's my mother. I heard her tell my brother once it was his responsibility. And Rosemary butted in and said girls always think it's their fault. So I didn't want you to think it was. Your fault, I mean. Bobby's such a jerk. I ought to know."

"It was my fault." Pause. "It was my idea. I just wanted to try it…to see what…"

After setting the crushed up ball of toast, cereal, and paper aside, Maureen took a cigarette from her purse and lit it. "All right," she said, waving the smoke out the window with her hands.

Joann took the wad of crumbled cereals from the breakfast room table and, shoving egg shells and cantaloupe rinds aside, dropped it into the garbage pail under the sink. "My stomach's been upset for weeks," she said. She sat down opposite Maureen and lit a cigarette of her own. "I think the smoke is making me feel sicker."

"Rosemary didn't smoke the whole time she was pregnant. She had morning sickness for three whole months."

"What's morning sickness?"

"It's what you get the first three months of being pregnant. It makes you vomit in the morning or when you get upset. I read about it in a little pamphlet Rosemary had. It's supposed to be normal."

Joann clenched the hand holding the cigarette so hard the end was crushed between her fingers. "I thought maybe it meant it was going away, that I was sick and it would…disappear or something." She took a deep breath. "Was there anything in the book about things that aren't good for you if you're pregnant?"

"Getting too tired, not taking your vitamins, things like that."

"Did you ever read about what happens when girls who were pregnant fell down stairs?"

"Like Scarlett in *Gone with the Wind*?"

"I was thinking of something like that yesterday, but it wouldn't have worked, would it? It's not straight down, not by the ocean."

Maureen slowly shook her head from side to side. "You'd be hurt, or dead."

"I wouldn't care."

"Everyone would think he wouldn't marry you so you tried to kill yourself. You might as well put a notice in the paper saying you're pregnant." After a moment she added in her most sensible voice, thinking, this is what I should say, this is right, so say it plainly so she'll pay attention: "And I would care."

Now and then in lonely or cynical moments, Joann recalls this moment, not as anything personal, but as a general affirmation of the truth that some people are willing to care for others in this world. She is not certain just when Maureen said these words to her that summer, but she remembers what she had been feeling before they had been spoken: squeezed down, crumpled, contorted, like a walnut in a shell; and she knows what she had felt afterward: a moment of hope, like the sudden burst of sun through an opening door. She has never experienced anything so richly comforting again, so she relies on this memory to deal with the ordinary outrages of life—the disappearance of her father in 1960, her husband's first affair, a difficult and dangerous surgery when she was fifty. For the extraordinary, like the death of a son, she has no defense.

What she does not remember: her relief at not having to take sudden, drastic, and solitary action and her discovery that she would be able to postpone decisions for another few days while she talked things over with Maureen. Combined with the comfort Maureen had given, these reminded her of a game they often played as children, and she had said in answer to Maureen, "I wish there was some kind of magic, like in that power game we used to play, only it would have to be the kind of power that could make things not happen."

At ten years old, Joann and Maureen had decided to believe that when they were together they possessed an extraordinary, possibly magic, power to transform the everyday world. Sometimes they played a "What if?" game: What if that car was a horse, what if that sign was a giant spider, what if that tree was a pirate ship? Afternoons in summer, when one of Maureen's older sisters had been required—as a condition for getting the car—to take them along on expeditions to the beach, they would each lie belly down in the sand listening to the waves. Suddenly one of them might sense the power and would instantly leap to her feet and dash into the water, swimming out beyond the surf where she could make the water warmer, turn her hands and feet to fins, disappear for half the afternoon. The other inevitably followed, and the water would turn warmer for both of them and they would both feel they could swim all the way to China.

"Like time going backwards?" Maureen at eighteen was not certain what Joann meant by "that power game," vaguely recalling only an afternoon when Joann's mother had scolded them for reading a pamphlet called "Powers of the Mind" that Joann's father got through the mail.

"No. If you went backwards in time, I'd still have to be pregnant, at least for a couple of months. But I just don't want it ever to be. Remember when my rabbit, Smoky, died? The morning I found him dead I wished that I could get up in the morning all over again and come out and find him alive, just like other mornings. You know what my father said? He hadn't started astrology yet, but was studying yoga, or something, and he said, 'Just pretend you never had Smoky.'"

4

Sheila, who has lived in Southern California too long, has been teasing me about the Marin County showers I take—the modified "navy showers" Chet and I learned in the drought of 1977 after she had been away from home two years. As I rub soap all over, I recall her cheerful voice asking, "Have you been wet all over even once, Mom, in thirteen years, just once? All those good hygiene lectures to your children gone to waste?" "Down the drain," I say to her shade, aloud, replacing the soap in its dish, turning the water back on, shuddering for a moment as a splash of cold hits the sag of my belly.

At least she doesn't have to worry about the old lady falling in the bathtub, I think, as I dry myself and pull on an old pair of striped pajamas that used to be Chet's. The sleeves have to be rolled up, the pants wrap around me like a skirt, but their soft folds comfort me. I had begun sleeping in his pajamas a month after his death, rotating the three pairs he owned until now, five years later, they are faded and threadbare.

Before I leave the bathroom I fill a hot water bottle to ease the stiffness in my shoulders and then swallow two aspirin. I put on my reading glasses, pick up the book I'd placed on the bedside shelf, and stand staring at the cover for a moment. No, I don't believe I'm going to be able to concentrate enough to read this night. Bare-footed, my long and knobby toes flexed upward to avoid the prickly carpet, I step over to the television set, search for a news station. At last, giving up, I turn off the lamp and lie down in the dark.

If I'd telephoned just because I thought I could return to the past hand in hand with an old friend, I was wrong. I repeat the words aloud, giving them the ironic twist I would have used if I were talking to Chet, then I add silently, the old lady is starting to talk to herself. I turn on my side, the hot water bottle under my neck. I pull the sheet and blanket up under my ear, pushing several strands of hair away from my face. If I'd thought Joann would be yearning to meet once she heard me speak, I was wrong. If I'd thought the two of us were actually going to talk about anything serious except grandchildren, I was probably wrong there, too.

Obviously, I'm not going to sleep soon. I uncurl myself, switch on the bed lamp, and sit up blinking. Am I imposing myself on Joann?

Barging into her town like barging into a house I used to own? But she could have said no; it's relatives who have a hard time refusing. Friends can always say, sorry, I'm not feeling well. If they're given time to think. So I am intruding, maybe not taking over someone's kitchen, but perching in the living room. This has been a bad habit of mine for—how long? When was it I began to establish myself in the margins of other people's lives? Certainly long after I knew Joann. I hope. More likely around the time I decided—could it have been as early as when I consented to be Nancy's Camp Fire guardian? I can hear myself saying, "Now we all have to earn money together so every one of us can go on the ski trip, not just those who have big allowances." All those little girls washing windows, and no one, no one, no one, ever left behind.

The words *left behind* remind me of an image that used to flicker on for the benefit of my internal behind-the-scenes commentator, the one who isn't happy when I congratulate myself too much. Usually it embarrasses me and I turn it off, but this time I try to let it run, listening for the voices. We are sharing a meal, my mother and father and I. It must be dinner because we are in the dining room, the grey kitchen door is behind my mother's head, and my father is carving a leg of lamb. The year has to have been 1950 or 1951 because we are discussing the Korean War, maybe whether my brother Bill's reserve unit would be called up. Suddenly my mother says something that flusters me: "Have you talked with Joann?"

I pretend to be puzzled. "I thought someone told me she left town. Why did you ask me that?"

I remember it is Dad who explains: "Paul Ridley's got himself in trouble picketing the draft board. He says he's against the war in Korea. With the new people in town, well, they don't understand him. Someone called the police and asked them to send him to the psychiatric ward. He had to go through a sanity hearing."

Then my mother reveals the real reason for her question; she is suggesting that I step in and help. She says, "I hear Joann's been down here for a few months to help her mother straighten things out. I saw her in the bank the other day, and she looked as if she needed a friend."

I always cringe at the memory of my reaction that day: for my mother's benefit, an indifferent shrug. Within myself I say, not this friend, I won't be friendly to someone as unfair and hurtful as Joann. My mother examines my face for a moment, turns to my father, changes the subject, and I am left to remind myself I have an excuse for such detachment. I had given Joann everything I could give, and her final words to me, what I thought I remembered of them, had gone something like this: If you ever see me again it will be like a betrayal. She had spoken them without anger, without caring what effect they would have on me, without any emotion, really, and that part of her message had been quite clear.

In the motel room, propped up by pillows against the head of the bed, staring at my legs stretched out before me under the faded stripes of Chet's old pajamas, I try to think what else Joann said to me besides "betrayal." She had made me feel abandoned by that word, all the pleasure I might have taken at going away to college and exploring the world collapsed. Did regret and guilt about the abortion overcome her? Suppose I had ignored what she said, come back, at least tried in other years, when we were younger? Sometimes I think the truth is, I went off and left her behind. Maybe I should ask myself why.

Once Maureen had an answer to that "Why?" but the sharpness of the insight has since become absorbed in a story she tells herself of how helpful she tried to be that summer, when she isn't blaming herself. One night in the late sixties, she and Chet had put the children to bed and were sitting in front of the television watching horror clips of the war in Vietnam.

"Do you remember the newsreels when we were kids?" Chet asked.

"Sort of—men marching to band music, bombers roaring over the English Channel, billowing smoke, soldiers walking through ruined towns, bricks all over the streets."

Silence as a burst of flame engulfed three buildings in a Vietnam village pronounced by a reporter to have "strategic significance."

Maureen continued after the commercials began, "But I'm not sure which were just movies and which were the real thing."

Chet smiled as Maureen took his hand, and they stared companionably at the set through one cereal commercial and one car promotion.

When a political ad came on, he dropped her hand and picked up the pile of history exams he was supposed to be correcting. "Being born a girl isn't all bad news, I guess," he said.

"What do you mean by that?"

"I was sixteen the last year of the war, and from the time I was fourteen I was scared shitless it wasn't going to be over before I was old enough to be drafted. I was sure I was going to be killed."

"Girls have other things to worry about."

"Like what?"

"Like getting pregnant."

"Don't tell me you lost sleep through your high school years worrying. Or maybe you did. You haven't told me all your past, is that it?" he teased.

Maureen had to admit then, while he sat with the first student paper opened in front of him, that she had lived through that period of her life as if she'd been locked within a blessed enchantment. No, she hadn't had to worry about getting pregnant; she knew the rules. As for the war, even when it intruded, as when her friend Keiko Matsui was taken away from sixth grade or her brother was drafted and then sent overseas, some part of herself never believed in its reality.

As Chet began to turn the pages of the exams, concentrating, a slight frown on his face, she thought, but I did believe it when Joann got pregnant. When I was little, our friendship, even her house and her parents, were a kind of retreat. The summer we graduated from high school I wanted the enchantment to go on forever, but having to cope with Joann's pregnancy frightened me. I realized I was going to have to live in that dangerous world, and I was terribly glad when I could leave Refugio and pretend again that everything was always safe and never any harder than I wanted it to be.

From the first day she visited when she was nine, Maureen liked the Ridley house, a small tan stucco imitation English cottage, with window nooks and wooden paneling, a living room crowded with old furniture, and two canaries in twin cages in the windows of its dining room. Joann was an only child, sharing a bedroom with no one. In one corner she kept a whole bookcase full of her own books, among them several Oz books Maureen had never read, and a chest full of toys bought just for her. In the backyard she had rabbit hutches, a big house for her dolls, and a tree house ten feet up in a sycamore tree.

Though the Lewis house was bigger, the carpets thicker, the furniture older, the neighbors farther away, it was filled by two older sisters, Marilyn and Rosemary, and a brother, Bill. Maureen couldn't play or read in any room in the house without being bothered by one of them or their friends. If he wasn't teasing her, her brother had boys over to visit who seemed to take up all the space outside, shooting baskets or working on noisy, smoky cars. After he went away to college, whenever he came home, he and his friends took over the living room and dining room, smoking and talking. Sometimes, especially when they talked about Hitler and the threat of European war, her mother joined them and smoked and discussed history. She would get so excited that Maureen couldn't even get answers to simple questions—her mother just didn't hear them. Marilyn and Rosemary were both in high school, and almost every day they brought their friends home to play music on the radio or phonograph and dance to it. Or they flirted with her brother's friends.

Maureen had loved Joann's mother almost immediately. She was a tall thin woman with a lopsided grin, freckles, and dark hair so curly she could never keep it sedately rolled. She had always wanted more than one child, but for some reason unknown to either Joann or Maureen, had not managed another one. They heard the word "miscarriage" once or twice but thought it was the name of a nurse at the hospital where Mrs. Ridley had to go two or three times with stomach trouble.

Mrs. Ridley believed that children were beautiful and naturally good and that it was society that brought ugliness and evil into their lives. Her belief allowed the two girls great freedom to come and go, for she held that they could not get into trouble unless led astray, and she didn't know anyone in Refugio who would lead them astray. She liked to listen to them tell her about what they were learning at school and what they were reading. She also liked to help with Joann's pets. One spring day before gasoline was rationed, she picked them up after school in the car and drove them up into a canyon not far from town where they could see poppies covering whole fields with orange. It had been an especially rainy winter, and they had never seen poppies in such profusion. Her voice trembled when she told them, "We'll have to remember this day for a very long time," and though Maureen thought she might have been a little silly, she liked thinking they were important enough and old enough to be told to remember a present experience until they were as old as their mothers.

The first time Maureen met Mr. Ridley, she thought he was Joann's big brother, another version of Bill. He was tinkering with his car on a Sunday afternoon when Joann took her outside to meet him, and he was wearing jeans and a blue work shirt. His hair was blond, curly, and unruly, and though he had smudges of grease all over his face, she could see that his skin was thin, lightly freckled, like a child's. When Joann interrupted him he left his work to stand before them and then made them giggle by bowing and pretending to lift Maureen's hand to his lips like foreign gentlemen in the movies. But unlike Bill, whose main purpose in making little girls giggle seemed to be to make fun of them, Mr. Ridley joined them, laughing as if his purpose was to give them delight. Unlike Bill, too, he let them stay all afternoon watching him sorting out the car's wiring, telling them how he felt about the car and the wiring without long explanations of how it worked.

"When I was a little boy," he said during one winter's walk along the beach at Silveira, "I read in my history book about how the miners found gold in river sand, so I was convinced that if I could get every piece of glitter out of a bucketful of sand I would be rich. I thought it was really important to be rich then, and I guess I still do."

"I don't need to be rich," Joann piped.

"But if I had got all the glitter out of a bucket of sand, I could take you and your mother to, let's see, where would we want to go? How about to India? I'd like to see a tiger in India. Would you?"

"And Maureen too?"

"Sure. We couldn't go without her."

"I'd like to go to Samarkand," said Maureen.

"Well then we'd go there too, on camels. I think they ride camels in Samarkand. Does either of you know?"

Then when they got back to town, they parked in an alley behind the cafe. Mr. Ridley opened the back door for them, and Maureen followed Joann, stooping under his arm, into the dark kitchen, between hot water heater and sink, steel cupboard and refrigerator, out to the front where the soda fountain stretched to the windows. Right there, right at the front he sat them on stools. "Now I don't want you watching

the folks walking by outside. They'll see us and think I'm open and
knock on the door to come in. Besides, you have to tell me how to
make it."

"What are you going to make?"

"Whatever you say, sweetheart." It surprised Maureen that he really meant it, it wasn't a tease.

"A Samarkand sundae then."

He laughed out loud, genuinely delighted with the name.

Judge Lewis had once walked with Maureen down the strand after
Sunday afternoon dinner at Hughie's Dinner House in Pismo Beach.
Although he allowed Maureen to take her buckle shoes and her short
white socks off, he kept his hat, his tie, his coat, vest, and shoes prop-
erly in place. (He wore slacks and an open-collar shirt on vacations on
the Russian River, twill pants and plaid shirts and boots in the Sierras.
His sport clothes were several years old because he wore them so sel-
dom.) When Maureen asked him if the sparkling bits of sand revealed
just when the wave receded were gold, he said, "No, just the sun
reflecting off the water left in the sand. The only gold along the beach
in this area was at Oso Flaco Lake, where it settled after washing
down from the hills."

At night in those days Maureen dreamed of buckets of gold, and in
the morning she kissed her father good-bye on the way to school. He
always wore his vest and necktie at the breakfast table and read the
San Francisco papers with a worried frown. Days could go by with just
a kiss at night and a kiss in the morning from her father. Her mother
almost never remembered to kiss her.

She did not notice the change developing in Mr. Ridley's behavior
through the three or four years she'd been close to Joann. True, after
the soldiers came to town in 1941 he no longer took them for Sunday
walks with a treat in the closed cafe afterward, but Maureen, if she
thought about it, put the lapse in the same category as some of the
other changes she had to undergo as a penalty for growing older—paying a quarter, not a dime, at the movies, for instance, or having to go to
dancing classes. On long slow Sundays when they were reading books
in Joann's bedroom, he was spending his time sitting in the dining
room reading and taking notes from a pile of books and pamphlets
while the radio played music and news. Then one Saturday when she
was accompanying her mother into the cafe to pick up a quart of ice

cream, she noticed he was not helping Mrs. Ridley, who seemed tired and tense as she waited on several people and cooked breakfast for them too. Instead he was sitting at a booth at the back of the cafe with his books, paying no attention to what was going on around him. Though he nodded a greeting to her and her mother, when Mrs. Lewis asked after his health he replied, "I'm so worried about evil and all the deaths in Europe I'm having a hard time staying in the present."

In later years, Maureen had disagreed with her mother, who claimed that Mr. Ridley had always been a bit "mad." Instead, she insisted that for all the years she had known him he had countered his wife's strong Catholicism with varieties of theosophical studies and experiences, but it was the war that had affected his behavior. She especially remembered what had happened to him on the day Japan surrendered, in August 1945. This had made her feel sorry for him as well as embarrassed, but vaguely guilty too, for she had watched and what she had watched she always thought of as his disgrace. She had never talked about what she saw to Joann, hoping that Joann did not know about it.

Once she told some friends about how Refugio had treated Joann's father the last day of the war. "I remember that day in August very well, but not because the war had ended, or at least, not exactly," she began. It was a monthly gathering of old friends and neighbors and fellow activists who had decided to meet at a restaurant on the Bay every once in a while just to gossip and be companionable. None of them had met Joann—nor would they ever meet her—though they had spent enough time together to remember the character when she came up in Maureen's discussions.

On this day they were all recalling how clearly they remembered the ordinary events of life when those events got tangled with great international events.

"I know Annette watched soap operas when she came home from kindergarten because it was when she turned on the television that I heard Kennedy had been shot," said one.

"The day World War II ended I was still fourteen," Maureen told them.

She had driven to town with her mother to pick up the groceries, both of them aware of the news on the radio. But they were not prepared for the impromptu celebration going on in the center of town, near the mission and the grocery store. No one remained on the sidewalks; men and women, girls, soldiers, dogs, little boys were leaping and shouting in the streets, crowding the few cars that tried to creep among them. Several soldiers had bottles of whiskey in their hands and were passing them around. Both Galetti brothers, the owners of the grocery store and bakery where her mother usually shopped, were stationed outside their doors shaking hands with everyone who danced or bounced or shouted past them.

Maureen wondered why everyone was so excited about something they had all known would happen for several days. As she and her mother walked from the side street where they had parked the car, she felt separate from the world, the sounds of the crowd seemed muffled, their antics disjointed.

"The war was over, I don't know why I didn't feel anything about it, or anyway I don't remember feeling anything," she confessed to her friends as she meditated on her reactions. "I felt insulated, as if I were wrapped up in cotton batting that day—you know, the way nursery school teachers used to describe shy children. But it wasn't shyness. Maybe if there had been a parade. But just people screaming and shouting and carrying on. I thought they were all crazy."

Suddenly, as they were making their way through the crowds toward the grocery store, Mrs. Ridley appeared running against the crowd toward them. She wore her white uniform dress from the cafe with a ruffled, blue half-apron, but her cap had fallen off, and her curly hair stood up around her ears. Tears streamed down her face, and she held her hands out as if seeking to grab someone to hold her up. Her hands reached up to Mrs. Lewis's shoulders. Maureen heard her cry: "Help me stop him; no one will help me!" As her mother's arm went around Mrs. Ridley's shoulder, she glanced up into her face and saw it clamp into a firm and righteous anger she recognized all too readily. Then she herself was grabbed and taken in through the door of the store by the senior Galetti, who was saying something like, "No place for a little girl." When she tried to push away, back toward her mother, she found she could not make her way out onto the sidewalk where a crowd of soldiers had formed a mob. Her mother had disappeared, and so had Mrs. Ridley, but the younger Galetti brother was pushing at the backs of soldiers, trying to break into their center. "It's all right, just a little fun, they won't hurt anyone," Mr. Galetti senior assured her. Above laughter and taunts, she could now hear Mr. Ridley's voice, "It's wrong, it's wrong, you can't celebrate, think of all the people in those burned-out cities. Their ghosts will haunt you." The voice, shouting, breaking, screaming, went on and on. The soldiers were yelling back, "Listen to the preacher," and "What do the stars say?" and more and more voices, "Roll him, hey roll him up the middle."

"It's all right, it's all right," Mr. Galetti kept saying until abruptly a scream, as if from a woman, and a husky roar, half laughter, from the soldiers. The roar followed Mr. Ridley, now pushed from the circle and stripped half-naked. He ran into the store, cowering, crying, "The dead children! All the dead children!"

Maureen remembered, always, the great fear that something would happen to her mother and Mrs. Ridley. "But everything else is blank. I don't remember how my mother and Mrs. Ridley got themselves out of the crowd or how we got home that day. And get this, instead of being angry or upset—well, I *was* frightened—I was mostly just embarrassed that I knew Mr. Ridley. It's the strangest thing to me now. I don't even remember thinking one way or another about the bombing of Hiroshima. I just didn't allow my imagination to extend to that kind of thing. But I was terribly upset about what happened to me. I dreamt about it and worried about Joann. I started worrying about all the bad things that happened to individual people, all the things I'd read about for years, things like assaults on people or murders. Soldiers from three army camps had filled the town for most of the war. They made everything dirty and beery, like a big amusement park, and I'd seen big bunches of them, crowds of hundreds, really, standing near the bus station or up by the USO. Suddenly I became aware they might do anything. It was like a nightmare sometimes. Lots of times I was afraid of them.

"I've often wondered why I didn't ask my mother what happened. Or, why it is I just can't remember if my mother did tell me on the drive home what had been going on and whether she had been able to do anything for Mr. Ridley."

These days when Maureen thinks of Joann's father, she classes him with many of the other attractive and hopeless idealists she has encountered in her active life. She realizes that Joann understood her father even when she was a child. She can recall Joann telling her several times, "We argue about religion sometimes, not because I'm such a good Catholic, but because some of his ideas are so dopey. Did you know he doesn't believe in evil, but because he doesn't believe in it, he has to fight for good all the time?"

It is because she recollected some of Joann's comments about her father that Maureen said, sitting in the Ridley breakfast room right after she had been told about the rabbit, Smoky: "Have you thought of telling your dad? He's not so strict as your mother, and he always tries to understand—at least he used to." Joann in her white cotton pajamas was leaning her head on the windowsill and did not answer for a while. Maureen reflected on how easy it would be if an adult could solve the problem, then continued, "He might know of some way we could change things, make it like it never happened, or so we could pretend that anyway. I could go with you."

Without lifting her head, Joann said, "He'd think it was the reincarnation of Buddha or something. No, I mean it. He wants me to stay home—I'm going to lose my spirituality if I go away to school. It's my mother who keeps telling him I have to, I'm grown up now."

She remained still for a long time, sunlight gleaming in the hair tumbling across her face and arms. "Anyway, he doesn't believe in getting rid of things or stopping them. Not even ants. You break the cycle of reincarnation."

"What do you mean?"

The voice was flat, almost sleepy. "If he knew about it, he'd think this thing inside me is supposed to have a soul already, from someone who's died. It's reincarnated. My mother too, only she's Catholic and the soul comes from God."

"Is that what you think?"

"For about one week, after I missed my first period, I tried." She sat up and reached for a cigarette, but just held it in her mouth for a moment without lighting it. "But remember that fairy tale about the troll or spider or whatever that jumps on the girl's back and won't let go, so that she has to die first before she can get rid of it? That's the way I feel if I think it's alive at all. Or like when you're sick, and all you want is to get well. If it has the soul of a spider I don't want it…and…I'm not a Catholic anymore."

"But it's not even a spider. It's not anything."

"I wish."

The last time Maureen saw Mr. Ridley he had arrived unexpectedly at the train station on the day they were leaving for San Francisco. He came strolling up just as Joann took her place in front of Maureen in the line leading up to the stairs into the train. He had a book open in his hand, and though Mrs. Ridley frowned at him, his mouth was fixed in that perpetual grin he had adopted—the beneficent smile in the face of corruption is what Joann called it.

"He's left the cafe with only the boy there doing dishes," Mrs. Ridley sighed. "I'll have to go."

Joann kissed her, accepting a hug without returning it, and then turned to say good-bye to her father. He took her by the arm, saying, "Something troubles me about this trip. I don't want you to go; everything's going too fast."

"No it's not, Daddy," she reassured him cheerfully. She turned away toward the stairs, but he wouldn't let go of her arm, pulling at her as she tried to step away from him. Maureen lunged ahead, up the steps. Mrs. Lewis tried to come to the rescue. "Come on now, Mr. Ridley, they'll miss the train." In the end it was the porter, pretending to be oblivious to the struggle and stepping between Joann and her father like a shepherd separating his flock, who freed her to climb aboard.

When the train slid northward through Refugio, and they were leaning back in green chairs and staring down the valley as the car crossed Dana Street, Maureen said, "You didn't tell him did you?"

"Are you kidding?" Joann said. "It's hard to tell whether he just doesn't want to lose me or whether he really does get some kind of sign no one else can see. Maybe he reads minds."

The Mr. Ridley that Maureen remembered in her childhood could have read minds—at least she would have agreed if anyone suggested it to her as a possibility.

In the late morning of the day they had been smoking in the Ridley's breakfast room, they were on their way to the beach, Maureen driving, Joann staring out the window.

"There was a book I read last year, there was something in it about a girl who gets...pregnant...and she gets her boyfriend to see about an operation. No, first there were pills, but those didn't work, then they looked for a doctor who would perform an operation that would get rid of the baby."

"You mean an abortion." Maureen had known about abortions since she was fifteen and had read about an "abortion mill" operating in San Francisco. She had asked her sister Rosemary, then expecting her second child, what an abortion mill was. The answer had been as hushed, but in the long run more satisfactory, than the answer to her childhood's question about menstruation. "It's against the law," she told Joann.

"That's what it said in the book. The doctor wouldn't do it because it would be killing a baby, he said. Everyone else was afraid of getting into trouble if they helped, but then the girl and her boyfriend went out in a boat, and she fell into the water and he didn't do anything to help her out. He wanted to marry someone rich, but he was executed for murder instead."

"What book was that?"

"*An American Tragedy.* I like Thomas Hardy better."

Joann shook her bottle of suntan lotion and rubbed some onto her face. She fiddled with her tube of zinc oxide, slathering the white ointment onto her nose, rubbing it into the skin around her lips and on her cheekbones, then reaching in her purse for a tissue to wipe the grease from her hands. "I don't care if it's against the law," she said.

Maureen's chest muscles constricted, and she clamped her fingers around the steering wheel. One day, searching in a courthouse corridor for her father, she had seen a young woman going into the Superior Court closely guarded by a sheriff's deputy. Had abortion been her crime?

"The operation's supposed to be dangerous. Rosemary told me girls die."

"My life feels pretty dangerous right now. My father will make me get married, I know he will, and anyway I can't keep hiding it forever."

Maureen does not remember this precise moment. For forty-five years she's thought she hesitates too much, though she has moved from stasis into decision, from a completed state into a progressive one, from self-satisfaction into discontent and action hundreds of times over her lifetime. These moments—when she sees a set of boundaries, tightens her fists, and then moves past the limits—have often been in the service of others, but not too often for herself.

For Joann the moment blended into many moments driving to Silveira, coming up the hill above the village, and catching sight of the sea. Bright. Blue.

At the crest of that hill, at the moment when the bright blue sea filled her eyes, Maureen said, "We'll have to find an abortion mill then."

"But where?" asked Joann.

5

When abortion became a public issue, Maureen used to amuse her friends with the story of how she and Joann began their search for an "abortion mill," and she still laughs out loud when she thinks of it.

"Here we were in a town where just about everyone knew us or our parents; we were part of that protected set of people, the 'good girls.' Not by choice, but because we hadn't learned any other way to live. Asking anyone for the information we needed would automatically keep us from using it. Besides, we'd been taught at home, at school, in books, and at the movies that just needing to ask would make everyone in the world treat us with scorn and mock our bodies. So what do you think we did first?"

"You asked a doctor."

"No. Anyone in town could see us going to the office and ask our parents what was the matter."

"You asked a girl who was not 'a good girl.'"

"If she knew, she wouldn't have told us—self-protection. Or, the other side of the coin, we wouldn't have trusted her not to tell, just to bring us down, make fun of us."

"You might've asked the boy involved to find out."

"That's not what we did first. As far as my friend was concerned, the less involved he was, the better. We did think about going to a coastal town ten miles south of us where we had heard that all kinds of vice flourished during the war, but we had both been in the town, and it looked normal so we didn't have the faintest idea where to begin. So we did what was logical for two bookish girls, we went to the library. Not to find an abortion mill, of course, but to find out more about abortion."

Then the rest of the story would come out as a tale of childhood adventure, exaggerated but with all panic and desperation drawn from it so that it was flat, like a cartoon. As Maureen told the story, Joann had a summer job at the library, though the truth was that she had worked there as a clerk two afternoons and all day Saturday for over a year. For some time Joann had been aware of a book called *The Science of Eugenics and Sex* kept behind the desk in a locked case among books with valuable color plates. In Maureen's version, Joann has never considered trying to sneak the book out by herself but decides that with the two of them, they could make a plan.

On Joann's regular Thursday afternoon shift she reports for work accompanied by Maureen. Unaware that Miss Bianchi, the inquisitive and kindly librarian, has spent her youth studying, pressing, and sketching California wildflowers, Joann asks her for the key to the locked case because her friend wants to look up a wildflower in the book with large color plates. According to Maureen, Miss Bianchi clasps her hands together with pleasure, retrieves the book herself, locking the case after retrieval, and, the ribbon to the key still in her hand, pores over the book with her, asking impossible questions like, "Was the capsule ovoid or subglobose?" While Maureen guesses at the answers to the questions, Joann hovers at Miss Bianchi's elbow, gesturing to Maureen to let the librarian turn the pages so she can seize the key the instant the ribbon is loosed—here Maureen sometimes makes her eyes as wide as she can to give the impression of how muddled she was by having to respond to the signals and answer the questions at the same time.

The story at this point changes from time to time because she has never known exactly what ruse Joann used to pry Miss Bianchi from her side. One version skips Joann entirely and has Maureen pretending to recognize the flower; by pure luck, one that happens to be common to the hills in midsummer. Then she asks for more information, thus persuading Miss Bianchi to allow a passive Joann to return the book at the same time Maureen lures the librarian into the stacks. Joann then returns the wildflower book and removes *The Science of Eugenics and Sex*, a ponderous black volume, and, according to plan, places it next to the collected works of Jane Austen.

"We chose this place," Maureen would explain, "because the A's were in a dark corner."

With her back to the entrance of the aisle, the pages of the book shadowed, Maureen checks the index for *childbirth* and then turns to the discussion where she gapes in horror at the pictures before she sees a reference to managing labor after an *abortion*. This clue sends her back to the index, where she finds abortion, and scrambling to the page—having first taken a look over her shoulder to make sure no one is sitting at the one library table from which she can be seen—she reads: "distinctly criminal" and "Various drugs are taken by women and too often their use results in death, or in dangerous sickness." She returns the book to the shelf next to Jane Austen and then shaking her head she whispers to Joann, "No help at all." Her story goes that then, of course, Miss Bianchi overhears her, comes forward, and pursues her with books on botany and wildflowers all afternoon.

She did not include the last part of the afternoon the first time she told the story because it did not seem important, and now she doesn't remember it at all. Joann, having sneaked *The Science of Eugenics and Sex* back to its place in the locked case, followed another avenue of research among the periodical indexes and stores of magazines in the basement, Miss Bianchi's training having been thorough. Eventually, her shirt damp from tension, her face pale, she came to the table where Maureen floundered, alone at last, behind a stack of biology and botany books and handed her a pencil, a notebook, and two news magazines, pausing only to point to the note she had written, "Pages 65 and 82." First placing the notebook so that no one could peek at what she was writing, Maureen took notes on the two articles in her round, careful handwriting, turning the magazine over to hide the topic every time anyone walked behind her chair. One, an article on an abortion mill in New York City, informed her that an operation cost $400. Another, an article on a patent medicine or salve the FDA had outlawed, told her that it was made of potassium iodide, iodine, and soft soap, and that it worked—though sometimes it was lethal. One girl had died from heart failure three hours after it was administered, and what others had died from was not mentioned by the article. She had returned the magazines to the desk and was reshelving the biology books when Miss Bianchi startled her, taking her by the elbow and whispering, her breath heavily scented with peppermint, "You have the satisfied smile of a successful researcher on your face. So nice to see young girls do something useful in the summer."

Joann remembers her descent of the library stairs in the late afternoon, the notebook she had provided Maureen in her hand. She recalls herself hesitating briefly at the corner opposite the mission before turning toward the town's business center where drugstores occupy three of the four corners. Although it has been a hot day, she feels cold, stiff, awkward, and she is not aware of passing Mrs. Lewis, who is entering Galetti Brothers' Market, or one of the mission priests, who is making his way back to the rectory from the post office, though each of them later asks, "Where were you going in such a hurry?" and she has to say, "When?" and then make up a lie. At Norton's drugstore, picked because her mother never went there, she can still hear herself blurt out to the older Mr. Norton, who is standing by the cash register in front of the prescription counter, "I need some potassium iodide."

"Are you asthmatic?" he asks raising his head slightly to see her through his bifocals.

"No," and she regrets saying this: "I fell and scraped my knee."

"You need tincture of iodine, then," he says, and shows her an amber bottle with a skull and crossbones in red ink on the label.

"Yes," she says firmly, handing him a dollar. But before he takes her money, he pulls a red-covered record book out from under the counter and tells her she must write her name and the purpose of the iodine in the book because it is poison.

Later, still cold, her heart pounding, her fingers awkward, she is trying to mix the bottle of iodine into a bowl with ivory flakes in it, a soap she foolishly believes she can make "soft." The white soap becomes sticky, reminding her of the consistency of the hamburger meat she has seen her mother mix up at the cafe, and it turns faintly yellow. The area around a hangnail burns slightly as she squeezes the mixture through her fingers, and her heart begins to pound at the idea that maybe the girls who had died—one of them in three hours—after using the paste had been badly burned first. But the sharp pain stops, and she tells herself it hurt just a little and for a short time and the flesh of her finger is only slightly red.

She also remembers a frantic search after she has become concerned she hasn't enough iodine in the paste. Checking the bottle's label for the strength of the solution, she perceives she has bought sodium iodide, not potassium iodide. In her mother's medicine cabinet she reads the labels on two patent cough medicines, but she finds none with potassium iodide. It is by this time almost seven. After hiding the bowl with the paste and the empty bottle of iodine under her pillow—her father is unpredictable, and can come home at any hour—she leaves the house, running, for downtown. She has almost a mile to go back to town and feels winded after half the distance, but she keeps on, a heavy pain in her chest and a sharp one in her side. Again at the central corner, she chooses a second drugstore, glancing first across the street in hopes that Mr. Norton is not peering at her out his window. She tells the clerk, her chest heaving, she needs something for asthma and her mother told her to buy something with lots of potassium iodide in it. The clerk retreats behind the pharmacist's high desk, confers, and a white-coated, curly-headed young man comes out to talk with her.

"That's a pretty old-fashioned remedy. We can do lots better nowadays," he says.

"But that's what my mother wanted."

He withdraws to browse among some large bottles filled with colored liquids on the shelves behind his desk. After a moment he pulls one down and calls out to Joann, "How much did she want?"

"The largest size, please."

She watches him pour a transparent yellowish liquid from the large bottle through a funnel into a smaller bottle. He turns to a typewriter, clacks out a few words, pastes a label on the bottle, and brings it to the counter for her. She looks at the label. "But it says hydriotic acid syrup," she protests.

"It's made with potassium iodide; this is how you take it when you loosen a cough."

"But does it have a lot in it?"

"If whoever has the asthma isn't better by tomorrow, send her to the doctor," he says, retreating again behind his desk.

At home it is past eight o'clock by the time she has the paste mixed up. When she was younger, she had made up a game to play when she was on her way to the dentist for fillings or to music lessons for which she had not practiced: *As long as I'm here, I'm not there.* By ignoring where she was going and what was going to happen to her, she could overcome her fears and be able to cross any threshold. Before this occasion she has always had someone to draw her over or force her over or applaud her over this threshold—her music teacher, or the dentist, or Maureen—but this evening she is alone with a slimy, sticky yellowish mixture, and her first thought when she realizes she is *there*, is that no one ever has to know whether she just throws this mixture down the sink instead of using it. No one will ever know that she is afraid of burning herself, or even killing herself. Calmed, relieved that she is going to be allowed to decide not to use the paste, she goes into the bathroom, takes off her underpants, and, sitting on the toilet with her legs spread, tries first a little dab of the paste at the opening of her vagina, and when the cold paste becomes warm, decides there is little burning. Then with the nozzle of an enema bag she shoves as much of the mixture from the bowl as she can into her vagina. She is frightened now because the nozzle scrapes her tender tissues—or is the mixture starting to burn? she wonders. But, "It's too late," she whispers, her heart pounding, and continues until she is all soapy and slimy.

Now and then in a nightmare she still feels that soapy, slimy, burning sensation, and her hands appear before her, slick and stained saffron.

Joann cannot remember how later that same evening she and Maureen argued on the phone. She'd described to Maureen how grateful she was for the help at the library, carefully veiling her language because she was convinced the operators were bored and listened in from time to time. "I'm feeling free for the first time in a couple of months," she said.

"I can't understand why. We haven't got anywhere."

"I'll let you know tomorrow if you're right."

"You're not doing anything tonight without my being there," Maureen said. She managed both question and threat in the one sentence.

"Why not?"

"You can't do that. What it said in the magazine."

"Why not?"

"You're always going off on these tangents by yourself, and then you turn around and expect me to follow."

Joann experienced momentarily an old childhood fear—that she would open her eyes alive inside her own coffin. "Do you really think this is a tangent? It's my life, maybe my whole life."

"That's what I mean. You could die. Tonight."

"How?"

"You could bleed all over."

"I'm not going to talk on the phone anymore."

"I'm coming over."

"No you're not. Besides, my mother just got home." Joann quietly put down the receiver.

Maureen's parents were already side by side in bed, her father with a mystery in his hand, her mother propping a large biography on her stomach.

"No," said her father. "You cannot spend the night with Joann. It's too late."

Her mother gazed at her face. "Is there something the matter?"
Maureen smiled and shook her head, "No."

"Have some hot milk before you go to bed," her mother said.
"You've been looking worried these days."

Maureen crashed at last into a restless sleep at four in the morning,
her visions of Joann lying in a pool of blood, the sensations of burning,
her uterus on fire, accompanying her into her dreams. By nine she was
knocking on Joann's door, and then the window of her bedroom, and
then going around to the back door and pulling its lock open in the
way she had learned as a child. When she entered the bedroom, Joann
was leaning against her pillows reading.

"Are you all right?" Maureen asked.

"Nothing's changed since yesterday, if that's what you mean. But
you shouldn't be here. If something is happening to me, if it gets into
my bloodstream, like with that girl, they'll arrest you for being an
abortionist."

Maureen had not thought of that possibility and it frightened her,
but still she said, "You're crazy. If you start to bleed all over, if your
period suddenly starts and won't stop, somebody has to save your life.
If I don't stay, I'm in trouble."

They argued for an hour, Maureen cross-legged on the end of the
bed. The rest of the day they spent lying side by side, Joann reading
Far from the Madding Crowd and Maureen trying to get interested
in *Aurora Leigh*. Occasionally Maureen asked, "Are you feeling anything?" and once in a while Joann got up, went into the bathroom,
and looked for blood, returning each time shaking her head, her eyes
averted from Maureen's. Every now and then they exchanged a
few words:

"Maybe it takes a while."

"It must, to get it into your system."

Late in the afternoon Mr. Ridley arrived home from a walk in the
hills and looked in on them. "I know you're both troubled, but it's not
necessary to feel that way," he said. "Your mother told me to remind
you to eat," he added, and then he left again. Without checking with
Joann, Maureen called her mother and asked if she could stay over.

That night in bed, lying curled on her side, her back against
Maureen's, her eyes open into the darkness, Joann thought, we have

not spent a night together since seventh grade, when we told stories until four in the morning to go with our spy game. Or was it the pirate game? Dolphin. Maureen's pirate name. Suddenly she was remembering clearly a conversation. She could almost, but not quite, hear Maureen's light, child's voice.

"Have you thought of your name yet?" she is saying to Maureen. "I'm Captain Terror."
"Dolphin, I already told you."
"You can't. It sounds like Hitler."
"Dolphin's not Adolph."
"Try saying it fast."
"Dolphin."
"I mean Adolph as in Adolph Hitler."
"We're not bad. That's what I mean. Dolphins are in the ocean and they're good fish, my mother said. They used to give people rides."

Joann heard Maureen take a deep breath, sigh. She felt tears fill up her eyes, begin to run down over her nose and onto the pillow. She reached for a tissue; Maureen had never heard her cry.
"Are you sick?" Maureen asked. She sat up and peered down into Joann's face. "Do you need a glass of water or anything?" She put her hand on Joann's face as if feeling for a fever.
Joann shoved her hand away and blew her nose. "No. Just nothing's happening down there. But my nose is running."
Early in the morning, when she had given up hope the homemade salve would work, Joann said, "We could, maybe, go to your mother. She might know what to do."
"I thought we already went over that. Remember?"
"But we were talking about just telling her I was pregnant. This is different."
"Well, I don't know," Maureen said.
"I always thought she was different from other people, more experienced, more intellectual maybe than the other people in this town."
"You didn't hear her fuss when Marilyn started going out with soldiers the last year of the war and coming in late. Or when Rosemary said she was pregnant and she was married. Don't make me laugh."

"What would she do if we just tried, or I...I could...I could go to her alone."

"First thing, she'd call your mother. Period."

Early in her separation from Refugio, Maureen had decided that she had been wrong, her mother might have helped. She had friends outside Refugio and would have known how to ask about abortions, maybe even whom to ask. She might, Maureen ventured to think, even have known girls who had had abortions in her own college days.

Nowadays Mrs. Lewis, who is almost ninety and living with her son, Bill, takes Amtrak down from Seattle to stay with Maureen in San Rafael. Maureen never has liked spending time with her mother, who has always been impatient with anyone not willing to act instantly. Bill is always having to go out and collect her from meetings in Seattle. Rosemary, who lives in Fresno, complains that if their mother sees a homeless person on the street, she has to stop and steer him to a hostel, whether or not he wants to go. Maureen has long ago given up expressing opinions about daily events to her mother when she visits, because she is always writing angry—though reasonable—letters to corporations, political organizations, magazines, and newspapers, and nags at Maureen to write also. Maureen remembers telling Joann when they were on the train to San Francisco that she was relieved to get away from everyone. It was the first real escape from home she'd ever made—at least the first escape from the guilty sense that she could have her mother's attention if she began trying to set the world right.

"All right, not your mother." Joann wondered whether, without telling Maureen, she might try it anyway. "There's no other adult I can think of except your father."

"But he's a judge."

"He'd know how to keep it secret then. I can't imagine him calling up my mother and—"

"Yes, but he'd get you to bring her to his office, and you'd all three have a chat. You haven't heard him on juvenile delinquents and children's courts."

"But I don't know anyone else to go to, Maureen. I could at least try. I mean I have to be brave."

"It won't do any good, I tell you."

"You're just afraid to have your parents find out anything. You're just as bad as me. You think they'll start treating you like a grownup instead of a little girl—isn't that it?—if they think you're associated with someone like me."

"Is that the reason you won't tell your own parents?"

"You know better than that."

After a while Maureen said, "I don't want to fight. Maybe we'll think of something tomorrow."

6

J O A N N

Immersed in immeasurable dark, and my nose is running—the cold
air. No tissue and so irretrievable. But not forever. A practical lady of
sixty years, I use my sleeve. When it trickles again, I stand up and
climb the path out of the black gulley I've been huddling in.

I could huddle at home tomorrow—phone the restaurant and leave
a message for Maureen. Tell her I'm sick. Lie. Risk having her break
my silence another day.

My path follows the southeast slope of a hill shaped like a breast
and named after the Virgin Mary—Nuestra Señora del Refugio. After
a steep climb it comes to a grassy bench where boulders once tumbled
from above and came to rest in synodic curves. I never forget the hill
is a volcanic cone, long extinct. I often reflect on what signs it might
give if the magma sealed deep below were to find a new crack, and
boiling, fuming, seething, fulminate to the surface again. The way I
like to imagine the process, it is excruciatingly slow, skin loosening
into wrinkles, hair drifting to grey. Great heaves go on for months, the
rigid boulders crack inch by inch, trickle in imperceptible increments
down the hill toward next century's housing. The birds would leave
first, black specks flying overhead, as if the soul of this valley were
dying. Then the deer, the raccoons, possums, skunks, and yes, of
course the cattle that graze in the pastures on the slopes above the
houses—all slip down through the gardens as the human inhabitants
grow old and die, their dogs, cats, even children fading into time as if
some Pied Piper were whistling the slow sounds of the earth. Those
old people who remain are unconvinced that any force could dislodge
them. No, that's wrong. They would remain because they have
nowhere else to go, no other hill where they can shelter because it
takes years and years to build shelters strong enough to live in.

A burrow, is that what we—I—have made of my life?

In spite of all the evidence, I am a practical woman, even here and
now as I climb, shivering, to an outcropping of granite in the dark.
That the stone faces the southeast, gathers the sun for most of the
day, and stays warm at nights is one reason for going there; take it as
another example of my practicality. The flashlight I carry is also practical, and I turn it on each step and handhold as I make my way
upward. Once long ago I surprised a snake, not a rattler, thank god,

but I didn't know that when my hand came down on it.

At the top of the path, where the rock flattens out, my breath is coming a little fast. I examine the grey surface with the beam of my flashlight and I toss, one by one, pieces from a small handful of pebbles to make the noise that will scare small creatures away. Then I sit down, leaning back against the warm rock. No one knows I come to this place, for I never climb up here by day and when I come at night I never tell anyone. I'm aware it's a bit dangerous. In spite of my cautious approach, I could fall, I could attract, with my practical flashlight, a predatory man. But I enjoy the prickly alertness I have to maintain. My head works with the pace of youth, which gives me the illusion of the peace of youth.

Or used to, for tonight I am staring out over the lights of the town waiting for the peace to come, and it hasn't. My nose has stopped running, I feel the warmth of the rock against my legs, I've stopped meditating on nightmare volcanoes, and I'm trying to attend to what I shall decide about Maureen. Instead, my thoughts circle, eddies of mud, whirlpools of sand, urgent reminders of the continuity between my flesh and the flesh of the earth. Maureen, what I remember of her—a stand of trees in thick fog—now you see one, now you don't, and you never know if the next one you see might not be the other side of the first one.

For several years I've caught myself trying to ignore change by refusing to observe what has changed, and this sin I must not commit again. I have changed, Gil has changed, Bobby Moss, god help him, has changed. Maureen has changed. Thirty years ago the valley where Refugio lies reflected the sky; I used to look into the center of a globe of darkness, scattered lights below, scattered stars above. I could, on nights when there was no moon, see the pattern as one continuous sky or one continuous town, and—because I loved to watch the darkness play mirror tricks on me and I couldn't bear the change when the night time surge of light bulbs blotted out the stars—I didn't look, or didn't notice, and sometimes I didn't come here. A mistake.

Thirty years ago, when I made the mistake of thinking I'd found my religious self, I would lie upon the rock, the words of a prayer upon my lips, "Our Father, who art in heaven," and—magically—translate myself to a world infinitely large and infinitely, lovingly small. Stars and human light. But now I haven't wanted to pray for several years. What I once believed made all the world sacred has turned out to be profane. The light of the world is about as luminous as processions of lights around the mission—too much light, too many rules, too many ideas made too much flesh—one hundred incandescent bulbs compared with a star. But these understandings I have also turned from. Can a whole life be a series of mistakes? Is this what Maureen wants me to tell her?

∞

For turning in a perfect paper one Friday late in May of 1948, Joann had been excused from her English final. That afternoon Miss Bianchi, working at her desk in the library, had lifted her narrow face, broken by a smile displaying pride and pleasure, toward Joann, who was reporting for work. "I hear you are to receive the Arbor scholarship this year."

"Yes, Miss Bianchi."

"We'll have to celebrate, then, of course."

Uncertain how to appear self-deprecating—the mode most adults seemed to expect of her—Joann replied, "But I have to pass my finals with good grades."

"Well then, we'll just have to arrange for you to take tomorrow off, so you can study."

She smiled gratefully at Miss Bianchi, who had described her once to her mother as an "angelic child." That evening she and Bobby planned a hike for Saturday up a canyon where she was sure the poppies and lupines were still in bloom. She hid her plans from her mother and next morning left the house wearing her jeans and carrying her lunch in a paper sack after both parents had gone to the cafe.

She remembers still the lie she told to Miss Bianchi, but she does not clearly recall the hour spent in Bobby's parked car, for it blends with many such hours. Now and then, even these forty-five years later, she tastes again the salty kisses and feels the sweet heavy ache of her belly, but that could have happened any time. Nor does she remember their walk up the canyon along the banks of a creek. But she remembers clearly and wonders occasionally about the lifelong repercussions of the moments when they had lain down side by side under an oak in grass so high that when she raised her hand above her head, the grass was still higher than she could reach. She remembers thinking, why not, why shouldn't I? as she unbuttoned her jeans and pushed them down her thighs, and she can still hear her own voice say, "Don't stop, I can't bear it if you do."

Sometimes she allows herself to recall this moment without internal comment, especially now when she and Gil have ignored each others' bodies for several years. Hers a scarred, thickened body, as broad at the waist as at the shoulders, unkempt, white-headed, careless of men.

J O A N N

If I lie down all the way, flat, I can fix my eyes and maybe my thoughts on the sky rising above the black mass of the Santa Lucia Ridge across the valley. Mistakes. Dad said it was a mistake to marry Gil. He didn't like Gil being Catholic. He cried at the wedding; the tears actually rolled down his cheeks. The priest, who had a gravy stain right where his collar met the black of his cassock, glanced over at him from time to time. Mom handed him a handkerchief.

When Gil and I were in Redding, I used to write to Dad about his crazy books. Buddhism and the nine steps—or was it eight?—it was so long ago. It was like dying, slowly, not to be able to catch what Dad was trying to tell me, and finally I had to make the process fast, and tell him I needed something present; I needed something like what Gil had, a tradition. It seemed so much more sensible. I needed someone who said he would love me forever and never leave me. I was so often trying to be sensible in those days I hardly recognize myself.

Paul Ridley sat in a booth at the back of the cafe, a thin man made even thinner by a heavy beard so long it seemed to pull him downward. He held a book, his arms outstretched and his eyes narrowed because he could not quite see the print without glasses and he refused to buy any. It was the same booth where he had sat with maps during the war, showing soldiers from the camps the astrological significance of what he had heard on the news the night before. The paint along the wall was no longer bright as it had been during the war. It was chipped, the wall scraped and spotted where food stains had been scrubbed. Joann leaned one hand on the table and awkwardly kissed his cheek. He didn't stir, nor did he move when Bobby walked down the passage beside the counter and extended his hand.

Joann had told her parents about Bobby Moss before she brought him to the cafe. "He's beautiful," she said. "And his eyes, they're soft and kind of sweet when he smiles."

"Is he a good student?" her mother asked, and Joann answered, "Yes," keeping back his excellence as a quarterback and a basketball forward. "He likes to talk about what his brother did in the war. He's very sensitive about that. We talk about history, books, things like that. Maureen Lewis went out with him last year."

"You've got time," her father had said.

"No, I don't."

"He's not the one." He had moved his head back and forth, his hair tumbling down into his eyes, no.

"They're going now," Mrs. Ridley warned from behind the counter. "They'll be late for the dance."

Mr. Ridley leaned his palms on the table and stood up, moving from the booth out into the passage. Though he was tall, he was slender, and Bobby hulked over him as they shook hands. "She's not your ordinary girl," he warned Bobby.

Mrs. Ridley ignored her husband; she often seemed to pretend he didn't exist. "It's not your fault," she said to Joann. "It really isn't."

Joann, her eyes filled with tears, seized Bobby's hand and left the cafe.

Joann hadn't gone out with boys during the first two years of senior high school. This puzzled the other girls because Joann fit their ideal of good looks: she had grown tall and she had a habit of sitting and walking gracefully so that her baggy sweaters made her look soft, and her long curly hair, now brushed into a neat roll, shimmered as she walked.

"You two used to be such good friends," a member of Maureen's new group said. "What happened?"

Maureen lifted one shoulder. "I don't know. I got interested in boys, maybe."

Her friends agreed. "Joann's too immature for boys."

Others said she had an inferiority complex, and a few, bent on carrying tales about her father, said Joann was afraid her father would get mad at her if she brought a boy to the house. One girl said her father was crazy and that was why Joann was too embarrassed to have any friends, boys or girls.

"Barry Farin was going to ask Joann to the prom, but he thought he'd better try to get to know her first. So he sat down next to her in the cafeteria and asked if she got the chemistry homework, and all she did was say yes, it was easy, and go on eating her apple."

"So he didn't ask her to the prom?"

"Are you kidding? And no one else'll ask her either. She's too much of a brain."

"Too tall."

Giggle. "Too innocent."

Giggle. "Too eth*eee*real."

Maureen's friend extended her arms as if flying. Everyone except Maureen laughed.

Maureen hadn't made any mistakes with Bobby. She and three of her closest high school friends all took boys to the backwards dance in the fall of their sophomore year, and by the spring all of them were going steady. Maureen had chosen Bobby Moss because she liked his willingness to express his opinions on subjects other than teachers and sports, she told her mother. She told her friends she liked his sweet smile and the way he kissed. Besides, his father owned the Ford agency, and he drove a bright red 1940 Ford convertible.

After they began going steady they took long drives into the country on the Friday nights he was free, holding hands, Maureen's head on his muscular arm, her half-open eyes watching his left hand spin the car around hairpin curves. Sometimes they drove as far as Encina. He made her feel comfortable and socially acceptable in the same way having wall-to-wall carpeting installed in her bedroom that year made her feel fashionable, and she had great affection for him. He seemed genuinely interested in learning about her family and how her sisters and brother always made her feel left out. Though he didn't read much himself, he liked to hear about what she was reading, and one glorious summer afternoon he listened to her read the whole set of Keats's odes. He taught her how to change the oil in the family car and how to throw a football and how to dance some of the jitterbug steps his older brother had learned in San Francisco when he had been in the navy during the war. She worked at getting him to talk about what it was like to play football and what he hoped to do when he finished high school. She tried to get him to take her fishing when the season opened, and her mother tried to get him to talk about what he thought of the atom bomb. Her father always went to bed before they came home from the show or their drives or a dance, so they spent an hour or so every Friday and Saturday night exploring how far Maureen wanted to go with French kissing and what her interpretation of the hands-above-the-waist rule was.

In the spring of 1947, their junior year, Maureen objected to his flirting with another girl. She cried. She got a B on a history test. She cut her hair to shoulder length and stared at the sharp ridge of her nose in the mirror every morning and evening. She tucked her blouses in more severely to show off her heavy breasts.

Bobby took her up to Corona Heights—where everyone parked on the first date or two—one April night, a Friday. He kissed her, lightly. He took her hand, he stared out over the city, and he said, "My mother wants me to see other girls, play the field."

Maureen bought a jar of the white, spicy-smelling lotion he used to keep his hair in place. She kept it open on her dresser for two weeks after they stopped going out together. On Friday nights she read books. On Saturday mornings she called several friends, trying to find a girl to go to the show with. She had little success at first because everyone else was still going steady. She missed going to the junior/senior prom—Bobby was going steady with someone else by the middle of May—and no one else showed any interest. Eventually she found one and sometimes two girls willing to go to the show on Friday nights. By June she had stopped looking at herself in the mirror and had begun to daydream about the kind of life she would lead when she left Refugio. She would never marry, she would have two dogs, she would live in a house filled with books. Sometimes on Saturday nights she baby-sat for Rosemary, whose husband had returned from the war and had been hired by the Bank of America.

J O A N N

I am becoming uncomfortable, there is a nipple in this rock slightly above my left hip. Could I have I pulled it into existence—flagellation, laceration, a bed of sharp rocks to atone for my mistakes? I'll just scoot over, hands flat on the rock, but first the flashlight in my lap. Damn, it's slipped; I can hear it rattling down the slope into the black depths of grass and scrub. I wonder if dropping the flashlight is a mistake for which I'll pay. Too bad. But Maureen, that's what I came up here for. Why am I rummaging in my own old boxes? Was it a mistake to break away from her? The only time I can remember her crying was on the phone that day. "What did I do?" she was sobbing. "Just tell me, please." And I hung up, burning myself, a shooting star, flaring out, seeking dark, silent waters.

I wonder what she looks like now. I hardly recognize some of us who drive past in cars or stroll down the street to disappear into the bank. Grey bouffant, double-chinned Dorothy. Maureen would not wear her hair like that. Russet curls, deep lines, velour jogging suit like Charlotte. Not the velour jogging suit, though she could dye her hair, not red, but blond. Jeans tight over a thickened stomach, plaid shirt, a thick bun like Jan, but Jan married a rancher. I can't recall their youthful faces. Layer after layer has covered them, layers as thick as clay. Can't recall Maureen either, even without the layers. The face peering down the well, the no-face, light behind it catching the fair hair, a halo of light: more symbolic than anything. I always had a sense of Maureen coming to help, to save. I had an explosive, a grenade in my hands once. I remember sand, we must have been at the beach, I can't remember how old we were. I wanted you to help me, but I was also, yes, I remember now, afraid you would see how afraid I was, so I pretended to be daring. I was always pretending to be brave for you, braver than you, that was the only way I could be.

In October of their senior year, Joann surprised everyone by asking Bobby Moss to the backwards dance, and he amazed everyone by accepting. People had thought he was going steady with a girl from a high school in another town, but Joann would not have heard that gossip. Some of the girls who had been out with Bobby Moss after he broke up with Maureen smirked. One raised her eyebrows and said, "I wonder what he sees in her?" after Bobby and Joann went to the movies together the next weekend.

Maureen, who had not gone to the backwards dance felt defensive and confused, for herself or Joann, she wasn't sure.

"He's not so bad," she said.

"You're telling me?" the friend replied.

"Maybe she helps him with his homework."

"I'll bet."

By Christmas everyone knew that Joann and Bobby were in love, not just going steady. Joann became instantly popular. She was surrounded by girls at the basketball games where they watched Bobby make one basket after another. She was telephoned before dances to find out what she would wear, consulted about what Bobby knew about whether Ralph or James or Leroy had said anything about a certain girl, sought after in the halls at lunch time and after school. Miss Lentz, the social studies teacher, invited her to join the group of senior leaders discussing ways that they as individual citizens could work for peace in the world—an after-hours propaganda course, actually, emphasizing how they would keep communism from spreading. Joann went to the discussions, held in Miss Lentz's crowded office with the one window facing east. She seemed to daydream through the conversations, her blue eyes either on Bobby or on the window where spring clouds drifted through the sky.

When she gave the valedictory address, she repeated much of what had been said in Miss Lentz's group, how the class of 1948 had a responsibility to make their highest aspirations reality by bringing peace to the world. The United States was the greatest and strongest nation in the world, made so by the moral fiber of their idealist youth, who three years before had won the war against the corrupt and barbaric nations of Germany and Japan.

Maureen had spent the year reading. She had begun with Shakespeare's history plays, gone on to Malory's King Arthur stories, and landed mid-January on *Sir Gawain and the Green Knight*. It was a short trip from there to the *Canterbury Tales*, and she fell in love with Chaucer, enchanting Miss Tynan, the English teacher, with her desire to learn Middle English. She read *Troilus and Cressida* all through May. The U.S. government teacher had a unit on the United Nations in May, and she wrote an essay on the knights of the Round Table. Listening to Joann's high-pitched voice in the auditorium on the day of graduation, she discovered that she was suddenly inflamed with a desire to take on responsibility for the peace of the world. Joann made it sound like a quest.

After pushing through the crowd of parents and black-gowned classmates in the hall after the ceremony, she reached Joann and said, "Great speech. It really was."

"Thank you." Joann looked bewildered.

"It made me feel like there's a real reason for going to college and getting things done."

Joann nodded, her eyes staring blankly. "I guess so. It was hard to write. I had a hard time thinking what to say." The corners of her mouth turned down.

Joann and Bobby were the focus of attention at the party after the graduation ceremony, though not in tandem. Perspiration from the effort of speaking had tightened Joann's curly hair, and it had left its smooth page boy, frizzing up around her face. She tugged at it nervously in the rest room, trying to wait out the congratulations and compliments of all the girls who had come in to put on makeup and chatter before the dance music began. When she came out at last, Bobby had already begun the first dance with another girl, and he continued with the same girl through the second and the third, while Joann leaned against the wall trying to appear indifferent. Maureen for a few minutes leaned against the wall next to her.

"Congratulations on going to Mount St. Mary's," she said. Joann's scholarship had just been announced that evening.

Joann opened her eyes wide as if trying to remember what it was Maureen had said and answer what she was expected to answer. "I guess so." Her voice was faint.

Her apparent inattention, or inability to hear, dampened Maureen's ability to think of anything else to say. Gazing out over the dancers, hoping for a couple to point out, conversationally, she saw only Bobby on the edge of the crowd. He had his cheek against his partner's cheek, holding her close in a series of turns. He is fun to dance with, was all Maureen could think of to say, and remained silent.

"We've been together since kindergarten," Joann remarked.

Maureen had no idea how to respond. For one moment she saw wildflowers covering a hillside and thought of Mrs. Ridley. "How is your mother?" Maureen asked.

When the party broke up, Bobby left Joann. Most of the class—girls who had dates and all the boys—were driving to the beach where a bonfire and beer party had been secretly planned. Maureen drove Joann and two other girls who had come to the party without boys home.

"Are you breaking up?" someone asked Joann.

"I don't think so," she replied. Maureen heard doubt in the silence.

"It's going to be cold tonight at the beach," the girl sitting next to her offered.

"And boring," Joann added, too fast, Maureen thought. Neither of the other two girls spoke.

Just as she pulled to the curb outside one girl's house, Joann said, "I know. Let's climb Refugio Mountain tonight."

"In the dark?"

"It's too cold and my folks won't let me."

It's joy I think I'm feeling, Maureen told herself, then said, "And we can wait for dawn at the top. I've got a blanket in the trunk. I can sneak into my house for shoes and sweaters."

"You're not going up in your good dresses?"

"Why not?" asked Joann.

"Why not?" echoed Maureen. She was already planning what she would tell her mother if she happened to meet her while she was for-aging: a perfectly safe trail, first, and second, Joann Ridley is going through a breakup and needs someone to comfort her. Third, and here she paused, for she could not articulate the need she felt for sharing again with Joann. She was excited—about what? There was Joann's speech about world peace, but that wasn't quite it, though she did intend to prepare herself for that mission as best she could. Something special about an arduous hike, waiting for dawn, exploring? As she pulled into the dark driveway of her house, the other girls safely dropped off and Joann in the front passenger seat, she repeated to herself what she could say to her mother. Just, it's perfectly safe and Joann needs a friend this summer.

At three o'clock on the afternoons she worked in the library during the summer of 1948, Joann adjusted the venetian blinds on the western side of the reading room. Each time she pulled one of the heavy cords, slowly, so as to be quiet and leave the patrons undisturbed, she turned her head to look down over her shoulder as the patterns of light on the dark tabletops narrowed then disappeared. One Saturday she noticed a man, thin, with a thick bush of brown curly hair over a narrow face, watching her. He was young, but definitely not her age, not a boy. The white shirt carefully rolled up on his forearms, the sharp angle of his jaw, the round, steel-rimmed glasses he wore, the wrinkles at the corners of his eyes, and the evidence of a carefully shaved beard under the skin of his cheeks made him look like a veteran. Some girls she knew dated the veterans who were attending the local college, but she had not. To her they were even more certainly another generation than to Maureen, with her older brother and sisters; they were as remote as the soldiers who had filled the streets during the war. Her mother had never let her come to the cafe when it was filled with soldiers waiting for the buses to take them back to camp. Her mother had said it cheapened girls to go out with these strange men, pointing out the heavy makeup, the overblown hairdos, the tight skirts of those who did. Once when she was sixteen she had gone to a dance at the college arranged by a school club, but she had stood at the side all evening watching. She couldn't understand how girls could dance so close to people they didn't know—some even kissed a little in darkened corners. The girls looked like the ones her mother had criticized during the war.

When the man came to the desk where she was checking out books at five o'clock, he introduced himself as Gilbert Henderson, a college student. Stiffly, he asked for her telephone number. She felt herself blush. She wanted to answer, "My mother doesn't let me go out with strange men," but dreaded sounding childish. Instead, too confused to think of a way to refuse, she assumed a manner she had practiced, playing games of sophistication when she was twelve. "Why do you want it?" Smile.

"Why do you suppose?"

"I can't imagine." Smile. The corners of her mouth felt strained.

For answer, he handed her a piece of paper and a fountain pen, and she wrote the number down.

"Why not go out with him if he calls?" Maureen asked.

"He must be at least twenty-five."

"That's younger than Bill. What are you going to do when you go away to school? There's lots of them there."

"How can I possibly want to go out with anyone when I've got this, this other problem?" She thought how strange it was not to want to be friendly with any man. Tears were stinging her eyes. Would it be this way forever? She could not bear Maureen seeing her cry.

But when Gil telephoned on Wednesday to ask her to a movie on Saturday night, she could think of no reasonable way to refuse. Or real reason to refuse, for that matter.

He wore slacks, a tweed jacket, and a necktie to the movie. She felt awkward in a dirndl skirt and blouse, flat shoes, and no stockings. The waist of the skirt was just the slightest bit snug and she felt nervous about that, pushing her hand down over her belly several times before he arrived. He complimented her on her hair, the long swoop of curls, and said she had the prettiest eyes he'd ever seen. "I like women who aren't afraid to wear their hair long," he said, reaching for her hand, which he tucked under his arm. Woman? she thought. Her cheeks burning, she removed her hand. He bought tickets for the loges at the Elmo, where no one from high school ever sat. He asked her, in sincere tones, how she liked her job. After the show, he walked her over to the Gold Dragon where they sat at a table near the window. He pulled a chair out for her. He asked her what her favorite courses in high school were, and she answered, watching the high school kids stroll out of the Islay Theater next door. Two or three waved hello; she wished they had not seen her. When Bobby, arm around a girl's waist, walked past, she was glad he had not turned his head to see her with someone so much older.

The next Tuesday Gil telephoned to ask her again, but she said she had a date for Saturday. "Friday then?" Yes.

On Wednesday he arrived at the library at four-thirty and waited until it was time for her to go home, then he drove her home. Thursday the same.

"What will I do?" she asked Maureen.

"Why do anything? You're not giving up dates forever, are you? Then why do it now?"

"I think he likes me a lot. He keeps talking about the kind of woman he wants to marry."

"Tell him a few of your crazy stories. That ought to fix him."

"Well one good thing, anyway, he always offers me a cigarette and when I take one, he pulls out his lighter. Just like in the movies."

The morning after her second date with Gil, Joann remembered the cause of the one major quarrel she'd had with Maureen: smoking. When they were thirteen and Joann had tried smoking, Maureen was convinced it meant she was ready to put on high heels, lipstick, and flirt with older boys, even soldiers. Joann had become so insulted at the accusation and had made so many accusations of her own that their friendship had broken apart, and they hadn't seen much of each other during their high school years.

This morning they were sitting on the back steps of the Ridley house. Maureen was staring out over the driveway at the grey boards of the shed where the rabbits used to live. Joann was twirling a glass ashtray that said Cafe Ridley against the cement, trying to control an urge to smoke again—the ashtray held four butts, three of them hers.

Each of them was smoking regularly by this time, had been since they were sixteen, hiding it from their parents. Maureen did it upstairs in her room where her mother never came. She had started after her sister Marilyn moved to San Diego to be with her husband, leaving a carton of Chesterfields under her bed. Maureen thought the smell made her feel less lonely. Joann had carried on defiantly for a week when she was thirteen. Then she was caught by her father, who noticed some were missing from the cafe's store. He was studying theosophy at that time, and told her how disappointed he was. He had thought she was an old soul—someone who had lived many lives on earth already and was almost ready to move on to another plane—but this careless pollution of her body proved him wrong. Joann stopped, then started again at the beginning of her last year in high school when he was spending long hours with a yoga teacher in Halcyon and her mother was running the cafe. She used to climb a tree way at the back of her yard above her old playhouse, the one she helped her father build, and smoke, usually with a book of poetry in her hand.

"Leslie Howard must have been about forty when I was dreaming about him," she said, lighting her fourth cigarette with a kitchen match.

"You mean the blond guy in *Gone with the Wind*? I don't remember you having a crush on him."

"It was when we started smoking and had that big fight. I'd seen him in a spy movie."

"The big fight. I can't remember anything about it except we had it and then I started flirting with Jack."

They were silent for a while. "The problem, I mean another problem," Joann paused pulling smoke deep into her lungs. "I mean, it's going to cost $400, the magazine said. I mean if I find someone to do it."

"How much have you saved from working?"

"About $300, but I need all of that for the fall."

"There won't be any fall if you don't use some. I've got $100 I can lend you. And Bobby, he should pay something. I mean, he's got to."

"But he doesn't even know."

"Then he'd better find out."

"No."

"You're being stubborn."

"I heard one time you could do it with a coat hanger, but I never could figure out how."

"I'd never forgive you if you tried."

"I could marry Gil."

Maureen made no comment, but struck a match, then another and another, blowing each one out as it came close to burning her fingers. "I heard one time there was a retired, you know, madam, living down behind Murray Elementary School."

"Who told you that?"

"I don't know, one of the Miller boys maybe. Anyway, they say people like that had certain methods. They had to, in that business."

"Do you remember which house?"

"No. I'm not sure they knew which one, exactly."

Joann put her cigarette out and stepped back into the house, heading for the bathroom. She shut the door, locked it, pulled down her underpants, and sat on the toilet. She did not urinate, but taking a deep breath, letting it out, she took toilet paper from the roll and wiped at the opening to her vagina. Then biting her lip, she looked at the paper and once again felt a coldness she identified as despair right below her heart—just a trace of clear and slimy mucous. Leaning forward to the basin, she ran water over the fingers of her right hand, then thrust one finger up as far as it would go into her vagina. Withdrawing it carefully, she looked at it. No streaks of blood. She had been checking herself this way several times a day for six weeks, and there never was.

On the way back outside, she thought about telling Maureen that she kept visualizing her uterus as wrinkled tight like a fist in its grip on her and she was folded over and over and over upon herself. But she said, "I thought I felt something, and I just went in and checked."

"Sometimes you miss a period for other reasons. Though I suppose you know whether there is a reason, usually," Maureen suggested.

Joann felt a surge of hope. "Was that something Rosemary said?" As a child she had relied upon Maureen's reports on Rosemary and Marilyn to provide her with information on everything female from fashion to physiology.

But Maureen, innocent of Joann's expectations, often carried information from magazine and newspaper reading or just made things up and let Joann think the material had come from her older sisters. "Yes," she said, and added, "But of course you have to ask a doctor. They have tests to be certain you really are pregnant."

"I can't go to a doctor here. Everyone would find out."

"We could go up to Encina."

J O A N N

It's about three o'clock in the morning. Fog has curtained both town and sky, and the rock feels damp now. One knee has gone stiff; I'll have to move awkwardly and extremely slowly so it won't give way on me. Damn it for losing the flashlight. I concentrate on the pitch of the path, the feel of it under my feet, don't slip, down into the oak glade now, where strangely it is lighter than up in the fog itself.

No lights in the house. Gil when he returned from his meeting must have assumed I was already asleep. Feel my way in through the door, into bed with my shirt and pants still on, my feet so cold I'll never get them warm, and here is Maureen again. I suppose I will really have to see her. I cannot possibly tell her my mistakes—it would take all day—I can't even remember all of them. A general confession, like when I first took the church seriously. "Is it a sort of autobiography?" The priest, that fat blond Irishman, answered, "You could see it as a summing up of the kinds of mistakes you usually make, what leads you into them, how you think you can improve, and so forth." That was easy, I'd made only two—no three—mistakes by then.

7

Occasionally Joann relives the night after she and Maureen had driven north to see a doctor in Encina. For the first time in her life she hadn't slept at all. She began to understand how solitary she was, what a shadowy, foreign place the world was, flat, grey, like a movie where she knew none of the people, but they all knew her, and the real people, the ones she had once loved, sat comfortably pink and wrapped in yellows, blues, greens, somewhere just beyond her sight. At the stillest, longest part of the night, between one and three, she had contemplated running away (but where would she go?) and the alternative, killing herself. She rehearsed the ending of *Anna Karenina*, and with tears soaking her sheet, mentally threw herself onto the train tracks, saw the great black front of the engine bearing down on her, felt the seconds of shrinking from pain, the fierce roar, then the terrible pain of being crushed, her arms first? her legs? At three she rose to go to the bathroom where she hunted through the medicine chest for the phenobarbital her mother took for high blood pressure, but it wasn't there. At five in the morning, lying on her side, knees drawn to her chin, she began to cancel events that had happened. She began with the trip to Encina.

If she hadn't told Maureen, being pregnant would not be real. She could have worried all summer and never found out for sure. She could have had whole hours, maybe days, of pretending she was in another game. She would never have gone to the doctor in Encina.

Maureen, that same night, curled up with her head under her pillow saw exactly how she was to blame for humiliating Joann and wondered if she would ever get over her urge to pose as an authority. When she said women might miss periods for other reasons, she was relying on what she guessed after reading a short story about a young wife hoping to please her husband with a baby. She really didn't know about her sister's periods or her pregnancy or what her sister might have noticed after she'd begun sexual intercourse. Rosemary had married a soldier from Camp Roberts she had known for six weeks, and when he had been sent to Oregon, Rosemary had followed him, and then she had come home and all Maureen knew was that she spent a lot of time sewing in her room, and seemed to need it because she was outgrowing her clothes. Not until she was four or five months along did Rosemary

tell anyone, and by that time her husband was in Italy with
the army.

"It's just I didn't think about those things," Maureen explained to
her lunch group once. Her friends were skeptical that she could be so
ignorant. "When Rosemary came home, let me see, I was in the eighth
or ninth grade. I was spending most of my time reading." "Reading
what?" "You're not going to believe this. Tennyson's *Idylls of the King*."
"What?" "You know, those long poems about King Arthur and
his knights."

"Oh yes," said one woman. She was ten years older than Maureen,
and in her day the *Idylls* had been required reading in high school.

A younger woman asked, "But how could you not think of these
things, as you call them?"

"Say sex, not things," said the older woman, flatly. She liked everyone to forget she was older. Everyone laughed.

"Didn't you think of things like keeping boys under control so you
wouldn't get pregnant and so forth?" the younger woman went on, not
quite as earnestly as she had begun.

"Sure I did. In the eighth grade I was sure that if I let Jack Ceedar
kiss me I might get pregnant," said Maureen.

In the movies, a woman who thought she might be pregnant went
to a doctor. After he examined her, a process withheld from the movie
audience, he spoke to her in an office where, fully dressed, she received
the news that she was going to become a mother. There was a variation
on this: the woman did not suspect she was pregnant and fainted during
a dramatic scene with her boss or her mother. When she woke up a
doctor surprised her with the news.

By the time she was fifteen, Maureen had read in a book just
exactly what happened and what their parents felt, physiologically,
when babies were conceived. She also knew that missing a period
might mean you were pregnant, but she didn't remember where she
had read this. Of course, she had also heard girls gossiping about
someone quizzed by her mother because she hadn't bought sanitary
napkins for a couple of months. She must have understood when she
heard them, for she certainly did not spend time trying to work it
out—the connection between the whispering about missed periods

and what the book said about blood and erectile tissue, eggs and sperm, and how the uterus acted as a cushion for the new life entering the world. Then in her senior year in high school everyone was required to take the class called Senior Problems where they saw a film about what happened to teenagers who had to get married because the girl was pregnant. It occurred to Maureen that maybe in the class discussions Miss Flaherty had answered a question: no, missing a period didn't always mean you were pregnant.

"You just get the doctor's name out of the phone book, and then you tell them you need a checkup," Maureen said when Joann looked hesitant about how to arrange the visit. The Ridley family rarely went to a doctor, and Joann had not seen one since she was ten.

"I'll say I'm Mrs. Moose," said Joann. "I've just come into town."

"And you live on Yellowstone Way."

"Seriously. We have to get a real street in Encina or they'll know it's phony."

They had worried at first about how to make the phone call at all, since they could not use a pay phone or the nurse would know they were calling from Refugio as soon as the operator came on the line and said, "That will be forty cents for three minutes please," and the coins went jangling in. Then Maureen said they would just have to take a chance using her parents' phone, hoping that when he paid the bill her father would think her mother had called Encina for the political campaign she was working on.

They waited until Mrs. Lewis had left the house for the afternoon before they went into the den where there was a telephone. Maureen poured them two glasses of lemonade, and they sat on top of the desk in the den, cross-legged in their shorts. Maureen, who could make her voice as deep as a man's, gave the number to the operator, then handed the receiver to Joann. She bent her head against Joann's, pale blond against brown, her ear on the receiver so she could hear too. Everything worked. The appointment for Emily Richardson was for two o'clock on Thursday. When the nurse asked Joann for her address and telephone number, Maureen had a moment of panic, but Joann knew how to play her part. With only ten second's pause, the kind people make who are not attending and have to be brought back to reality, she said, "35 Auburn Road, 1685-W."

That evening Maureen asked permission to borrow her mother's car Thursday afternoon. They did not worry much about having the use of the car because Maureen's mother was spending most afternoons that summer typing campaign letters for the Democrats down at her father's office, and Maureen had been using the car most of the time for trips to the beach. This time they decided to tell Mrs. Lewis where they were really going, in case they had a breakdown or a flat tire. If discovered, they would have a cover story—the small department store in Encina was having a sale of underslips, and they thought it would be a good chance for both of them to see what was around in other towns for their college clothes. On Wednesday they withdrew twenty dollars from Joann's college bank account to pay for the visit and twenty dollars from Maureen's to pay for the underslips they would have to buy. The only thing they had not been able to manage was the wedding ring they felt Joann had to have.

Early Thursday afternoon they sat side by side on the plush car seat, Joann dressed in a pale blue dirndl sprinkled with tiny white flowers and a sleeveless blouse buttoned up to the neck. Maureen was wearing a cotton plaid dress. Both wore pale beige stockings and Joann white sandals with heels. Maureen drove without shoes, her long thin legs slightly separated as she pushed her left foot down, changing gears and keeping up speed on the steep grade north of town.

They had driven through the pass at the top of the grade and had curved around behind the ridge into a valley. Maureen slowed down passing through the village of Las Virgenes, then without warning pulled the car off the highway to a stop just short of a gas station.

"I'm sorry. I almost forgot." She rummaged in the black purse she was carrying, an old one of Marilyn's borrowed to make her appear older.

"Here." She dropped her mother's engagement ring into Joann's palm. She had sneaked it from the drawer where it was kept and forgotten, too small for her mother since before Maureen's birth. She had sneaked it before, long ago, for games with Joann, who recognized it and knew instantly what it was.

"It fits me now." Her voice was so faint Maureen could hardly hear her.

In the doctor's small waiting room at two o'clock they sat side by side on a hard brown leather couch. Every time Maureen reached forward to a coffee table where the magazines rested, the legs of the couch skidded a little on the beige-and-red linoleum floor. An old man with a cast on his arm smiled at her whenever she looked up from her magazine. She wondered whether he knew her, maybe had seen her in her father's office in Refugio. A woman so heavily pregnant she could hardly hold her three-year-old in her lap read softly from a book of nursery rhymes. Her little boy stared at Joann instead of at the pictures in the book, his thumb in his mouth, his heels in scuffed white ankle-top shoes kicking his mother's leg.

When Maureen's eyes were on the magazine, she could see Joann's left hand clenched knuckle down in her lap, hiding her ring finger, the arm not moving, not even to turn the page. For a second Maureen envisaged her with the protuberant belly of pregnancy, then retreated, as if she'd walked in on her in bed with someone or caught her eating some loathsome food.

After half an hour or so, the nurse called, "Mrs. Richardson." Maureen was momentarily startled when Joann arose to follow a white dress down the corridor behind the desk. The old man grinned again, more intently it seemed, and she determined to read the article she had found in *Woman's Home Companion* about women's basic need to feel dependent on men. One of the women used as an example went out to work like Rosemary, leaving a baby-sitter with her children, but found that she was really happier at home with less money. There was a psychological quiz running down one side of the page, and Maureen took it, answering as if it were for Rosemary.

Half an hour later Joann, accompanied by the nurse, stopped at the desk. Maureen noticed her blouse was not quite tucked in at the back and that her cheeks were faintly pink.

"Just a minute, I'll get you a kit—those vitamins and so forth—just in case. They're free, compliments of the drugstore."

"I'd like to pay," Joann said in her little girl's voice.

"Oh, we bill you, and—just a minute, let me see—in cases like this the office call is part of the price of delivery."

"I better pay," Joann insisted. "We might be moving one of these days."

It was hot in the car. "There's another test. He took blood for it, but he could feel it. It's there."

"Feel it? Are you kidding? How could he feel it?" Maureen had seen pictures of embryos, and they were just too small for anyone to feel through the stomach wall.

With the windows of the car down, her hair blowing in the hot summer air, Joann shouted at Maureen, "With his hand, what do you think?" She was angry, near tears. "He puts his hand up there."

8

MAUREEN

I wake at five in the morning, startled momentarily by the blackness and stuffiness of the room. I'm accustomed to the sun shining through tree branches onto my blanket when I wake. Or, if I wake in the middle of the night, to the faint glow of street lights and city lights reflected in the sky. My eyes wide open against the dark, I see that pale grey is edging the motel curtain. Then I recall where I am and without moving toe or finger consider my plans for the day. I'll walk, I'll eat breakfast. I'll meet Joann. She'll come—I'm sure she will, or at least send her body. Together with a script? If she does, how will I break through? Not by thinking "break through." What's happened to all the wisdom and sensitivity I've gathered to carry me through my old age?

For a moment I stretch my back and leg muscles, still stiff from that awful couch at Sheila's house the night before last. Today I'll probably be too tired after lunch with Joann—I'll have to stay in Refugio one more night. I'll talk to the desk clerk after breakfast. Nothing at home but a committee meeting tomorrow afternoon. I'm just about to turn on my side and thrust my legs over the edge of the bed when I remember Sheila's not-quite-hidden concern at my confession that I plan to run for city council in the spring.

"You'll be so tied down if you win."

"I plan to win."

"A city council's no place to carry on crusades."

"What about Berkeley? They condemned apartheid in South Africa and declared themselves a nuclear-free zone. What about something as positive as rent control? The city council is a good pulpit."

"In Marin County?" She giggled at the idea.

"What's so funny?"

"Seriously then. You always think everything's great or you're going to fix it, no problem. Presto chango, Maureen's here!"

"Why, that's just not true." It has never occurred to me that a child might observe, then judge me. I have always assumed both Nancy and Sheila would see me the way I see myself. "That's your view of me. I thought you knew me better than that. I'm a very practical person, and I've had enough responsibility in my life to know you don't win every battle."

"This isn't easy for me to say." Sheila paused and I prepared to debate. Unlike my concern about saving water, this was not a laughing matter. "People are always able to lead you into some unreal place, where everything works just because you've given your all to make it work. Even when you haven't won, you think you've at least taken a few prisoners. Have you ever felt helpless, really helpless?"

"Of course I have, a lot of times." But only because of my age and the narrowing of the range of choices, I should have added. But I would have lost my point then, wouldn't I? "I'll admit, when I was younger I thought I could fix everything, but you didn't know me then. And optimism is not a character flaw," I added.

As I prepare to take off on my daily walk, I muse on the term *character flaw*. It's an old-fashioned concept, no doubt thought up when people considered character as one whole piece of you, like your nose, and a flaw was, what? Like a bump on it? Nowadays it's all in the flow from synapse to synapse, and what is it we call it? A personality disorder? A negative behavior pattern?

If someone had asked me forty years ago what Joann's worst character flaw was I'd have said without the slightest hesitation, and I could sound really judgmental, "She takes too many chances." But even while the words were coming out, I'd be telling myself I missed some quality, something essential—whatever it was that made it *seem* like Joann took crazy chances, when maybe, inside herself, she wasn't.

That doesn't make much sense, Maureen. What was my biggest flaw at the same age? Ages? Forty years ago I would have answered, "Irresponsibility," though I knew that was just not true. Fact is, I wanted to be free of all the responsibility I took for everyone, even for pollywogs, now I think of it. So I made sure it *seemed* to people and pollywogs that I couldn't care less what happened to them.

Accordingly, maybe there is someone who said, it *seems* like Maureen is irresponsible, but maybe, inside herself, she isn't.

So here I am, beginning my walk. Sunny, swift, and honest, forthright and, at least this morning, responsible Maureen, striding (more or less) down Valencia, contemplating what? Love. Yes, love. Was I really in love with Joann that summer? Curious, if she'd been a boy, I'd probably answer that question, Yes. Because the way I felt about her that last summer was the way I was expected to feel about boys: one, yearn to be with him; two, be happy and excited when in his presence; three, talk with him for hours on end; four, admire him infinitely; and five—go lightly on the sex. Except I desperately wanted to help her, and I did wish she hadn't taken risks and had stuck to the rules and then I wouldn't have had to be responsible for her.

And right now the rule is that I'm supposed to be concentrating on what I'm seeing here and now, and obviously I'm not. What do you think of Refugio? Joann will ask, and I'll have to tell her I walked all over, seeing nothing and doing character analyses. Well, the railroad tracks still cross over the street in the same place, I'll tell her, and the Ford agency is still where it was after the war, but everything else this end of town has changed. That is, I recognize the buildings but the shops are different.

No, not the Ford agency—it's the Moss Motor Company, same building. I might as well ask her how Bobby is these days. Do they bump into each other on the street? And what do they say to each other when they do? If only we could laugh about some of the things that happened, like the night I persuaded you to talk to him and then couldn't leave you alone and popped up between you like a computer's help message. Laughter. Did you send me away because you foresaw the possibility of laughter forty-or-so years in the future?

I'm turning up a street that used to be called Seeker. I've decided to go this way partly because the hill is steep, therefore good for me, and partly because I want to see Murray Elementary School, which nestles—used to nestle?—just where the top of the hill slopes down. Actually, it was what the others didn't like about Joann that made me wish during high school we could be friends again. Her strange father, for one thing. Her way of telling about books and movies until we could turn them into games. The imaginary questions, conflicts, and challenges she was always thinking up to take the place of the real problems everyone wanted girls to be ignorant of. The risks she took, these and her imaginary undertakings allowed me to make plans. I've really always liked making plans.

I remember now that on the way to Encina to see a doctor, Joann had said, "I'd rather not know. Until a doctor tells me absolutely I'm pregnant, I have hope."

"But we can't make plans unless we know," I said.

I am at the top of the hill when I recall this exchange—it jumps suddenly into consciousness—and I consider the possibility that Joann's true, deep-down flaw wasn't that she always took crazy chances, but that she refused to make plans. Every girl has to learn to think ahead; it's part of survival. Like taking care when you go out at night, making sure your car's in good order when you go on a trip, using birth control, bringing tampons in your purse. Thank god that's a worry I don't have any more.

As a child Joann used to make Maureen angry when she refused to yield to interruptions. If Maureen came over when Joann was reading a book or listening to a radio program, she would have to wait until the chapter was finished or the program was over before Joann would play. Sometimes she went home, and Joann didn't notice. Mrs. Ridley used to say, "She's just too intense," or sometimes, "She's just too imaginative." Maureen never believed these were good excuses. She thought it was selfish, and often told Joann so, and Joann, with perfect sincerity, would apologize and then do it again.

Not many people noticed this fault. At school most teachers appreciated Joann's ability to stay fixed upon her work for much longer than anyone else. Outside of school, she seemed mildly irresponsible to most adults. She might keep off the grass if there was a sign and maybe not even put her finger on wet paint—she had an unbending way of walking right past this kind of temptation, a kind of stiffening of the back, and a holding of her head slightly tilted away, as if she were too dignified to get her hands dirty—but only if she was not at play. Nothing would be permitted to interfere with her imaginative play, when no rules not in the game mattered. She might run or sneak through anyone's yard, balance herself on others' trees, fences, ridgepoles, smear herself with mud, draw on the pavement in front of others' houses, start fights in the school yard and out, as long as it served the game she was playing.

To Maureen's older sisters, Joann was unreliable. "A spoiled brat," Marilyn called her. Rosemary sat Maureen down one afternoon upstairs in her bedroom so Marilyn wouldn't interfere. "Don't you have any other friends you really like?" she asked, and, "If she really liked you, she wouldn't keep on reading when you come over. You were supposed to go the show, so how can you go, if she keeps on reading? She's not fair to you," she said.

Maureen was embarrassed Rosemary had found out about the failed plans for the show. She worried Rosemary might think she cared, when she didn't. She was used to Joann, and if she had wanted for sure to go to that movie she would have asked someone else to go with her. So Maureen shrugged and frowned and said, "Can I go now?"

Rosemary continued. "This is serious," she said, looking solemn. Inwardly Maureen squirmed, but she made her face serious, her eyes attentive.

"What were you kids doing down on Valencia Street after dark the other day?"

"I don't know. What day do you mean?"

"The day you were half an hour late for dinner. I didn't tell Mom where I'd seen you, but I almost told Dad."

"We must have been on the way home from Camp Fire." Maureen knew they were not, but said this anyway.

"I saw you following a bunch of soldiers who got off at the bus depot."

They had been following three soldiers. Maureen had been a bit nervous, but they were playing a game of spies then, day after day, and they had a theory that an Italian butcher was sending messages to the Japanese. One of the soldiers might have been the messenger, so Joann had said when she heard his foreign accent as he got off the bus. The three had not boarded the army bus that would ordinarily have taken them out to the camp. She had wanted to get close enough to hear, but the soldiers had turned into a bar just as the girls had managed to catch up to them. Joann had slipped inside the open door of the bar, but a man on his way out had told her she had no business there, and had taken her arm and put her out. Maureen wondered if Rosemary had seen that much.

"We didn't," she said.

"I'm telling you this because you could get into big trouble doing things like that."

Maureen's skin felt itchy and tight, the same way it had when Rosemary noticed her breasts had begun to grow and said she was going to have the curse soon.

"Only cheap girls go into bars."

"So what?"

"You ought to tell your friend Joann about that."

Rosemary could not tell she had already won. She pressed her point. "And haven't you seen in the paper about the girl who got raped by a soldier just the other day?"

"What's that mean?"

"Sexual assault." Rosemary lowered her voice as if the whole family were standing outside the door listening.

Maureen knew how to take revenge. "What's sexual assault?" she asked in her loudest voice.

"You'll have to ask Mother if you don't know."

This was the end of the discussion, though not the end of the spy game. Maureen and Joann did look up *rape* in the dictionary, learning little more than they already knew from increased attention to the newspapers. Eventually, some well-placed eavesdropping on the ninth grade girls after gym class told them what they wanted to know. All the same, Joann could not be persuaded to give up the case of the Italian butcher. They argued day after day as Joann tried to plot an elaborate scheme to sneak into his house one afternoon and Maureen—unhappy about feeling she had to be sensible—tried to dissuade her. They still hadn't settled their argument when they quarreled about smoking and then let their friendship die. Maureen never connected her conversation with Rosemary and that final quarrel with Joann, though when Joann had confessed she was smoking, she experienced the same feeling she had felt when Rosemary talked about "cheap girls."

Maureen's tendency as a child to think ahead, encouraged as it had been by a mother who allowed her independence—but always required an accounting—had been considerably strengthened when she was twelve and her periods began. She was one of the women who had severe cramps with menstruation, the kind of cramps she later realized were as bad as labor, minus only the wrenching back pains.

She began to menstruate a full year before Joann. Her sisters had been open about having "the curse," so open that Maureen had looked the word up in a dictionary when she was seven, and then, puzzled and disturbed, had gone to her father about the problem. Should he take steps to save Marilyn and Rosemary from whatever evil was coming to them? He puzzled her even more by behaving as if he was a little embarrassed. "This is something you should take up with your mother," he said. Her mother was out at a book club that evening, so Maureen couldn't say anything to her, and the next morning everyone overslept and Mrs. Lewis was so rushed she pulled Maureen's hair three times while undoing the rag curlers. Maureen spent a total of twenty hours thinking that her sisters—and eventually she, Maureen herself—would live on this earth under some evil eye, and no one in authority, like a father, could do anything about it. Her dreams that night had clothed her sisters in long white robes with sashes, reminiscent of the muslin togas they wore for Latin Club dinners, but had added tall hats like those of the witch Mombi in *The Land of Oz*, at that time her favorite book. At school she missed two problems in subtraction drill, and Joann got one star more than she did on the class achievement chart, and though that seemed to be curse enough, it didn't compare with the possibility that one day soon her sisters would be snatched away. They might be turned to stone or wood and never move again.

When at last Mrs. Lewis explained carefully, with diagrams of the uterus and ovaries, Maureen thought the picture her mother drew looked like a cavern shaped like the mask of a sheep with big curling horns. Her mother also said it wasn't really a curse at all, but that when it began she would feel it was a bother, but not much more than that. She didn't really know how the word *curse* got started. She would have to look it up and then she would tell Maureen, but she never did. Gradually, the idea of a dreadful future disappeared from Maureen's view into boredom. But she still had the nightmares.

When her periods did start, she understood the second time why it was called "the curse": the pain, of course, but the embarrassment it caused too. Not only did she suffer endless nights wrestling with hot water bottles and struggling to keep aspirin down long enough to get it into her bloodstream, but she had to hide the paraphernalia in her closet, the carefully rolled up and bagged balls of blood and paper in wastebaskets. One night early in 1942, just a few months after her periods began, she tried to overcome the pain by turning on the light and reading in bed, the hot water bottle packed hard against her belly. She had no idea what time it was when the telephone rang downstairs over and over again. After a while the door to her bedroom opened unceremoniously, and her father appeared to ask her what she thought she was doing. "Just reading," she said, too embarrassed to tell him she was in pain because of menstrual cramps. "Don't you know there's a war on," he scolded. "They telephoned here to say we were breaking the blackout rules. The Japanese are off the coast." He had already turned off her light. With his last words he shut the door and she heard him descending the stairs, his slippers going scuff, scuff. She rolled herself into a ball and opened her mouth against her knees, wishing she could scream. She would welcome the Japanese if it would stop her pain.

Planning began soon after this incident. If she had term papers or book reports due the day after she expected cramps, she had to plan to finish her work early. If she hoped to go to a football game or a dance, she had to count out the days ahead to see whether she would be able to go.

She rarely talked about her periods or her cramps, just said she had an upset stomach. That's what girls said when they had to stay home from school because of cramps. The school nurse never raised an eyebrow when those with that excuse went to her for readmittance slips. Maureen was embarrassed, though, when she had to miss school every fourth Thursday and present herself and her readmittance slips to male teachers.

Mrs. Nevins, the young, married physical education teacher at the junior high told all the girls in the ninth grade that cramps were in their heads and that maybe those who had them were suffering from an unhealthy focus on another part of the body. In any case, people like Maureen should drink plenty of water and not let the pain keep them from pursuing their normal daily activities. Mrs. Nevins did let her pupils stay in their regular clothes instead of changing into gym shorts if they asked for an excuse, but Maureen never asked for this privilege. She was always too sick to go to school.

She never told Joann she had started to menstruate, preferring to behave as if the days of childhood extended indefinitely in spite of the changes in her body. Once, before she had learned to plan, her period began while they were at the afternoon movies. She felt a funny sticky sensation in her underpants as she wriggled in her seat, then went to the rest room, and sure enough, the blood had started. She'd spent all her money on two Milky Way candy bars before the movie, and had no money for the dispenser. She went back into the theater and asked Joann to lend her a nickel.

"What for?"

"Do you have to know everything?"

"No, but I don't have one anyway."

"I've got to go home."

"Why? This is a good movie. I'm not going with you."

"I've got to go."

In the lobby Joann grabbed her arm. "You can't go now. Are you sick or something?"

"My stomach hurts."

Joann walked her to the cafe, sat her down in an empty booth, and asked her mother to call Maureen's mother. Later she called to find out how Maureen felt and the next day said she herself didn't feel so well, she must have caught the flu also. Maureen didn't tell her what had really been the matter until one day not long after Joann's period started.

When her elder daughter began to have cramps at the age of twelve, Maureen felt helplessly depressed for days. "Why does it hurt so much, Mommy? Please hold my hand, make it go away," echoed in Maureen's consciousness long after Nancy was up and about. Darkened rooms, hot water bottle, aspirin, vomiting. Doctors who said there was nothing physically wrong, other doctors who said cheerfully, "It will go away as soon as she has a baby." How can a girl accept herself, her own body, when it does this to her every twenty-eight days? she asked herself. To Nancy she said, "Well, everything does some good; it helps to teach you how to plan." "How?" asked Nancy, who became a rebellious skeptic, it seemed from that moment. "Girls never win at anything," she said.

M A U R E E N

I cross Pacheco Street, glancing down the rows of camphor trees that arch over the pavement, then turn my gaze forward, to where the kindergarten and first grade wings of Murray Elementary School should be, a short block away. The school is changed, I decide, and then walk a few steps forward: No, it's gone. I turn back. I refuse to view this new building, whatever has come to take the place of the school.

I wonder which house it was where I thought there might be a retired madam. One afternoon we did go, didn't we, and ring door-bells? Joann was certain she had spotted the house—one with curtains pulled across the windows and an old, square-topped black Lincoln in the driveway—and she insisted on going to the door herself. She was going to pretend to be a reporter for the *Bulletin* and ask for an interview about prohibition days. A woman wearing several rings on her fingers did answer the door, heard her story, and just shook her head no, then closed the door. She was quite polite, Joann said, but didn't seem at all interested in discussing prohibition, so she couldn't have been the madam.

In the bedroom in San Francisco Joann played solitaire one night. Maureen, waking up once, could see the yellow wallpaper with white sprays of tiny flowers above Joann's hands and, under the light on the dressing table, the surface where Joann was laying out the cards again and again.

"Why are you playing solitaire?" she murmured when she noticed the clock said three-thirty.

"Because I can think and not think. Because I keep thinking I might just win. But I never do."

When she recalls this moment, Maureen can still hear Joann's voice, lilting. As if the words had turned into a lullaby.

They were playing games with rules, the summer of 1948. Cards or board games, usually, but sometimes hopscotch when they were alone together, and once when Maureen found an old bag of marbles they drew a circle and tried, but they couldn't remember how the game went, whose turn was lost, which marble was taken.

Once, at the beginning of summer, just after they had recovered their old friendship, they were reaching for the same book in the city library, and Maureen said, "Do you remember when we played pirates?"

"Vaguely," Joann replied and let the subject drop. Sometimes in later years Maureen recalled having been hurt by this response.

Another afternoon before Joann told Maureen about being pregnant, they had driven to the beach with Wendy, someone Maureen felt sorry for because she was so tall and heavy. Wendy had brought a deck of cards. As soon as the blanket was spread, she insisted that they all play hearts. After a while two other girls they hadn't seen since graduation joined them.

"How's Bobby?" one of the new girls, Donna, asked while Wendy shuffled and dealt the third hand.

Joann sat cross-legged on the blanket, leaning her elbows on her knees, staring down at the backs of the cards piling up before her. Maureen lay on her belly like the others, in a position to examine Donna's face. The new girl was watching the cards flap down on the blanket in front of her.

"They broke up a month ago," Wendy spoke to Donna kindly, not as if she'd been a fool not to notice or a malicious tease if she knew. Yet Wendy is wary, Maureen thought, for she held the deck of cards still in her hands for a moment.

"I'm sorry."

"It's okay. He's going with Anne. He says he's really having a good time this summer," Joann said in a tone that sounded falsely bright to Maureen.

"And you are too," said Wendy, the last card dealt.

They all laughed.

"Bobby's not so bad as a friend," Maureen observed as Donna led the first card.

Though the others gossiped and giggled, pointing out new arrivals at the beach, commenting on tans, sunglasses, new pairings during the play, Joann did not speak any more, dealing swiftly when it was her turn, playing her cards so fast after Wendy played hers that the girl apologized almost every round for holding up the game.

When the wind came up at two o'clock, Donna had to go home, and the game ended. Joann asked whether she could borrow the deck of cards for the rest of the afternoon. While Maureen and Wendy swam, Joann played solitaire.

A week or so later, after Maureen knew about the pregnancy, she said, "I wish you remembered the pirate game."

They had been playing Ping-Pong in Maureen's summer house, and Joann had begun to let the ball hit the floor, then sweep with her paddle to send it back. "What for?" she asked.

"Because even that game had rules."

"But it was fun to break them, and allowed."

"One rule about this summer you're ignoring. You've got to see Bobby."

"I want to win this game without him around."

"But it's not a game."

"I know that."

"And we can't win. We don't know how."

That summer Joann taught Maureen ten different games of soli- taire. Afterward, Maureen never played a game until one day, during the time she was cleaning out Chet's desk after his death, she found a box with two unused decks of cards in them. One deck had poppies on its back, the other lupines. Pleased by the soft orange color of the poppies, Maureen laid that deck out in front of her. The pattern reminded her of the solitaire games, and recalling the rules of one of the easy varieties, she began to play.

The game was deeply satisfying. I can think and not think, she was saying to herself after she had played for an hour. Feel and not feel. Postpone everything for the turn of the card. That evening she went to the library to find a book that would help her with the rules of all ten games. Next day, she played five games of each of the ten. Then the next day more, the next day more. Every time she finished a game, she told herself, "I must finish this packing away of Chet's things. Then I'll get on with my life." Every time she ended a game, she began a new one, telling herself, "As soon as this one is over." Every time she felt sad or angry or depressed about Chet's death, she picked up the cards and said, "I'll feel better when I've played a game."

Sheila came to San Rafael three weeks later to discover Maureen had made almost no progress: her father's coats still hung in the closet, his sweaters and underwear still filled the chest of drawers she'd planned to take home with her, his papers stuffed the file cabinet she'd been promised.

"Why are you just sitting there playing cards?" she asked her mother. It was Sunday morning, the chest and the file cabinet had been loaded onto her trailer, and she was about ready to leave. Maureen sat at the kitchen table, sipping coffee, arranging the blue lupine cards.

"I can think and not think. Feel and not feel. And every once in a while I have hopes I just might win. A friend of mine said that once." She smiled at Sheila, holding back her next thought: when she was in a lot of trouble.

9

The first time Joann saw a sanitary napkin, she and Maureen had been playing pirates, a game of the imagination that they'd complicated with as many rules as Monopoly and as many moves as chess. One rule held that, once they were up in the old Monterey pine in Joann's backyard—their ship—they could not touch the ground without ending the game for that day. Another rule was that they had to use the nautical language they were learning from Sabatini's books. A third: they had to use the names they had chosen for themselves, preferably the names of animals in English or Spanish. Maureen claimed the third rule was silly, but Joann convinced her that it would be even sillier if they were trapped in a cave by the incoming tide after they had buried treasure and she'd have to call out "Maureen" and be answered by "I'm over here, Joann."

"I don't see it's any better to call out 'Lupo' and have me answer, 'Yes, Oso.'"

"The names put us inside the game. We wouldn't be in the pirate world without the names. We'd be half here and half there. Besides, the names will remind us of how the pirate we are—is?—I mean how he acts all the time."

For days Maureen considered possible names for herself, rejecting Joann's suggestion—Red Hawk—as too cruel to bear. It made her think of the day she had seen a red-tailed hawk tear up a baby rabbit in the fields across from her house. She asked her mother one evening what animals were kind to each other, letting herself in for a lecture on the habits of bees and ants, but finally hearing what she wanted— whale, or better, dolphin. The name made her not quite so ruthless as Joann would have liked.

The game began during loquat season, when the tree in the opposite corner of the neighbor's yard filled with yellow fruit. They had piled the ship high with plunder and were circling the globe to get home without meeting the Royal Navy. But in the Straits of Magellan an enormous wave had ruined their food supply, so they had to land on Loquat Island and revictual. Several afternoons they walked one at a time, Joann in the lead, along the top of the fence until they reached the loquat tree. Once an old man, limping around the corner of his house, shouted at them two or three times, and when they heard him say he'd tell Joann's parents, Joann called back to him, "My parents have both been dead since I was very small."

Another day, when they were at the top of the tree, hidden from the ground by the thick, heavy foliage, some old friends, the Rendez girls, strolled by. Lena and Josie Rendez were then in the seventh and eighth grades. On this occasion they had been downtown shopping and Maureen, wise to the ways her older sisters dressed, thought they were hoping to flirt with boys in their pleated skirts, white shoes, and cardigans over white blouses. They wore bright red lipstick, they combed their hair back from their faces in soft rolls, and they carried purses bulging with lipsticks, bright compacts with mirror and powder, bobby pins and combs, and fat wallets filled with snapshots of their friends. "I'll bet they're wearing brassieres," Maureen whispered when she saw them coming.

Lena, the elder sister, circled out from under the tree, away from the sidewalk littered by rotten and broken fruit. But Josie still had a taste for the plump, sour fruit, and passing under the tree, paused long enough to pull a branch down so she could tug a cluster off.

"Invader," Joann called.

"I know that's you and Maureen up there," said Josie.

"It's ours."

"Who said?"

"It's ours by right of conquest."

"What silly game are you playing now?" scoffed Lena.

With all her strength Joann threw the softest, brownest loquat she could reach at Josie. It landed with a tiny plopping noise on Josie's white blouse, leaving a brown, wet scummy piece of its flesh on the starched white cotton. Josie shrieked. Then she looked down at her blouse, wiped at it, and shrieked again, as if a spider had been crawling on her. Lena picked up a mushy piece of fruit, slinging it with her best shortstop's overhand upward, but it hit a leaf and fell apart. She took the cluster of loquats Josie held, tore one off, and tried again. To Joann's taunts, the two of them threw several pieces up into the tree, but all lost force, spattering harmlessly against the heavy leaves protecting the pirates and falling down on the heads of the attackers. At last, enraged, Lena grabbed the branch hanging down over the sidewalk, pulled herself up on the fence, and reached up and grabbed Joann's foot, tugging her down, wrestling with her, forcing her to jump down to the sidewalk.

Everything moved so quickly Maureen had barely time to wonder whether she should keep the game going by shouting something like "Man overboard," when the red-faced Lena, good clothes and all, had Joann flat on her back, sitting on her and holding her down with her weight.

"Surprise attack. Just like Pearl Harbor and look who's winning," she crowed.

"Lena, stop it, your purse," Josie said.

The purse, which Lena had put down next to the fence, was not far from Joann's head. Seizing it, Joann clutched it to her chest, squirming around and away from Lena at the same time. Then she opened it, emptying it item by item, in spite of Lena's hands tearing and pulling at her. "Musket balls," she said, tossing a lipstick out to clatter and roll on the sidewalk. "Gunpowder, shaving mirror, and three combs," she sneered, tossing a compact and then the combs one by one at Josie. "A money bag. Pictures of slaves they've sold, and, at the bottom, a big wad of bandages for severe bleeding. Or something," she said, unfolding the ends of a sanitary napkin, feeling its gauzy material, staring puzzled at its oblong folds of absorbent tissue. At this point Lena removed her hands from Joann's shirt and stood, tears rolling down her face, hands at her sides while Josie scrambled for the lipstick and one of the combs. "You're crazy, Joann Ridley, just like your parents," Lena sobbed. Joann dropped the purse onto the street and sauntered toward the corner. The back of her yellow overalls was stained with the crushed fruit. Maureen, scrambling down the tree, found herself in the old man's backyard and had to escape down the driveway.

When they met at Joann's back door, Maureen spoke angrily. "You didn't have to do that," she accused. "You're always getting us into some kind of trouble." Joann's wide blue eyes retained the unblinking fierceness she assumed when she was playing Captain Fox Terror.

"Why are you worried? We had to protect the island. Anyway, I don't know why she had to get so upset," Joann replied.

"You embarrassed her."

"What does an invader have to get embarrassed about?"

"You know. It was something private."

"I didn't see anything private."

Maureen forgot the incident within the year. Joann remembered it all her life. In the summer of 1948, they met Lena Rendez passing the library one afternoon. She was pregnant, her legs moving unsteadily with the crablike stride of someone very close to giving birth. Her delicate face was rounded and pink. She leaned against the grey stone wall surrounding the library lawn while they talked.

Maureen had become adept at all the appropriate questions from listening to her sister's friends and rattled them off with confidence. They discovered the baby was due in August, Lena was hoping for a boy, her husband was working for the railroad, and Josie was working for the county as a file clerk. Josie would be married next year, too.

"It's so heavy carrying this load around, I can hardly wait till it's born," Lena said, but the expression on her face showed contentment and pleasure at the thought of having the baby.

"We're going away to college in the fall," Maureen told her. "I'm going to Cal and Joann's got a scholarship to Mount St. Mary's."

"That's great, for you. But I'm so glad I'm out of school, I hated all that studying. I don't know how you can stand it. But I always did admire Joann's brains, especially since she's not stuck up about it, like some others I know. Even if she didn't speak to me for three years." She grinned, looking up at Joann from the corners of her eyes. "But that was because I called her names, wasn't it?"

Joann's narrow cheeks reddened. "No, that didn't bother me. It's because we were a pirate ship, we weren't playing war."

Lena turned from Joann to look into Maureen's face, her eyebrows slightly lifted, puzzled.

"Remember how we used to play those made-up games, really live them, when we were little kids?" Joann explained. Maureen wanted to add, and you and Josie teased us all the time, but decided to be tactful.

"Oh," Lena said, smiling. "We used to think you guys were nuts."

Afterward Maureen asked, "When did she call you names? I don't remember that."

But Joann would not answer. "I've never seen anyone that pregnant before," she said. "It looks awful. It's like an albatross, only hanging down inside you somewhere, haunting you for your mistakes. Only it's not a spirit, it's real."

Joann was unprepared for having her period. Not that she hadn't had the usual hygiene lecture at school, and her mother had explained when she was about ten. Mrs. Ridley had begun the discussion,

"When girls grow up, they have the special privilege of becoming mothers. There's this little vessel in their bodies where darling little babies can grow." This didn't seem to concern Joann, so she hadn't paid much attention to the rest of the talk. If someone had asked her whether her body would change as she grew older, she would have answered, "Yes, of course." But that was in a world her mind didn't really inhabit, a world where she might grow up to be like her mother, who dressed everything up in old-fashioned, flowery ways. When she was thirteen, her mother, preoccupied with the stresses of the war upon Mr. Ridley and the cafe, had not noticed the physical changes in her, and Joann had just ignored them. The hair in her pubic area and the softening breasts had not come upon her suddenly, after all, and she had grown to accept them as an ordinary part of herself.

Not so ordinary, though, that she was willing to expose herself to other girls when she was at slumber parties. Not even with Maureen. On the occasions when they stayed over at each other's houses, Joann took her pajamas into the bathroom when it was time to undress for bed, avoiding all opportunity to notice Maureen's small pointed breasts and her lightly curling triangle of hair. Maureen was thus as surprised as Joann that her friend's first period began during a Camp Fire overnight.

The summer grounds of the Camp Fire Girls had been closed during the war—too close to Camp Roberts, the training ground for tens of thousands of infantrymen preparing for combat. But enterprising Camp Fire groups from Refugio went on overnight camping trips with their leaders to earn their ranks, badges, and honors at county parks, the lands of agreeable ranchers, and in large backyards. The group Maureen and Joann belonged to went to the park at Venado Lake for a weekend in the spring of 1943.

They were sleeping in bedrolls made of old blankets on the lawn above the lake. No one had settled down early. After the recitations and songs around the fire, the leader, Mrs. Fairchild, had to scold, threaten, and finally separate groups of girls who couldn't stop teasing and giggling. During the whispering period that followed, Joann had told a story to two other girls besides Maureen. It was about a spy who had tried to recruit her father because he was able to send messages by mental telepathy. She had admitted the story was made up, but when the two other girls had insisted there was no such thing as mental telepathy, she had gone off with her blankets to the outermost fringe of the group, leaving Maureen to close her eyes, listening to the derisive comments about her friend and wishing she was asleep.

It was quiet when Maureen woke up, feeling a hand on her shoulder. She opened her eyes to a full moon shining from the west right into her face, and Joann, her face in shadow, squatting beside her.

"Let's go swimming," Joann whispered. "I'm too hot, I can't sleep."

First making sure that Mrs. Fairchild had her back turned to them, they crawled slowly out of the circle of bedrolls into the deep shadows made by the trees that grew close to the lake. Then scampering from shadow to shadow they made their zigzag way down the slope toward the water's edge. Once, edging around the pit where they had lit their fire earlier, smelling the slightly charred sticks on which they had roasted marshmallows, Maureen thought, just for an instant, she heard voices. Again, when they had waded side by side up to their knees, she was sure she heard the husky tremble of a man's voice, the responding laughter of another coming from—could it be the center of the lake? the other side? She tried to see out over the water, but near the surface everything was black except for the flash, flash of the moonlight caught on tiny wavelets thrown up by the wind.

As Maureen stood listening, Joann pushed forward up to her waist, a glimmer of white against the heavy blackness of the water. The darkness reminded Maureen of the muddy color of the lake's depths in sunlight, where every now and then, one year or another, someone had drowned, caught in reeds or mud or decaying limbs of trees—snares, so far under the surface even expert divers had trouble finding them.

"Come on," Joann urged. "It's not too cold."

"Listen."

The lap, lap of the water suggested to Maureen the sound of ducks splashing down from flight. Then the voices, more like high school boys than men, the deep one cracking slightly, thin.

"Someone's out on the float."

Joann had sunk down into the water, only her face, a tiny triangle of grey showing.

"Wait, I can't see where it is." The patch of grey disappeared. Maureen had more to say, but was ashamed of the panic now attacking her. She took a few steps forward. Her feet were sinking into the mud at the lake's bottom.

Suddenly, Joann was standing at her side again. "Come on, Dolphin. I can see in the dark. Let's hold hands and we can paddle out. Come on, trust me," she coaxed.

Maureen took another step forward, down. She was up to her waist now, her hand and Joann's white on top of the water.

"Just pretend it's another world we're going down into, a forest world. We'll fly above a dark forest world. Come on."

The last words were a rhythmic chant, the strokes of an oar, the beat of her heart. Maureen lowered her chest into the water and together they pushed off, gliding through the suddenly cold water.

"We're like spirits. No bodies, they're gone," Joann whispered.

Stirring the water as little as possible, they paddled slowly in the direction of the voices until Joann squeezed the hand she held and pushed it down through the water so that they had to stop. Several feet to the right and slightly behind them was the dark mass of the float, three pale shadows on it. Three voices. To Maureen and Joann they became like the voices of a radio drama.

"You going to do it or not?"

"Give me a chance."

Laughter. "He wants a chance. Must be a girl."

"No. He's afraid of catching his balls in the branches."

"Let's push him."

"Cut it out, I'm going."

"You got to bring back a piece."

Laughter, a bit more deeply voiced, as if at a dirty joke.

"What if I can't find one? It's dark."

"Just point the old rod at it."

"We're waiting."

"Maybe he's got one already. A piece."

"You got a piece, chicken?"

"Don't push."

"Hey that's right, don't push."

A ragged, heavy splash, head and shoulders probably hitting first, followed by awkward, dangling knees and thighs.

"Shit, what a dive."

"He'll never make it down to the tree."

"A buck says he will."

"First try?"

"You kidding?"

Silence.

"Where'd he go?"

Silence.

Splashing and heaving.

"You got the branch?"

"The piece."

"No-o." The sound of panting.

"Give him a beer."

"Try again, lardass."

"Don't." Cough. "Push." Cough. Cough.

"How's that champeen swimmer down there? You going again or not?"

Splash and silence.

"How far down is that tree anyway?"

"I thought you been down there."

"Didn't take no measuring tape." Laughter. "Not fifteen feet, I guess."

"Have you been down there? Tell the truth."

"Nope."

Shouts of gleeful laughter. "Shhh. There's a bunch of girls over there."

"Well fuck my ass. What are we waiting for?"

"Little girls."

A low glug sound, like air heaving up from a drain pipe through a full basin, rapid, harsh panting.

"Got it?"

"No, he don't."

"Send him back down again then."

Gasping. "Can't."

"Hey, help, he's trying to get back on the float, hey, help."

The two on the float, giggling and pushing, managed to send the diver down once more.

"It's getting cold," Maureen whispered. "I'm getting tired of treading water. Let's go in before we sink."

"Let's wait to see if he gets it this time."

"This is crazy. How's he going to find a tree fifteen feet down in pitch black? If it was me, I'd swim to shore and go home."

"It's important."

"What?"

"He needs to get it to prove he's one of them. Like sailors or soldiers, fighters."

"But not to those guys. They're too young to be in the army or navy. I bet they haven't even done it themselves."

"He thinks they have. Wait, listen. There he is."

"I'm going back." Maureen took a stroke back in the direction she thought the shore was. Turning, she could no longer see the dark outline of Joann's head.

"Joann." No answer. "Joann." Nothing. Then she felt a tug on her ankle, and a second later another pull on her wet hair. Then Joann was puffing again at her side.

"I can't get down far enough." She took a deep breath, and her head disappeared again. When she came up again, she held on to Maureen's shoulders. "It's very strange down there, I can feel reeds all around me. It's like feathers, it's like diving into the past, dark, you can't see anything, just feel feathers. Like flying."

"You're going to get stuck, and I'm not going to be here. I'm going in. You better come or I might tell someone."

She swam off, no longer trying to be quiet, and when she reached the shore found Joann had followed. "Tomorrow night," Joann said, "when they aren't there, I'll dive from the float. Maybe I can find the tree."

In the morning, her damp pajamas a cool corner under her bedroll, Joann felt dampness between her legs and wondered whether she was perspiring, or whether she could still be wet from the swim. She touched a sticky place with her fingers and brought them up out of the blankets to look. Blood. She must have cut herself scrambling back to bed or squatting among the pine trees. Reaching to the end of the bed for her shirt, she pulled it on, and noticed that everyone in the campground was still asleep except Mrs. Fairchild. She took her shorts from the box beside her blankets, pushed them under the covers and wriggled into them. Then she climbed out from under the covers, pulling them up to keep the wet pajamas hidden. She was putting on her shoes, bending down to tie them, when Mrs. Fairchild came over to her and spoke softly, "Do you need a sanitary napkin?"

In the sixties, when she first noticed her daughter's small breasts

beginning to bud and determined she must prepare her for menstruation, she recalled the enormous embarrassment of that moment with
Mrs. Fairchild.

"No," she had said to the leader.
"You've got your shorts all bloody."
"I must have cut myself."

As she bought the junior napkins and the small belt in the drugstore for Brenda, Joann had to thrust from consciousness the image of
Mrs. Fairchild's narrow face and the red patch of sunburn on her
cheeks. That evening when she sat down in Brenda's bedroom to
explain everything to her, she was flustered, almost ashamed that she
had to talk about this burden that women carried. It's almost as if I
were responsible, she said to herself, like the women who had to bind
their daughters' feet in China.

"Your mother didn't get you ready for this?" asked Mrs. Fairchild.
"It's only a cut." Joann was angry. She had heard people criticize her
mother before—for working too much in the cafe, for letting her play
in the fields and down in the creek—and she always defended her.
Mrs. Fairchild had been a teacher before she married. She began
the lecture she used at school for girls suddenly caught there with the
onset of the menses. "This is the most important day of your life. A
special event has happened, and it's a perfectly natural one. It just
means you have grown up to be a woman."

"We had that in fifth grade," Brenda said when Joann tried to tell
her how wonderful growing up was for girls. "It grossed me out."

Joann never forgot how she hated this "becoming a woman." It
meant, among other things, she had to go home without ever trying
the long dive into thick blackness she had planned. When menopause
came, at age fifty, she rejoiced. But it was too late, she sometimes thought.
It came too late.

For Maureen, who had fallen asleep in her damp pajamas thinking
of the long slow slide of a pale naked foot down a pale naked thigh,

memory of the night was special. Years later, she would insist to Chet they have a swimming pool and a float in the pool, and on hot nights they would walk out when the children were asleep and glide into the water, naked together.

Maureen had been unprepared for menopause when it came, a sudden frightening flow on the second day of a regular period when she was forty-five.

"Yes," she told the doctor when she asked whether or not the flow had been heavier for a while. "Well, I think so." She was lying on her back, knees bent and feet in stirrups, legs separated, and the doctor had one hand up her vagina and the other pushing on her belly.

"I can tell more after a D & C," she said.

A week of worries later, with three of her friends assuring her that it was either (a) a fibroid tumor, (b) just hormones, but the D & C would be curative, or (c) cancer, but uterine cancer was usually not very serious and several aunts and cousins of the friends had survived twenty years, Maureen went into a hospital after a sleepless night spent gripping Chet's hand and wondering how he could snore so when she was nervous.

The D & C proved all her friends wrong; she had a precancerous condition, and her uterus should come out since she was past child-bearing age. It did. She had a peaceful recovery, and three months later eight hot flashes spread over two months signaled to her that her ovaries had given up also.

10

The house is quiet. I heard Gil leave in the pickup at seven while I
was curled, cold, under my quilt. If I were a bird this bed would be
my nest, long and tubular, hanging by two or three strands, and deep
in the shrubbery. A tiny tunnel opening at the top, where I would dive
when anything threatened. I would sway, nestled in the dark.

To eliminate the possibility of eggs, I'd be as old as I am today,
a bird who had no more hot flashes! And not particularly hopeful of
attracting males, a bird who closes her eyes, dreaming. A bird who
believes in the soul. I have to believe in the soul, but not the rules
any longer. Perhaps a swallow, my house made of mud—not swaying,
solid, my body secure inside, my soul in my eyes, peering out
through the aperture at the sky, the hills, the earth. Unable in that
moment of clear presence to divide my mud house or me from
the universe.

Until I'm hungry, as I am right now. Careful. Be still. The house is
empty, Gil really gone and Andy, the son to whom I cannot speak, not
here (is he at Sally's?), no one to break into my thoughts while I make
coffee. No Andy to argue with me again about my quarrels with Gil
over city development. No Gil, poor hairy little man, pleased with all
the money he makes, so pleased he no longer tries to please any other
human. Has he changed? Not really. Pleasing others to please yourself
is a good commercial practice. Better question—was I ever pleased?
No. We came back here from Redding because small town real estate
business used to depend on everyone knowing who your family was,
and he figured my family was known. No Gil, so I will rise, not at all
like a bird, find my slippers—yes, there they are beside my chair—
and go to the bathroom for my shower.

Like warm rain, the shower melts the cold pain in my calves and in
my arms. The ache that seeps in from the well. Hello, Maureen. Is
that really you up there? I don't really know what warm rain feels like.
Can it wash out mistakes?

I will recognize Maureen, of course I will, no matter how she's
changed. Those round blue eyes, and if her hair has greyed it will not
be far from the color it always was. A doll's hair, like silk, my mother
said once. She must have combed it for Maureen when she stayed
over those many times, but still, I cannot see the face in the mirror.

High cheek bones, yes, but I remember talking about them. I can't visualize them.

I can't visualize my mother's face, either. I have to look at pictures, and then the grey face in the picture becomes what I remember. There is one almost-glimpse, from the side, the day we closed the cafe. Winter. She had a black coat on. Her hair was grey. There was a comb on the side, loose. In the morning light, she bent over locking the door. Her voice, gone. Funny, I remember what she said, but not her voice. "Time. Now I'll have all the time I want. I hope the place is clean enough." She'd washed, then painted for days to get the place ready for new tenants.

I'll dress in white today, white cotton slacks, white overshirt. My lined, but not yet wrinkled neck framed by the collar. The blouse like the white sweatshirts everyone wore for gym, even the sleeves pushed up. I could sit downtown and gather a reunion of my generation by tapping every woman with her sleeves pushed up her forearms and smoking.

Mom often wore a white starched dress under a blue or green apron as her waitress uniform. She hated white.

Maureen is the only person I know of in the world who will remember my parents when they were both young, as I do. For both my parents, I will tell Maureen, it was difficult to stay out of others' minds. "What will they think?" guided my mother's life. "I plan to change what they think," my father's. If I'd grown up the way they wanted me to grow, I'd have been a leader of some kind, or a teacher. My mother's face at graduation—no I still can't see it.

My mother, I will say to Maureen, always loved my father, but as he changed it was difficult for her to be at ease in her love. Even though she couldn't understand what he was trying to do with his life, she pretended he was behaving like normal people. The times he caused trouble, even the time they kept him for observation in the psych ward, it was as if what had taken place occurred outside her universe. When she died it was like a pond, a small clear tidy pond gradually evaporating, drawing in upon itself. In the light of the sun. Morning light.

I was never sure you understood why I couldn't tell them, I'll say to Maureen.

Bobby's father owned half of the Ford agency, an old-fashioned garage
with a domed interior, metal rafters, and dirty skylights that made pale
blue shadows on the cement floor. Built in the twenties, it stood near
the middle of town, not far from the county courthouse. Though
Bobby preferred sports to mechanics and perceived a car only as a
handsome and powerful showcase for himself, he had been required
by his family to work at the garage every summer and weekend from
the time he was fifteen. He had never been able to concentrate on a
car engine particularly well, preferring to stand ready at the entrance
to greet people who brought their cars to his father's master mechanic,
write out the work slip, and then with an exquisitely athletic grace
sling himself into the driver's seat to speed it back into some narrow
cranny of the garage. True, he did look a bit overpowering in the
Model A's some people had stubbornly held onto through the war
years, but in his white mechanic's uniform, strategically spotted with
grease, sleeves rolled up at the wrists to show lean, powerful forearms
under thick blond hair, and with his tanned nose and cheeks and
uptilted blue eyes, he convinced almost everyone that he was competent
and had a bright future.

Maureen's father had become one of the few skeptics during the
period his daughter and Bobby were dating. He brought his 1940 Ford
into the garage one day with Maureen beside him. She had been
going with Bobby about six weeks, and when she saw him snake
between the front fender of her father's car and the rear end of a pickup
truck, lifting his legs together and over in a final gymnast's motion,
she thought her whole pelvis had melted. This was a Saturday morning,
that night was the night for the movies, and she could imagine that
arm at her waist, about two inches under her breast. During the time
her father had been telling Bobby the car was making a grinding noise
in second gear, the boy was grinning and saying, "Yes, sir," but he was
staring at her. Later that day, when Judge Lewis picked the car up,
expecting to drive north to make a speech at a dinner club in Encina,
he discovered that Moss's mechanics had greased it and changed the
oil. That's all. They had noticed the noise as they drove it around to
the rear parking lot, but hadn't seen anything on the work order.

Bobby genuinely liked girls and enjoyed long conversations with them. He was willing to describe how it feels to be a football player or to tell them stories about his exploits at Boy Scout camp. Every girl he dated heard about how he felt the night he won the game with Santa Rita High School. He had been supposed to pass the ball, and he'd called for that play, and then suddenly he thought he saw a way to make it over the goal line on a run. So he ran. Everyone except the receiver, even the coach, thought he should be praised for quick thinking. But he hadn't been able to sleep that night. He told Maureen he felt so bad about being thought something he wasn't that he almost quit football. He said he liked Maureen because she understood. That summer after they broke up, other girls told her he often said he liked girls because they understood whatever he felt. They claimed he used it as a line, that he'd picked it up from his older brother who'd been in the navy during the war. One girl, Julie, said Bobby confessed, "My brother explained that women are better about people than men, so you can tell them how you really feel."

On the day Maureen drove the Lewis family Ford into the garage with the intention of cornering Bobby for an interview with Joann, she saw him smiling happily as he grabbed his clipboard and came over to the window she had rolled down. She was smiling prettily herself, though her stomach had been in knots ever since she had left home.

"It's only me," she said before he could mistake her for her father. "It's not about the car."

He bent down, leaning his bare forearms on the window frame. His shoulders and face were so close to hers she felt uncomfortable about turning her head in his direction. She was gazing at the wheels of a black car on the hoist, speaking as quickly as she could. "Joann needs to talk to you." Then she turned to catch his reaction.

He blinked, pulling his head back, but the faintly flirtatious tilting of the corners of his mouth remained. "I'm here every day, eight to five, except Sundays. I don't call that hard to find."

Maureen laughed nervously. He widened his smile to a grin, dropping his eyes to her mouth.

"She needs to see you when there's time to talk."

"I'm pretty busy this summer." Grin.

"I'll bet."

"She'll understand."

"I don't really think so."

Preliminaries over, he stopped grinning and talked too fast, explaining. It made Maureen think of how people talked when they don't have a school assignment ready on time. He had a new girl. He didn't like anyone to pin him down. He was at the garage every day, why didn't she just drop by? Why didn't she come herself today instead of sending her friends? Is there something the matter with her? He meant to call her after graduation night, but Anne was a little jealous. He was playing tennis every night with Anne. That made it a little hard to talk to any other girls.

Maureen flushed red with anger and embarrassment. He thought Joann was making unfair claims on him. Maybe he even thought she wanted—an image came into her head of two people in the back of a car—she couldn't think the words. She pushed down the clutch and geared into reverse, but the decision had been made, she would have to go through with it.

"I said she *needs* to see you, not she *wants* to see you."

In the evening Maureen borrowed her mother's car so she wouldn't have to say where she was going. She stopped downtown at the cafe where Joann was expected to eat her dinner that night. After parking around the corner, she walked back to find Joann waiting for her, but looking out the window in the opposite direction. She had to go all the way in through the front door and say "Hello" to Mrs. Ridley before she could get Joann to see her.

"Hey, Joann, I'm here." She waved her hands back and forth as if trying to snap someone out of a hypnotic spell.

"She's always daydreaming," said her mother. "But then you know that already."

Mrs. Ridley wore a faded yellow uniform dress with Ridley Cafe embroidered in red on the right breast pocket. Her cheeks and forehead were grey and shiny, and when she smiled Maureen noticed a blackened tooth. She was behind the counter, scraping the damp remains of food from a pile of plates into a reeking garbage can. Joann's father sat at a table in the back, in his shirtsleeves, writing in a small notebook. He didn't turn his head.

Joann kissed her mother's cheek and waved her hand at her father. "I'll be home before you are, probably."

"I'm so glad you girls are best friends again," Mrs. Ridley said to

Maureen. She started to say something else, but Joann was out the door, Maureen, after an apologetic smile, following.

They picked Bobby up on the corner a block from the garage, where he had parked his car. He slipped his legs in their crisp khakis into the backseat and leaned back, silent. Joann said nothing, though Maureen ventured, "Hi, hope you don't mind riding in an old car. It's my mother's."

"I've seen her driving it around."

Maureen could smell his hair cream, all spicy and sharp, and the knot in her stomach tightened.

They drove just a few blocks with Bobby in the backseat and parked the car near the playground at Jackson Park in the center of town. Her hands on the steering wheel, Maureen sat while the two climbed from the car, Bobby opening the door for Joann. They walked across the grass toward a bench under a tree, separately. Joann went with her head down, her shoulders slightly stooped, Bobby with his hands tucked into the pockets of his khakis. When they reached the bench, neither sat down, but stood, facing one another from opposite ends.

After a while, as she and Joann had planned, Maureen left the car to join them. Neither of them looked at her as she sat down on the bench, wiggled a bit, then put her feet on the seat of the bench and lifted her bottom to the back rail, so that her face could be approximately as high as theirs. Their lips were compressed. Joann's hands were clenched at her sides, Bobby's deep in his pockets as he rose to his toes, came down, rose, came down.

"I want to have an abortion," Joann was saying. "I thought I explained that to you already. I don't want to be a burden on anyone. But we don't know what to do."

"What is it you want to have?"

"An abortion."

He frowned. "What don't you know about doing it?"

"Finding out who, or where. I've got to know soon. I'm supposed to be leaving here mid-September."

He stared hard at her face, a pair of lines between his eyes, trying to figure something out. "I need a little bit of time to think about it."

"But you don't have anything to do with it. Just help me find out where I can go."

"He doesn't even know what an abortion is," Maureen broke in. "It's getting rid of it, stupid."

He swung his body toward her. "This is none of your business."

"I told you it was no use," Joann accused Maureen, calmly.

"I always thought boys were supposed to know all about sex and could help with all the problems. They always pretend they do, anyway." Maureen sneered.

"I didn't say that, did I?" said Bobby. "I just need some time, that's all."

Silence.

"Come on, it's time to go," Joann turned away.

"I don't want Anne to find out about it, that's all."

Maureen laughed, a short sarcastic bark.

"How am I supposed to decide anything right this minute? I don't even know whether my football scholarship's coming through, and to tell you the truth I don't even know whether I want to go to college. I was thinking of enlisting and getting out of this town for a while. Joann understands." He tried to catch her eye, smile his most sincere smile. She refused to look in his direction. "You do, don't you?"

"What I said I wanted was only whether you knew some way I could get rid of it, that's all."

"It's your turn to understand, Bobby," Maureen added. "She doesn't want to marry you or wreck your football scholarship. She just wants to know if you know anywhere she could go. And she needs money too. To have an abortion, to get rid of it, so we can all forget about you permanently." Having to explain and insist made her want to put her hands over her face. Only sisters had ever done this to her before, pretend they know what you really want and ignore what it is you say you want.

"I'm not sure," Bobby said at last. "I think my brother might know. He said something about a buddy during the war having to get one, I mean his girl. I'll find out."

"You can't tell anybody," Joann's voice was breaking.

"Are you kidding? How am I supposed to find anything out?"

Never before had Maureen seen Joann cry in front of anyone. "Can't you see how you're hurting her, you jerk."

"Well what else can I do? She doesn't want to marry me or anything."

"Can you blame her? Who would?"

Joann turned away as their voices rose, stepping quietly off across the grass toward the car. She paused for a moment, then said between clenched teeth, "If my dad finds out or my mother, I'll kill you."

"You think I want your dad after me? He'd put some crazy curse on me."

Maureen jumped down from the bench to follow Joann. Bobby caught her arm, "I have to get hold of my brother, you understand."

"Same old Bobby."

"No, really. I'll ring you up as soon as I know."

He broke into a run, an easy graceful lope away from them.

J O A N N

Walking down the hall to the kitchen, I notice Andy has been home after all, has left his bed unmade. In the kitchen I find he has left a pan caked with the slightly scorched remains of his egg, a dish on the counter, a glass coated with milk. A thin dry boy, like his father. A reedy voice, piping out the epistle at mass. Loose blue jeans, genuflecting. I saw him one day picketing a doctor's office with Sally. They were carrying a sign that said "Abortion Kills." Do they plan to marry when she is pregnant? Surely they cannot be using birth control, because the church still forbids it.

The coffee has grown cold, the toast I was so hungry for has gone dry in my dry mouth. The paper does not want to fold, the egg remains stubborn in the pan, and I am out of wire scrapers to pry it out lump by squishy lump. *Snow White and the Seven Dwarves.* My mother took me to see that movie when I was eight. We had ice cream at the cafe before we went home. She was humming that song "Some Day My Prince Will Come," Dad laughing at her. It must have been on the way home she said how sorry she was for her mother, how like Snow White's life hers had been, with the men leaving the house before dawn, and she busy with the cleaning and cooking all day— without any birds to help either. Then the men would come home at night to dirty everything and eat all she had cooked.

"I feel like Snow White," I confessed to Father MacKinnon when I was trying to find out about the religion my mother wanted me to keep. There were the barren, white stucco walls, adorned only with a picture of the bishop squarely above Father MacKinnon's head. The oak desk between us, the priest's hands folded on the green blotter. My hands hold my purse and a book, *A Guide to Catholic Doctrine*. He doesn't understand. I explain, "A princess condemned to housework, yearning for a witch with an enchanted apple to arrive at the door."

I sometimes believe now he was the only man who ever understood me. But it took me several years to understand him. He said, as if revealing a discovery of infinite value, "Let's look at it this way: the apple is the globe, the great universe. The witch is the grace of God to understand. And there you stand, the princess in rags, ready." So I bit into the apple and fell into a sleep where I dreamed that the universe was enclosed in a globe no bigger than an apple.

You ask me what I am doing these days, I will say to Maureen. One word tells all: separating.

She might not understand, though. I'll say, No I don't mean I'm leaving Gil. It might, yes, it might come to that, but that's not what I mean. For a long time, I'll say—I have to get this right now—I believed I had some grave defect, some basic misunderstanding with the world. I wanted to see past the veils.

My father, bearded, leaned one shoulder against a doorframe. He said, "I once thought you would see through all the veils of reality." "But I do, I do," I insisted, knowing I did not even understand what he meant. Veils?

No veils for Maureen. A "basic misunderstanding" will have to be the words I use to explain the mistakes I've made since she left me. There is such a difference, I used to think, between the chaos in my head and the world outside, and for a long time I thought it was important to have something symbolic to make order out of the chaos. Yes. I'll say that. I'll also tell her about my decision to marry Gil and to stay with the church, so then I can tell her how I've been separating from that specific vision. "Well then, tell me the new vision," Maureen will ask. She always wants in.

11

The phone rings. It occurs to me it might be Maureen, wanting to change the meeting place or the time, a habit of hers I have not forgotten. I hesitate for several seconds before I pick up the receiver. Suppose she's decided not to come at all. As I begin to speak, I find my throat has tightened, and the word comes out in an unintended squeak, "Hello."

"Joann?" a woman asks. "It's Mickey." I have known Mickey for almost thirty-five years, ever since Gil and I moved back to Refugio. She believes she's my best friend. We lived next door to each other when our children were young, served on the same school committees, and joined the dance club within a year of each other. Over all these years we have managed to develop only two subjects for genuine conversation, though to be honest they used to be long, exploratory, and stimulating: children and the educational policies of local schools and individual teachers. Recently most of the talk about children has to do with how successful hers have been. She has also added her experiences as a deliverer of warm meals to elderly shut-ins, and I've been trying hard to listen and praise for as long as she wants to go on—in Christian charity, even though I'm not certain I'm even Christian any more. That set of symbols is good only for people willing to spend their lives as if outside in the dark yearning in through a window. Then I remember, that's how I have spent most of my life.

I'm disappointed when it's apparent Mickey has not called to talk. I could have eased myself with the stories she has to tell. She is hoping Gil and I can come to bridge next Friday, just a reminder, it's a week early this time. I hardly know what to answer. It is expected that I know Gil's plans, but I do not. What shall I tell her—that I can only speak for myself, that Gil may be taking another woman to Santa Maria on Friday, that I am not supposed to know, but that I do, I have for two, maybe, really, I've suspected for three years?

I become impractical, the lovable (I hope) scatterbrain who thinks that Gil has to be somewhere important, but I've misplaced the calendar.

"I know it's really rude of me, but can I call you back later? I promise, I really promise, I have it written down on a piece of paper and I'll put it up on the refrigerator, 'Call Mickey about Friday.'"

She tells me that with this delightful weather she's planning to set the tables up on the patio. She wants to hear me rave about her flowers and her view, say I just can't bear the thought of missing the party.

I say just what she expects.

I am growing tired of the person everyone believes I am; it's like flying about in my mother's body. At times I ask myself, was the person I knew as my mother hiding behind a similar shield? Not scatterbrained—she had to work too hard to afford acting that part—but the person too easily thrilled, too quickly roused to praise of others, too falsely kind. After her stroke, this person disappeared. She became critical and demanding. "I'm surprised at you," she said one day, leaning on her walker in the kitchen when I was rushing about preparing to entertain the bridge club. "Going to such trouble for a stupid game. I suppose you're good at it."

I ignored her sarcasm, replying while I cut a cheese, "Yes I am."

"I'm glad you have the..." She paused for the word, her mouth an inverted bow, her eyes squeezed almost shut with her scowl. I knew the word was *time*, part of a sentence that went on, "I never did." After a moment, she found it, and finished the sentence. Usually I allowed her pronouncement to be the final word, but on this day I asked, "How come you never asked me to help out at the cafe?"

"In those days girls were supposed to be protected. I wanted you to be as good as everyone else, your friend Maureen for instance."

Her anger after the stroke no longer surprised me, but I had always taken it as part frustration at her condition and part inability to regulate her voice. On this day it occurred to me it had always been there, waiting. I asked, "I thought you liked Maureen?"

Her answer told me nothing: "You and Maureen, everything always a game. As bad as him and his religions."

The first week in August, Joann and Maureen were huddled in the late afternoon under the arbor behind Maureen's house, playing Monopoly. For some time they had been aware of the cold wind blowing fog overhead, but neither had been willing to stop the play. Finally at four-thirty Maureen went to her room to pull a pair of jeans

over her shorts. On her return she brought a sweatshirt and another
pair of jeans to Joann, who took the shirt but refused the pants, pulling
her legs up under her for protection instead. Kneeling forward, thighs
white and tiny blond hairs sticking up from cold, she was about to throw
the dice when Maureen's mother opened the French doors and called
out, "Bobby Moss is on the phone."

Joann started to rise, the dice cup still in her hand, but Mrs. Lewis
explained, "It's for you, Maureen."

"Come on in with me," Maureen said.

Joann shook her head no.

"It's cold out here."

Joann threw the dice, picked up her man, the top hat, and began to
count off. "It's double sixes," she said.

Maureen's mother had returned to the kitchen, where she was
chopping vegetables. The open phone sat in the hall, just outside the
kitchen door, its long extension cord looped on a hook beside it.
Taking the loops of cord in one hand and holding the phone in the
other, her ear jamming the receiver down against her shoulder,
Maureen stumbled as far down the hall as she could, at last squatting
on the hardwood floor, curving her body away from the kitchen door.

"How is she?" Bobby asked.

"Okay. Do you have a name?" Her voice was as soft as she could
make it.

"I mean, really. Is she really okay?"

"Not okay the way you mean. Just the same as the other day, if you
want to know."

Pause. "I've been sort of worrying."

Bobby's voice slipped down an octave, his sincere and earnest voice.
Maureen recognized it as the one he most often used when asking to
copy a page of math homework. Anger warmed her cheeks. "Have you
heard from your brother? What have you found out? We need a name
and an address, pretty fast too."

"Look Maureen, it's against the law. We could get in big trouble."

"What do you think she's in already?"

"That's what my brother said. He said I might even go to jail if we
tried to get an, you know what I mean. He said the best thing...the
best thing...he said we should get married. I mean at least consider it.
I've been thinking I might be willing to, I mean I could, we

could…and then get divorced later. But I don't know yet. Anyway don't say anything to her."

"I wouldn't want to insult her."

"What do you mean?"

"Look, I don't want to fight. The point is, did your brother give you an address?"

"He didn't really know anyone nearby. He says there used to be someone in Pismo during the war, but not anymore. But there's this guy he knew in the army, he used to know everything. He's up north, going to Cal or something, he might know someone, up there I mean."

"How are we going to get up there?"

"I don't know. I'd offer to drive, but what could I say to Dad about taking two days off?"

With as much contempt as she could express in a whisper, Maureen said, "Don't bother thinking about it. What's the name, just give me the name."

"You're talking as if it was all my fault. It wasn't, believe me."

"Just tell me who your brother said to get in touch with."

"Charlie Lapp's the name."

"Do you have a phone number? And some money. It's going to cost money."

On her way back through the kitchen, Maureen stopped for a drink of water and a glance at her mother's face to see if anything had been overheard. But Mrs. Lewis was pouring boiling water over a pan holding the vegetables.

"Your father's just closing the garage doors. Is Joann still here? Tell her she can stay. You've got to set the table now."

Maureen found Joann casting the dice again and again, shaking the cup then throwing the dice from one edge of the board so that they rattled explosively across it.

"Has he found anything out?"

"There's someone called Charlie Lapp. But he lives in Berkeley, and we've got his address."

"What good would that do? We can't very well write him a letter."

At the table Mrs. Lewis questioned Joann politely about her parents' health. When Maureen and Joann had been young children, she had enjoyed finding out how Mrs. Ridley managed her only daughter, ignoring politely any embarrassing revelation Joann might innocently make. Though she had learned to be somewhat cautious, she saw nothing disastrous in asking, "And is your mother going to miss you this fall when you leave for Mount St. Mary's?"

Across the table Maureen saw tears well up in Joann's eyes as she struggled to answer. "Yes. No. Not really. She never had a chance herself so she's proud of me. She wants me to be..."

"A high school teacher, or maybe a librarian, isn't that it?" Maureen filled in.

Joann nodded, then bowed her head to her plate. Judge Lewis had enjoyed reading Joann's columns when she was editor of the high school newspaper.

"What about journalism?" he asked. "There are some fine women reporters these days."

"I might," murmured Joann. A tear was by this time rolling down beside her nose.

"She's been reading psychology books this summer," Maureen lied. She herself had been looking through Rosemary's old college texts, especially the parts on sex. "So have I," she added desperately into the silence that fell as her parents at last noticed Joann's distress.

"Well," said her father, turning to her with a heavy attempt at humor, "Maybe you can tell us what the psychological drive behind eternal Monopoly games is?"

"Escape from depression, maybe?" said Maureen uncertainly. At the word depression she felt her face flush, and she took a large bite of meat loaf.

"The Depression you mean," her mother corrected. To Maureen's relief, her mother and father then slipped into a conversation between themselves about old friends from the thirties.

Neither she nor Joann paid attention. Joann wiped her nose on a tissue Maureen handed her under the table, then tried to eat, but the food on her plate was turning her stomach—she had been unable to stand the smell of meat for several weeks. So far she had been able to hide nausea from her parents by biting her tongue, almost until it bled, and holding her breath. She had not yet lost any weight, and she cultivated a sunburn to hide the pallor.

During her later pregnancies Joann remembered the extreme

discomfort of maintaining secrecy with this one, and the memory itself often made her ill. But in spite of the discomfort and the weight she lost in the first few months of these later pregnancies, she did not tell anyone, not even Gil, about them until the bulge below her waistline began to show. As long as no one knew, it didn't exist, she used to tell herself.

Specifics like the Monopoly game under the arbor or sitting at the table with the Lewises and crying, biting her tongue to disguise her nausea, she forgot. But the Lewises from that day forward made her uncomfortable. One time when she was visiting town, she turned away from Mrs. Lewis in the bank, pretending she did not recognize her. Later, when Gil and she had moved back to Refugio, she might meet one or the other of Maureen's parents at a dinner, or a movie, or in the library. Mrs. Lewis, always intent on her own thoughts and activities, seemed a bit uncertain of who she was: "Oh-hello," she would say as if greeting a stranger on a hiking trail. Judge Lewis recognized her, and if he was by himself asked after her parents and told her about Maureen's voyage through college, her year in England, and her marriage to Chet.

J O A N N

That last summer we were together, I will tell Maureen, I learned how to hide. What it means to hide, even from her. I had to hide how frightened I was, for one thing.

One morning, I will tell her, it was terribly hot; it must have been the middle of a heat wave. Mom's phone call awoke me. I stood at the phone in the kitchen—it was eleven o'clock. I felt awful, a headache, dizzy. I hadn't eaten anything. "Do you need anything from the drugstore, honey?" she was asking me. "Shampoo? Tissues? I'm going across the street to get my prescription filled."

So quick I wonder at my deception, I answered, "Sanitary napkins. I'm just about out."

Then in the dimness of my curtained room I pulled the box from the closet, counted out all but two, and stuffed them into a paper bag. The bag and all its contents I burned in the fireplace until nothing but white ash remained. It took a long time, and my face ran with sweat, my nightgown was wet. In those days I wasn't a skillful liar, was I Maureen? I never thought what the neighbors might say, seeing the smoke go up the chimney in the middle of summer.

Sometimes I wonder, if I had a stroke like my mother's, whether that wild, proud—and yes—frightened creature inside me would emerge, just as the harsh and critical woman inside her all those years surfaced after her stroke. If there is a wild creature left inside me. If I was ever anything but a game player.

I've been finishing the dishes, and now I'm about to begin the rest of my housework. I decide I will not make Andy's bed, though I will straighten Gil's, throw his dirty towels and shirts into the laundry, put his shoes out where I'll see them and remember to clean them. There was never a good enough reason before to leave Gil, I will say to Maureen.

At the beginning I think I was honest with Gil, and for a long time that blessed the marriage. Now I know he liked gratitude too much. I was honest with the church too, and I needed it, but for at least the last seven years it's been nothing but a retreat behind ritual. I wonder what Maureen will say to that. I don't remember we ever talked much about religion. My dad's crazy quest made it a forbidden subject, too embarrassing maybe, or maybe in those days I was too ignorant. I didn't even know the church for sure forbade abortion. They didn't talk about it at mass the way they do now. Or at least the Irish priests who were all we ever heard never brought it up. If you don't talk about it, it doesn't exist is what I suppose they thought—no wonder I'm the way I am. Come to think about it, I don't believe I ever considered the act of abortion itself as wrong. I thought I had done a bad thing with Bobby, that much I knew, and I was being punished for it, but after that I was just trying to repair the damage I had done to my parents. I don't even think I thought about the damage to myself. Or did I?

My mother had bought me a set of suitcases, one big, one small. They were beige, with a red stripe and burgundy pockets and lining within. After I came back from San Francisco they stood in a corner of my room. Every morning when first light came, I saw them. I closed my eyes, turned away, and then I'd try to sleep some more. My mother had ordered name tags for my blankets and towels. Every night she asked me if I had sewn them in. Every night she asked me what had happened between me and Maureen. Every night I went out with Gil so that I didn't have to see her or my father when they came home from the cafe. Every night I stayed with Gil as late as I could, necking in the front seat of his little car so that I would not have to go home, go to bed, and lie sleepless. Without Maureen I had no one to talk to about it.

Maureen and Joann began washing the dishes while the Lewises were still drinking their coffee and arguing about a book on the Roosevelt administration.

Maureen's voice dropped softly under the rumble of Judge Lewis's passionately held opinion. "Maybe Mrs. Fairchild would help." She still saw Mrs. Fairchild from time to time when asked to help out with a group of young Camp Fire Girls.

"No."

"Why not?"

"Just not the type."

"What do you mean?"

"I mean she's too much like our mothers." Joann could still recall her mother's chagrin that Mrs. Fairchild had rung her up to come get her daughter because she had come to the camp out without being prepared for her period. She had never told Maureen how ashamed her mother had been when she came to pick her up.

"How about Miss Flaherty?"

"She's always going on about her responsibility to our parents."

"Tynan then."

"Too old," said Joann.

"There isn't anyone else to ask for help. All the other teachers are old maids, except the married ones."

"And Tynan's not? An old maid I mean?"

"I don't know. She's always talking about the cruelty of love. Remember when she read that poem of Millay's and got tears in her eyes?"

Miss Tynan was a sharp-faced, shy, cringing woman, who wore her greying hair in a girlish page boy. Maureen resented the obvious favoritism she showed to boys.

"I can't imagine anyone loving her. It must have been unrequited."

J O A N N

When I have her looking directly at me, tilting her head, curious as ever, I'll say, Maureen, you always thought you had a right to know everything that went through my head. But there was so much you didn't know, for example, my trying to find the words in the doctor's office in Encina. "I'm not sure, I mean we're not sure, we want it," I stammered to him, and I think, even now, I think he didn't hear me.

The young doctor frowned, handed me the name of the vitamins he wanted me to take. "I'll want to see you again in a month," he said, opening the door of the examining room for me.

You wanted to know what he said, you wanted to know if he would help, you kept asking me, and all I could think of was how awful it had been. "Did you ask him?" you said.

"Of course I did." I was so ashamed I was angry with you for prying. "Do you think I'm a coward?"

"Well, what did he say?"

I stared at your hand on the gear shift. "No," I lied.

They had begun to argue when Joann insisted they park down on Valencia and walk the rest of the way. Maureen understood. Nobody visited teachers; that is, none of the students did, unless specially invited, and even then they tried to cover up for fear of taunts that they were teachers' pets. The unmarried women teachers—all but one of the high school staff—were entitled to their own lives as long as they went to church on Sunday: this is what the majority of parents said. In practice, everyone watched their out-of-school behavior without having to feel too personally involved. If the Lewis car was recognized near the house, people would speculate about what business Maureen had visiting a teacher, especially after she had already graduated.

"Look." Maureen stopped the car near the curb on Valencia without turning the motor off. "I'm going to have a harder time telling my mother what the car is doing here if somebody sees it. We're supposed to be going over to Darlene's house, remember."

Joann answered by stepping out of the car, pacing down the sidewalk with a long, bent-kneed hiking stride she had practiced ever since she had read about Indians covering dozens of miles a day in James Fenimore Cooper's books. She didn't look back, her white sweatshirt disappearing into the twilight. Maureen turned off the motor, jumped from the car, and ran to catch up.

"What if someone sees us walking up here? Isn't that worse than driving up and parking the car?"

"The point is, it will be dark when we finish so no one can see us when we leave."

"They'll see us getting into the car."

"Use your head. We could be coming from anywhere. Just went for a walk at night."

"You don't have to talk to me like I was stupid or something."

Half a block on Joann said, "Sorry. I just don't feel good most of the time."

Maureen fell silent, trying to imagine what it would be like not to feel well, not to have any hope of feeling well the next day, or the next, and to have to hide it from everyone.

The sun had gone down about half an hour before. By the time they reached the street where Miss Tynan lived, the world had turned purple and dark blue. The slope of the hill itself was black, the avenue of camphor trees lining the street like the roof of a cave, the garden hedges and bushes its walls. From the sidewalk, they glimpsed across the street a shimmer of white here and there, bungalows glowing through the foliage.

They had both thought they knew which was Miss Tynan's house. Like the location of doctors' houses, the places where teachers lived was part of local lore. But in the dark they were no longer certain, especially since the houses on their side of the street, where they had assumed she lived, were set back and protected by high hedges.

Maureen stopped beside the shrubbery guarding the second house up. "I think this is the one," she said. Sensing an opening in the hedge, she stepped onto a path that seemed to lead into the garden. Ahead of her she could see a light glimmering through a pane of glass in a door.

"Don't," Joann whispered, grabbing at her shirt.

"Don't what?" she replied, startled, turning her head. At that, she stumbled down two steps she hadn't seen, fell, and skidded on her hands and knees over brickwork. "Ohh," she groaned out loud. "God damn you, what is it?" Her knee burned, her wrist ached. She stood slowly, taking her time to make sure nothing had broken, then limped back up the path to the sidewalk.

"I cut my hand, I think," she said, trying to find enough light to see it clearly. "I think it's bleeding." With her left hand she groped first in her left, then awkwardly in her right pocket for a tissue. Nothing but the keys to the car. "Joann, where are you? I've cut my hand. I need a handkerchief." No answer. "Joann." Not a sound. Frogs in someone's backyard pond. The distant sound of a baby crying. The crying stopped.

Oh well, she thought, these jeans don't matter. She wiped her hand on her thigh, felt moisture welling up again, then pressed it down hard. The bleeding would stop in a minute, but what was she going to do about Joann? She would wait here for a while, but how long?

Someone began to play the piano in the house across the street, a faint intricate tinkling, the patterns of lace, she thought, touched momentarily by a surprising sense of being blessed by who and where she was. She was still warm from her walk up the hill, the pain in her hand was receding, and she didn't have to go see Tynan. It was Joann who was in trouble, Joann who had to find the house, go in, explain, ask for help. She could wait for a long time, lean against the trunk of the camphor tree, and listen to piano music. She had never felt so free in all her life.

Nor did she ever feel so free again. At first, in her twenties and thirties, when she thought of it, she labeled it, romantically, as a summing up of childhood. "Did you ever feel a moment of complete irresponsibility?" she would say in long sessions of talk with roommates or lovers. "A perverse sense of freedom from everything, from having to do anything but just be? I had this feeling once, that I was lucky, that I was well off. I was always going to have choices and be able to make them, and no one was ever going to take that away or make demands on me I couldn't fulfill."

But later in her more realistic forties, she was driving down a road in San Rafael on her way to an afternoon of volunteer work at a women's shelter. A Mozart sonata began to come through on the radio, and she flashed back on the moment under the camphor tree on Sonora Street in Refugio. With the vision came a new insight. She had really wanted Joann to disappear. The tranquillity she had felt had not come from comparing herself with Joann and feeling how much better off she was, the child's moment of freedom, but from understanding that all she had to do was quarrel with her friend, and she could be released from worry, concern, and yes, corrective action. After that, all her concern for Joann had been tainted by the possibility of pretense. No wonder she felt guilty.

Once a year Miss Tynan still telephones Joann to ask whether she wants to buy tickets to the women's club tea and fashion show, held annually to support a music scholarship for a local student. Since her husband has prospered, Joann always buys several. In the 1960s she actually used to attend the event with a few wives of her husband's business associates. Then one year, the year Andy was born, she didn't, and she learned that missing the tea didn't damn the family business or keep her off the lists of people who hosted important events.

Nor did it keep her from maintaining a loving, though distant friendship with Miss Tynan.

"Hello," Miss Tynan says on her annual call, adding shyly in a bright lilting voice, "It's that time of year again."

"Oh yes, the scholarship tea," Joann replies. She has begun to feel, whenever she responds to the social demands of the town and Gil's position as if she speaks with her mother's voice. Her mother's voice, as it would have been if her mother had not spent half her life in a run-down cafe. The resemblance makes her squirm, and she tries to shift to another mode but does not succeed, in fact, has never succeeded to her satisfaction. Her tongue is not her own. "It's so great to hear your voice. I wish you wouldn't wait until tea time rolls around to call me. It's been almost six months since we last got together."

Then Miss Tynan asks her to come by some evening. She goes and drinks two glasses of scotch, laid in especially for her by her hostess,

who has always drunk brandy. Miss Tynan says gently, as if she were
still one of Joann's high school teachers, "Now you must tell me all
about what you've been reading." Joann's answer never comes out
sounding as if she were still in high school though. It is her mother,
exclaiming about how exciting a description was or how fascinating a
simple discussion of some scientific discovery has been.

"You must get lonely, here in this town without anyone of your
caliber, with your interests," Miss Tynan says. "You should come to
see me more often."

The piano still vibrated in the darkness when Maureen heard the
slap and thud of Joann's feet trotting down the hill toward her. "I've
hurt my hand," she called out. Instantly she realized she meant the
words to explain why she had dropped back, and immediately she
resented her need to apologize.

Joann stopped several feet away, and Maureen could not see her.
"Come on, I've found the house, at the top. I went around to the
back, and I could see her through the window, reading."

"I cut my hand. It's bleeding." But Maureen was speaking against
the rhythm of the footsteps hastening up the hill again. Just another
game, she thought. I'm tired. She considered staying right where she
was, then realized Joann would come back down and urge her on, and
she had promised to help. She would have to go, whether she wanted
to or not. Holding her hand fingers up and at shoulder level to stop the
flow of blood, she followed the sidewalk up toward the top of the hill.

"Come on this way. The front door's at the side of the house." Still
almost blinded by darkness, Maureen turned toward the voice, felt an
iron gate, felt Joann's arm holding it open, and entered a garden where
the shadow seemed lightened a bit by the grey siding of a frame
house. Together they walked down a cement path to white stairs leading up to a black doorway. There was no light over the door, no light
in the hall beyond.

"Are you sure she hasn't gone to bed?"

"I told you she's in the living room reading. I saw her through the
window. Can you see a doorbell anywhere?"

Joann ran her hand up the wall of the house. In the end she knocked,
her knuckles managing only soft thuds against the heavy wood of the
door. After a long time they heard footsteps in the hall. The footsteps

reached the door, the light went on over their heads, and the door swung in a crack. Miss Tynan, wrapped up in a quilted, flowery robe and smoking a cigarette remained in the shadow. "Yes?"

Joann said, "Hello, Miss Tynan, I came to see you about something, only Maureen fell and hurt her hand."

There was a moment of confusion. Maureen, amazed to hear Joann speak as if she had been fussing over the injured hand, stepped back involuntarily. At the same time Miss Tynan opened the door and stepped forward, Joann moving to the side. Maureen backed down a stair, almost losing her balance. Joann and Miss Tynan grabbed her, one on each side, and they entered the house, Miss Tynan and Joann each holding to one of Maureen's arms, talking across her about how she injured herself and whether a doctor should be sent for. Maureen allowed them to lead her down the dark hall beside the staircase to a large bathroom. At the end of the hall she could see a room full of soft furniture and books. An old woman, a magazine open in her lap, slept in a chair under a dim lamp. That must be Miss Tynan's mother, Maureen thought. She must be deaf.

In the bathroom they seated Maureen on a low stool near the sink, Joann taking her wrist, pushing back the blood-soaked sweatshirt and thrusting her hand over the basin while Miss Tynan stared down at the cupped palm of Maureen's hand. More blood welled up from the jagged edge of the cut.

"I don't think it needs stitches, do you?" Miss Tynan was addressing her question to Joann.

"No. See it's almost stopped bleeding, and there's been so much blood we don't have to worry about tetanus." Joann was squeezing her wrist so hard Maureen wondered whether any blood could get through.

"Oh, tetanus, yes." Miss Tynan mused. She turned the faucet on and Joann moved the hand under it. Pink liquid rushed down the sink. Maureen gazed around the bathroom, noting how the space over the bathtub was festooned with stockings, how the bathtub itself had a grimy ring around it, and how there was an overflowing ashtray on a low cupboard near the toilet. A heavy smell of alcohol filled the room, as if someone had spilled a bottle recently.

"Do you have some peroxide, or mercurochrome, or something like that, and some gauze?" Joann asked. "I have a first aid certificate and I can bandage it."

"You do?" muttered Maureen. Joann gave her arm a quick squeeze.

"Oh yes, of course, of course." Miss Tynan fluttered about the cabinet over the sink. "Nothing here, just let me go upstairs, or maybe the kitchen." She rinsed a drop of blood from her fingers under the tap, then left the room.

"I'm okay, it doesn't even hurt much," Maureen muttered.

Joann whispered her reply. "Don't you remember that movie where they want to get into a house to find out how they can steal something, and they pretend someone sprained an ankle?"

"No." Maureen spoke out loud. This was silly. Why not just tell Tynan what they wanted and be done with it?

"It had Barbara Stanwyck in it, I think, or was it Bacall?" Joann was refusing to notice how she felt.

"But we're not…" She was going to say, "stealing anything," when Miss Tynan returned, her hands full of bottles and packages. In the next few moments, Joann carefully wiped all the blood away from the cut, poured peroxide over it, and then bandaged it, as Maureen gritted her teeth to keep from crying out. As white gauze pressed down on the torn skin and Maureen watched her friend's tanned and slightly dirty hands wind round her wrist, Miss Tynan said, "I suppose I should have taken first aid courses, but I never did. It seemed kind of silly for an English teacher. But my, isn't that beautiful. You should study to be a nurse, Joann."

Joann also smelled the alcohol, but she didn't think much about it. She had smelled alcohol on Miss Tynan's breath in school, a stale sweetish odor she had noticed on the breath of soldiers during the early days of the war, the reason her mother had stopped allowing her to come to the cafe except for dinner in the evenings. When she had peered in through the window of the living room she had observed a glass half full of a brownish liquid next to the chair where Miss Tynan had been reading.

After the hand was bandaged, Miss Tynan offered Maureen a warm washcloth and a towel for her face. Joann took her other hand and wiped it off for her. With a little hug for Maureen, Miss Tynan then led them down the hall through the open door of the living room. They sat down, side by side, on a dark brown sofa covered with stiff plush. Joann felt the prickles on the backs of her bare thighs, and squirmed a bit as they were introduced to Miss Tynan's mother, a small, bent woman with a tiny face carved by hundreds of deep lines.

Mrs. Tynan expressed her delight at meeting them in a strong voice, though as she talked on, the tones of some of her words were reedy and quavering. She had heard much about her daughter's students, even corrected a few papers, but she'd never had an opportunity to meet them. So different from the old days when teachers used to have little gatherings of their best students. But that had been in San Francisco, of course, where Margery had taught before she came here. Such interesting discussions, too.

Miss Tynan remained standing at the threshold of the living room, her hands in the pockets of her quilted robe, her eyes on the carpet, waiting for her mother to finish talking so she could show the guests the door. No one could ignore her apparent discomfort and impatience for long. Mrs. Tynan fell silent, looking up into her daughter's face. "Margery," she said at last, "Come sit down here and entertain your guests. I'm going up to bed now. Now don't get up," she said to the girls, who had begun to rise with her. "You could make them some chocolate and give them some cookies. You could have chocolate too," she said with some sharpness as she left the room.

With both women gone from the room, Joann, her hands folded severely in her lap, her back rigid said, "Are you okay?"

"Sure." Maureen held her bandaged hand stiffly at her breast to keep the damp sleeve of her shirt from the arm of the sofa. "Don't worry about me."

"I'm afraid she won't be any help."

Miss Tynan returned with sodas and a plate full of sugar cookies, set them down in front of the girls, picked up her highball, and settled down into the chair her mother had left. She looked from face to face, uncertainly, then raised her glass to her lips, took two swallows, and then put it down to light a cigarette she had pulled from her pockets. "Of course. You did say you wanted to see me about something." A blue haze surrounded her head. "I suppose I shouldn't smoke in front of you. They'd have my job, if they saw." She made a nervous laughing sound.

"Oh no, Miss Tynan," Joann said in her light voice. "We've graduated, and besides, I have my own cigarettes in my pocket."

She took the pack out of a pocket in her shorts and offered one to Maureen, then lit them both from a lighter she found on the table.

Maureen noticed a mirror behind Miss Tynan's chair, Joann's childishly flushed face, her long tumbling hair, the smoke pulsing from her pursed lips—the head of a wind sprite or fairy in the page decorations of children's books, except she was gazing downward. After a moment she looked upward, her wide blue eyes catching Maureen's in the mirror, and then lowering to Miss Tynan's. Maureen shifted her eyes to Miss Tynan's face, waiting for Joann to speak.

"We came to ask for your advice," Joann said in a low voice.

Miss Tynan swallowed and stirred in her chair. Her narrow brown eyes looked from one to the other. "I'm not much good at giving it," she replied, without a smile. Maureen suddenly recalled how some of the boys drew pictures on the board one day of Miss Tynan leaning over, a great big target made like a heart in her rear. For the first time she understood what the picture meant and why the teacher had been so upset she could hardly carry on the day's lesson. Joann should not go on, she felt this strongly, but could think of no way to stop her.

"It's about last year, Bobby Moss. We were in love, or thought we were. I don't know how it happened, but it did." She paused, trying to find the words to tell what "it" was.

Miss Tynan filled in for her, "Oh, love. We never know where it comes from or how it goes away. But it always does go away. I always try to be thankful that I had it for just a little while."

Maureen yearned to break in and tell Miss Tynan that was not what Joann meant, but she knew she could not.

"I know it goes away. That's part of the problem, I guess," Joann sighed.

"And college, and the career you hoped to have. What was it you planned to study?"

"I'm not certain, yet."

"You have plenty of time. My father insisted that I not decide until late in my college life. Maybe he was hoping I'd get married, but I was glad for the chance to learn history and philosophy as well as liter-ature. Here I've had to support my mother all these years, and I would never have had a chance to read or study what life was all about if I hadn't taken the courses at college."

"Yes, that's what I'm planning to do. The trouble is…" Joann paused again.

"You're in love. But learning is so much more important. It is something within yourself, something you can count on."

She does not want to listen, Maureen thought; she is afraid of hearing something she has no speech made up for. She put her cigarette out. "My hand is beginning to bleed again, I think," she said. Neither Joann nor Miss Tynan looked at her—Joann intense, groping for the words she felt she must say, Miss Tynan concentrating on what she believed was appropriate advice for young women capable of high academic achievement.

"I loved Bobby so much," Joann was saying in her high-pitched voice of utter seriousness, "that I..."

"But you simply must use your scholarship, you mustn't give up your chance to get out of this small town, you must learn. Love means nothing, really, just a few moments out of a life."

"I'm pregnant, Miss Tynan," Joann said at last.

Miss Tynan's face froze, her shoulders hunched, she pulled her legs together; her reaction so strong neither girl was able to look at her. "Well," she said. She picked up another cigarette, her hand scrabbling in her pocket for matches.

"I know what I want to do about it, but I can't find out where to go."

"But this is terrible news."

With the secret out, Joann gathered strength. It's the valedictorian's voice now, thought Maureen. "I want to get rid of it."

If Joann had come in weeping and saying she didn't know what to do, Maureen supposed Miss Tynan could have handled it in the traditional ways, fixing some warm chocolate, holding her in her arms, giving her tissues to blow her nose, and offering to do anything she could to help. But she really didn't understand. She didn't know what to say. She kept smoking and looking at Joann, as if waiting for an explanation of what getting rid of it meant.

"I want an abortion."

"But that's terrible. You don't want to do that. It's against the law."

"I'm so glad things turned out the way they did," Miss Tynan said to Joann the first time she invited her over to the house in later years. "Aren't you? I take a lot of credit for it."

What she meant was that she had spent almost an hour after Joann had told her she was pregnant trying to convince her that she must tell her parents and let them help her. Marriage to Bobby would not be the worst thing that could happen. She herself had never married, though she'd had the opportunity, and she always regretted it. "My life with Mother has been, well, all right." At this point she rose from her chair to walk out into the hall and peer into the darkness upstairs. Before sitting down again, she went to the kitchen and returned with a replenished glass and some ice for the girls to put into their glasses. They felt like prisoners of her sometimes rambling admonitions, and wrapped in their own stunned disappointment, they had left the cookies on the plate and the sodas untouched. "I just had to make sure she's in bed. I wouldn't want to hurt her for the world." Miss Tynan resumed, arranging her robe carefully over her pajama leg. "But you miss certain excitements. I don't mean, well you know what I mean, but I've never had a chance to be really close to anyone, living with Mother this way. It's hard to have intimate friends, they always have to ask Mother every time they ask me out, and of course she's always here. So I've been alone all my life. I don't want this for you." She went on to describe her disappointments with several people, men and women, in Refugio. Much later, after she had finished her glass and had filled herself another, she came back to a discussion of college for Joann. If Joann was really set on college, really wanted to pursue learning, she knew of a home for wayward girls where the child could be put up for adoption.

Joann, disguised as her mother, smiled, and asked for the name and address so she could write. Miss Tynan said she would find it and let her know.

On the way down the hill in the dark, Joann said, "Okay, you were right. There just isn't anyone else."

"What about this home, I mean, if it's the only thing we can do."

"I'd have to tell my parents. I've told you, I'm serious, I'd rather die. I would, too, if I could think of a way to do it without anyone knowing. Like falling off a cliff. Or walking in front of a truck."

Or exploding a grenade, Maureen thought, resentful and silent.

J O A N N

And now I'm ready, hair brushed, pulled away from my face on the sides, light lipstick. I've never worn makeup, not even powder. Does Maureen? Lines down my cheeks almost as plain as the lines in my palm. Keys. Burglar alarm. Garage door whatsis. Car. White-haired lady slips quietly down silent residential streets. Ominous. Will Maureen ask about Bobby, do you think? Answer. I rarely see him. He's fat, bald, very rich, and everyone in town seems to know him, the perfect host at the hotel where he sinks his millions. I pretend not to know him when I meet him accidentally. Another cover-up, have you been keeping score?

One question for you if I get to the part about lying and hiding. I remember you were terribly insistent about trying to think of ways of telling my parents, telling me that if they loved me they would understand and try to help. But I was so certain my mother, already defeated by my father's strangeness, would shrink away to nothing. I even had a picture of her in my mind all thin, curled up, shriveled by my failure. Now it seems to me that I didn't want my mother to know because that would make what happened to me real. I'm wondering whether you too wanted me to end the game.

12

Of course I'm early. I'm always early. I think I must have a defect in my sense of timing. Anyway, it amazes committee colleagues, lunch friends, groups expecting me to speak, even Nancy and Sheila after all these years. "What, you here already?" people say when they enter a room to find me already in place, holding up the book I brought or the papers I was working on as tangible explanations, excuses, or apologies for my unexpected—sometimes, I'm sure, unwelcome—presence.

"You shouldn't be making excuses for being on time," say friends who assume promptness is a symptom of morality. But I do apologize. I hate even to seem to put people in the wrong. And who knows, maybe those who question me want only a minute alone in the meeting room to plan a vote or gossip or just breathe and relax without company. I've taken the advantage (haven't I?) coming early and seeing their faces before they see mine.

My kids warn me my promptness will get worse with age, that it foretells dinner at five in the afternoon, a table set three days before Thanksgiving, three-hour waiting periods in airports, not to say cars parked a block away from a dinner party so no one will notice how you take up the fifteen extra minutes you've given yourself. Even income taxes paid in March. They say it goes with slower reflexes, reading speeds, and memory retrieval systems and comes with greater fears of making mistakes—the more-failures-fewer-risks syndrome. I don't think that's me; I think I've always been that way. Maureen's biggest flaw: her sense of timing.

If I'm wrong, I expect they'll put me away.

Today I'm pleased with myself. I'm just early enough. At twenty to twelve the restaurant ought to be finishing up late breakfasts. Most of the tables will be set for lunch, and I can choose the place I want. Outside, overlooking the creek, shaded, at the edge of the courtyard so I can look down at the paths. Yes, that one.

I like the young woman who shows me the table: "You picked the second best table in the place," she says, as if I've won a prize to go with it.

"I'm meeting an old friend."

"You can sit here all afternoon talking, as far as I'm concerned."

I like her style and I grin at her. "I'll bet you've lived here all your life," I venture. She reminds me of Sally who worked for Mrs. Ridley during the war. Sally told me once she knew the first names of over a hundred customers and what kind of sauce they wanted on their hamburgers. I didn't believe her then, but Joann's dad said she had the kind of spirit that yearned for the great ocean of other spirits and therefore what she said was always true. He said this kind of spirit often settled in small towns like Refugio.

I hope I didn't giggle when he said it. I'm amused now, remembering, as she tells me no, she comes from LA. "They like us to pretend small town manners here, though. It makes the tourists think they've traveled."

Like Marin used to be, I think, when every other restaurant had waiters dressed in blue jeans and cotton shirts, saying hello, I'm Jack and I'll be taking your order today. Refugio was always five years behind the fashion.

I choose the chair facing toward the building and the entrance to the deck so I can watch for Joann, then I order iced tea. When the waitress brings it, she tells me to watch for a pet blue jay who comes down for bread crumbs about this time. I nod, turn toward the creek where there isn't a trace of a jay, but where several children in bright-colored shirts stand or squat on rocks, stir the water, peer into it, dip toes or hands, leaves or sticks into small ponds and miniature falls. Above them on the opposite bank, morning strollers meander under the trees up toward the mission or down toward the Corcoran Boulevard Bridge.

I try to figure out where the path used to be, behind the houses that used to be, on the street that used to be, in front of the mission. Lena Rendez took me back here once. I don't remember why or when, just that I followed her lead one day when she turned off from the street across from the mission. "This way," she said. I saw a low building of white-painted bricks, her yellow dress, her tanned arm. Then there was a road—an alley, she called it—and a bridge. I leaned over its cement rail, surprised to see the creek coming out of a tunnel underneath Colgador Street. Then I slipped on a steep path beside the bridge, bumping into her. Her brown hand pointed to tiny fish flickering through a shaded pool.

Was that the day we climbed stairs into the building at the end of the bridge? We ran through dark corridors to another flight leading

down and out, and there we were on Dana Street right outside the
five-and-ten. Or was I with Joann that day, the day we ran through the
building, on a spy mission, disappearing because we thought we were
being tailed?

The truth is, I remember two experiences: that feeling of surprise
at discovering the creek behind all those houses, my feet on the slip-
pery path, and Lena's hand swimming above dark pebbles; and then
another: excitement at trespassing, the dark corridor, brown linoleum
on the floor, the clatter of my running feet, the sudden grey, safe light
of Dana Street. Connecting the two experiences is an interpretation,
not the memory itself. Did it happen the same day? Could Joann have
been with Lena and me the time I visited the creek, only I don't see
or hear her there any more? Could Lena have been playing spies this
one time? Was this the only time I ran through the building? Or was it
one of many? Even if today I asked Joann and she remembered a spy
mission, what I remember could still be what happened the day I
went with Lena.

It's like when Rosemary and I get together and talk about Dad, the
actively recalled experiences never quite coincide, just sometimes
the interpretations.

"One night Dad said Mother was a damn fool for supporting Henry
Wallace and his progressives," I say to Rosemary.

"Why then did he stuff envelopes for her?" she answers back. "I can
still see him sitting at a table with her stuffing envelopes."

"Christmas cards, maybe?" I suggest. "Mom swears he always disap-
proved of her politics, even when they first met."

"It wasn't Christmas cards—they were single sheets of paper. I
remember it was after the war because Debbie started to color on
them. But maybe you could be right, and Dad was just being nice,
helping her."

"He did like to help her," I agree.

"As long as it wasn't housework and it was night, when the curtains
were drawn."

So I don't really expect my recollections to coincide with Joann's,
and she may not even remember she sent me away. Why did you send
me away, Joann? What? she'll say, her eyes wide, I've wondered what
happened to *you*. And I'll swallow and frown and decide my uneasiness
about her will just have to shadow my personal image forever. I might

even grow to like it: notice that aura of world-weariness in the line of the brow, I'll say when I look in the mirror.

But if she doesn't remember, shall I tell her how I felt about her? Honor that friendship somehow? If she had been a boy, and I felt about her the way girls were taught to feel about boys, all that would be left would be a name and maybe a memorable junior prom; the feelings would have disappeared fifty years ago. It would be like coming home from a day on the beach, nothing left but sand on your feet. Yet the scattered memories I have of Joann come together like a year of full glorious days. Even the water I remember is warm.

Two men a good fifteen years older than I are sharing the other table overlooking the creek. I can hear their amiable voices, baritone, just slightly blurred and softened by age. They're dressed in straight-cut denims, deck shoes, cotton plaid shirts, everything well-worn. Their conversation moves slowly, as if they're pulling on pipes between thoughts, but of course they've given up the pipes. Like my brother, Bill, they would have given up tobacco years ago on doctors' orders, sensibly, part of a rational life, and like Bill, it leaves them just a bit pompous, as he is, especially when he talks about his legal work for the environment. Forty years ago men this age, especially those who sit in dignified, quiet ways as if they're at a meeting, would never wear jeans to lunch. They wouldn't be out to lunch in Refugio anyway, unless it was the Rotary Club or Kiwanis; they'd be sitting at home, coats off, with their wives serving them. Their wives would be wearing stockings under slips under dresses under aprons. When I was very small, my mother used to wear a hat when she went to town in the afternoon to buy groceries.

Mr. Ridley might have fit in with these men. Maybe if he'd known people with a kind of easy, rational understanding of different ways of thinking, he might not have been driven to express the most eccentric parts of his religious notions. All he had were the practical merchants and workmen and farmers to talk to, and later the soldiers. No dreamers. If those men dreamed, it was the way prospectors dreamed—how to make money. Men like my father never saw people like Mr. Ridley, except in their offices, on business.

Here comes that blue jay and yes, they're going to scatter crumbs from their bread basket for her. Good, kind men. The man not facing me is having trouble standing up. His cane—he has a twisted knee. I turn away, shuddering from the pain that transforms his face, but not too soon to see that his friend also turns away his face, scattering the final bits of a piece of bread to the bird. He waits, not helping. His grace, his sense of timing when he busies himself through his friend's painful struggles pierce my heart. How often have I rushed in before anyone has asked, knowing the dreadful future, planning to forestall it, only to stop, frightened of the burden I'm taking on. Damn it. Bad timing, always.

The morning after the visit to Miss Tynan, Maureen telephoned Joann's house as soon as she woke up. No answer. She pulled on jeans and a sweatshirt, grabbed a banana and started the walk over to the Ridley house. No one answered the doorbell. She knocked. The house remained still. She hesitated for a few minutes, knocked again, peered through a window into the living room, tried the special catch on the kitchen door but found it locked, and finally tapped insistently on Joann's window. "I know you're there," she called, though she really wasn't sure.

"I'm not."

Laughing with relief, Maureen called out: "Let me in. We've got to plan."

"I need some time to think."

"Okay, but let me help."

"No, not now."

"You've got to let me help. Please let me in, please, please."

"Why?" Joann asked when she opened the front door. She still had her pajamas on, short sleeved, white, faint blue sprigs of flowers dotted here and there. "I don't understand why you're so frantic."

Maureen knew instantly her answer to the why: because I'm sorry I want to be free. But she could not speak it, and not speaking it soon forgot it, and remembered it only many years later.

"What about the young women from small towns, young girls, really, who can't tell their parents and have no way to get help locally?" Maureen in 1989 addressed a meeting of women concerned about the

Supreme Court's decision allowing states to put restrictions on abortions. "When I was eighteen and abortions were forbidden by law, my best friend got pregnant and we just really didn't know what to do. There was no one to turn to, no one to ask, and we didn't know anything—I mean anything—about where to go or who to ask. Sure there are— were—must have been people in the town who knew what to do. But everything about sex was secret, especially kept from girls. So we were frantic. Then finally I got the idea of going to San Francisco. It was the only thing I could think of, but that wasn't so easy either. Money. How do we get there? What do we tell our parents?"

"What did you do?"

For a moment the intent faces of the women listening to her faded, and a visual memory superimposed itself: Joann, eyes closed, lying on a couch in her pajamas, telling how they could manage the trip to San Francisco. Maureen bit her lip, then she went on. "The first problem was the money. We'd counted on using my friend's college savings— her clothes money—for the abortion. But that was only three hundred, and we couldn't use any of that to buy train tickets, or meals or hotel rooms. I had about a hundred dollars I could use without being found out, but that wasn't enough. Then we asked the boy involved, and he said he could put in fifty."

Two or three of the middle-aged women in the group made noises halfway between a groan and a boo. A few of the older women and the young ones grinned at the interruption, but most remained intent, waiting for the rest of the story.

"He said he'd just bought new tires for his car and that was all he had left."

"Why couldn't he sell his car?"

"Then what could he tell his dad? Besides, we didn't have time. We decided to tell our parents we wanted to go see a play from New York running at one of the downtown theaters; I think it was *The Winslow Boy*, Terence Rattigan's. We thought we might be able to talk my parents into the money for my tickets, and then my friend could persuade her parents. My mother thought it was a good idea to go: the trip might teach us independence and our going to the play appealed to her. But she thought we should stay with relatives, and when I said I didn't want to, she said my father would insist and she wasn't sure anyway that hotels would keep two girls as young as Joann and I.

Which was true, by the way, though I'm sure if she or my dad had called for a reservation they would have accepted us.

"Having to stay with my aunt and uncle finished any hope I had, but my friend was desperate and she insisted: 'Tell her we'll stay with your aunt and then after a couple of days we can find someplace else to stay, I mean for the abortion itself, or I can. Anyway, we can figure something out.' My friend's mother was very reluctant to let her go, but my friend lied and said that it was my mother's idea and that the librarian she worked for was excited about our going.

"Then there was the problem of time, as serious in its way as the problem of money. We were to be allowed to go for only five days. We begged for more, telling more lies—to see the museums and visit Berkeley we said. But five days was the limit. My father set that. He was a judge, and it was like a sentence.

"But our spirits soon rose. We thought we might have a hard time finding the man Bobby had told us about, and we wondered about having to make an appointment. Still, five days was enough time. We had no idea how an abortion was done, but thought it could take no more than an hour or so out of one of the days. I figured it would be rather like starting a period, and that my friend would go home wearing sanitary napkins. We even made sure she packed a bunch of them in her suitcase.

"I feel terribly sad when I think about those children, such innocent liars." Maureen sighed the first time she gave this talk and felt her vocal chords constrict with pity. Other times, at rallies and in classrooms, she has felt constrained to drop this last sentence, but she has always thought the words, "innocent liars."

M A U R E E N

The old men are leaving, trailing slowly through light and shade among the tables. The light is almost green, winnowed through the leaves of the trees. The voices of the children rise and fall; the jay is screeching from the low branch of a sycamore. I fold my hands on the table, one over the other, trying to focus on my plan for our conversation, but I am drifting, gazing at the freckles, tiny leaves among the veins on the back of my left hand. I cannot visualize my hand at eighteen. The long fingers were slimmer, of course, whiter, weaker. I know that, but I cannot—strange, this is just the opposite of the way my face appears to me in the mirror. Oh, I know I've aged, I know the lines and sags, the red or grey that was once a gentle pink. But long ago I must have made my mind up to see only the outlines, the shape of my eyes, the curve of my jaw, the span of forehead, and never allowed what I saw in the flesh to change. The grand illusion. Who was it who said that once, approaching a mirror from a distance, she saw a stranger and only recognized her by her clothes?

Come on now, Maureen, you're supposed to be making plans. Developing strategy for this reunion, reviewing why you need the answers to questions. Okay, one: the consequences of keeping what you remember to yourself are that it becomes unreal—only flashbacks, no stories, nothing coherent. I need to spend time with Joann comparing—reconstructing the story of my youth. Two: I've built my life on a foundation that defines me as a generous and caring person, but I'm afraid the foundation has cracks in it, like a cement slab on adobe fill. Did I fail in one of the most important tests in my life? How?

Where will I begin? With gossip about the present, of course.

At the 1989 meeting the women were sitting around a long, black-topped table in the meeting room of a bank. Many had nodded in sympathy when Maureen stopped to clear her throat after describing how she and Joann had managed to travel to San Francisco.

"The awful thing is," Maureen began, then paused again. The faces were blurring as she concentrated on what it was she wanted to say next. She placed one hand on top of the other on the table before her, tried once more. "Within six months of this time I knew what we should have done, just six months out of the small town, living among older women, dating a veteran, or two veterans, and listening and asking questions in the discussions you have late at night. Questions like, What happens if you get pregnant? and answers like, I know a nursing student who knows a doctor. Or, There's a woman at the hospital who helps if you go to her. It all seemed so easy, if only we'd tried harder in Refugio, maybe in Pismo, but we just never thought of it. I suppose the way some young girls today never think of using condoms. So for those reasons or maybe some other reason as I grew older I became angry with myself for not being more sensible. I thought then it was my fault we'd gone to so much silly trouble. I thought it was just as if I'd been playing another game with my friend, having an adventure we'd both made up, like pirates or spies."

On Monday morning, the day they were to leave for San Francisco, Joann was packing rows of sanitary napkins into the bottom of her suitcase when Maureen telephoned. "My mother had to go over to pick up Rosemary's kids. She promised they could go to the train with us, and Rosemary decided to take half the morning off," she explained before she gave the reason for her call. "So I just thought I'd find out how you are and if everything's okay."

"Yes, I'm almost packed."

"Is your mother around?"

"No, she had to go down to get things going for the lunch time crowd."

"Well, then, how are you feeling?"

Joann flattened her hand on the napkin she'd brought with her down the hall. "Okay."

"Just okay?" Maureen sounded disappointed.

"Sometimes I wish you'd stop wanting me to be ecstatic about everything. If you need to know, I'm convinced I'm doing the right thing." She paused. Though she'd tried to speak in a frank and casual way, Maureen wasn't responding. "I'm sorry, I'm really grateful to you. I'm not mad or anything. I guess I'm just trying to let you know that I'm sure we'll find an ab... someone to help. And it doesn't matter we have only five days, we'll do it."

"That's right," Maureen said. "I just know we will."

"Where did you put the money?" asked Joann.

"Half in my purse, half in my suitcase."

On the train, the good-byes over with, Maureen settled into an aisle chair with a sigh of relief. Joann stood uncertainly in the aisle beside her. "Go on, you get the window seat, you've never taken the train before." Made clumsy by her high heels and the narrow skirt of her suit, Joann stepped over Maureen's legs and dropped down beside her. Soon after the train rolled forward Maureen removed her cigarettes from her purse, touching first, for reassurance, the thick roll of folded bills she had zippered into a side pocket.

When they had both lit up, exhaling a cloud of smoke, she said, "That's better."

"Haven't you told your parents you smoke yet?"

"No, have you?" They grinned at each other.

The train had reached the edge of the valley and begun the long slow ascent of the surrounding hills. "I feel like a snake shedding its skin, finally," said Maureen. "All those secrets."

"For me it's more like an explosion, a great burst, and I'm sent flying off into the stars, nothing to hold me down anymore."

"You would have something that sent you shooting off, while I'm just a lowly snake slithering along. Are you ever afraid, I mean really afraid, not just, well, wondering whether things are going to work out?"

"Sure," Joann said.

"What of?"

"You have to tell me first. I mean what you're afraid of."

"Okay. Let's see...I'm afraid I'm going to get caught and because I'm an accessory they'll put me in jail."

"I'm afraid of getting caught, I mean that after all this trouble they find out about it anyway. But you know, it's somehow different if they catch you after; that way, I mean if they catch you after, they can't punish you by making you have a baby. It's gone."

"My turn," said Maureen. "I'm afraid, I'm afraid, well, I'm not really afraid all the time, but once in a while I get panicky thinking what if something bad happens to you in the city. I know it won't, but sometimes you can't help thinking about some of the awful stories."

"I know. What I'm afraid of is if you find out I'm really afraid. That is, if I ever am afraid." She tightened her jaw, narrowed her eyes, lifted her chin. "Which I'm not, usually."

Maureen gave a snort of laughter. She called this Joann's Errol Flynn look. "Why?" she asked.

"Because if I'm not afraid you can't find out that I am afraid, because I won't be." If I wasn't afraid I wouldn't have secrets like the one that I *am* afraid, all the time, she was thinking, but she wouldn't tell Maureen that.

"I meant, why are you afraid of me finding out?"

"I don't know."

They both laughed, and Maureen proposed that now the train had come down out of the hills they could get up and walk around, maybe go all the way to the first car. They started out, wobbly on their high heels, catching themselves on the backs of seats when the tracks curved and they lost their balance, almost collapsing with giggles when one sharp turn threw Maureen against the shoulder of a boy wearing a letterman jacket from San Jose State.

Back in their chairs, Maureen proposed a game of battleship; she'd brought the paper and pencils in her purse. Joann said no thanks, and handed over the women's magazine her mother had bought for her. It reminded her of the color crayons and comic books her mother used to supply on the few trips the family had taken before the war. As Maureen flipped through the pages of recipes and clothes, Joann said, "You know what, the trouble with the snake idea is that you shed your skin, but you're still the same person underneath. Your name doesn't change. I think I want to be a totally new person, nothing under, no old secrets hanging on, just everything new."

"Miss Joann Snake," Maureen turned the magazine back to the table of contents.

"How about Miss American Eagle?"

"Miss Bald Eagle."

"Allie Batross."

"Allie Batross and Miss Ann Mariner."

Joann turned to the window. They were passing through a town with one main street and several rows of houses, most of them wooden bungalows built in the early 1900s. If I'd grown up here, she thought, and if I were leaving now because I want to, not because I have to, who would I be? If I could choose, right now, a different person to be, I suppose, yes, I'm sure whoever it is would have an open and therefore a dangerous life, leaving all secrets behind. She began to enumerate the secrets she had left behind. The way she'd let Bobby make love to her because she couldn't stop herself; the book she'd hidden under the library desk about prostitutes; the crushes she'd had on movie stars and teachers; her shame about her father's public preaching; her scorn for her mother's humility in front of Mrs. Lewis; her determination not to be like Lena Rendez; her pride at being smarter than anyone else, even Maureen, in school; the daydreams she had about building houses or learning about stars; wishing she could be an astronomer; longing to be brave enough to tell her mother and father all the secrets she had, the secrets she carried with her. She recalled once having dived down deep in pitch black water trying to find—what was it?—anyway, she had shut her eyes for security, it was so black. She remembered the confidence and the excitement of that dive. Black, that makes you invulnerable, she thought, and shut her eyes on the passing fields and hills.

A few miles south of Salinas, the train's speed diminished until the clackety-clack on the rails was just a rapid clack, clack. A family group taking up several seats behind Joann and Maureen prepared to disembark. Two women strained to pull several small suitcases from the overhead racks while three teenagers picked up the smaller children's sweaters and bags. A baby woke, cranky, crying.

Distracted by the family's noise, Maureen turned around to stare. "I'll hold the baby," she offered to a girl about their age, but the girl said, "Thanks, that's all right. She doesn't like strangers anyway."

"You must have found something in the magazine. What did I miss?" Joann asked.

"Nothing really. An article on college dating tells you what to wear to concerts and things. I'm just about finished with the detective story in the back."

Joann returned her attention to the window. She had never been in Salinas before, or at least didn't remember it. The one trip out of Refugio County she did remember was over to the central valley, to Fresno and Yosemite. There wasn't much to see in Salinas: vegetable fields and highway replaced by streets and stores, in turn replaced by sheds and railroad freight cars on sidings. The family had advanced to the front of the car where one of the women struggled with the door to the vestibule. The porter pushed it open, brakes squealed, and a dull silence followed, pierced by an occasional voice.

Outside on the long cement platform, among waiting businessmen and pairs of women wearing hats and carrying their coats, stood knots of soldiers dressed in neat, trim khakis.

"Is there a camp still open up here?" Joann asked.

Maureen didn't look up from her page. "I think Fort Ord is around here somewhere."

Joann had not seen soldiers in groups since right after the end of the war. She remembered how after the Greyhound buses came in, soldiers stood around on Valencia Street waiting for other buses to take them back to camp. Sometimes on Sunday afternoons she and her mother went to the movies, and when they came out they would have to walk through the crowd. Her mother would put her head down, walking as fast as she could, and the soldiers, some of them smelling of wine or whiskey, called out things like, "Hey baby," and "Hubba-hubba." This was after the spy period, and Joann had learned from these experiences to avoid soldiers altogether. But now, years older, she felt nothing of the old tension. Had she really begun a new life, she wondered, or was she happy to be reminded of the old? There was something, too, of Gil in the soldiers, his way of standing as if contained in some rigid mold, all the space around him tidily controlled.

One of the soldiers was standing directly under her window. She could see the faint wrinkle where his overseas cap flattened out at the top to accommodate the broadest part of his head. Then, tapped on the shoulder by another waiting soldier, he tilted his head up. Their eyes met, and though it was her custom to turn her eyes swiftly away when caught staring at a man, she kept her gaze steady. He was wearing heavy, horn-rimmed glasses. Ugly, he's really ugly, she thought, noting his wide frog-like jaw, thin lips, and narrow forehead. When he gave a little nod before moving forward to the stairs up into the train, she nodded back.

Mariner, Miss Ann Mariner, would be her name, she decided as the train nudged forward, then settled into a smooth, slow acceleration. With her eyes closed, she developed her game. Ann Mariner was on her way north to begin her career in San Francisco. She had been sent by her college—Vassar?—to a job at a hospital in Los Angeles—she was a lab technician—but then she and her friend heard there were openings in a criminology lab in San Francisco. She was really a lie detector expert. They were a lie detector team. She'd majored in psychology, and it was her friend who was the technician. She was reviewing all she had read or heard about lie detectors—would they be carrying their own? she wondered—when she heard a man's voice, quite near, "Hey there. Hello. Is your friend asleep?"

She opened her eyes to see the ugly soldier leaning against the chair in front of Maureen, peering down at them.

"If she was asleep, she isn't now. Hi," he said.

Maureen diligently read her story. Joann hesitated for only a few seconds. "Hello," she said.

"Say, my name's Tom Stedman, and I know you don't talk to strange soldiers. Especially now the war's over. But my buddy and I are on the way to the club car, and thought maybe you girls might join us for a beer."

Maureen still pursued her story. "We'll think about it." Joann made her Miss Mariner voice friendly but brisk, as if she really might decide not to go. When the two soldiers had moved on and Maureen had said, "That's the ugliest guy I've ever seen," Joann said, "Let's wait ten minutes."

"And go?"

"Why not?"

"I don't mind, and with them we probably won't get asked for IDs, but it's just...I didn't think you did that kind of thing."

"I don't." Joann opened her purse to retrieve her compact, a comb, and lipstick. "I'm Ann Mariner, by the way."

Maureen grinned. "That leaves me Allie Batross." She too reached into her purse for her lipstick, and touched the bulge of money zippered into her purse as she did.

They had bumped and stumbled through the club car earlier that afternoon. Only three men had been near the bar and a few couples faced the windows, small circular tables rising between them. This time when Joann opened the door the blast of voices and thick cigarette smoke startled her. She paused, searching for a way through the crowd that might provide them a few handholds if they lost their balance.

"Over here, over here." Tom and his friend had found a cushioned booth and a table near the door. Both were standing, one on each side of the booth, so that Maureen and Joann had to slide into the inner seats. Two bottles of beer stood on the table and a pack of cigarettes rested beside an ashtray. The friend remained standing while Tom took his place close to Joann.

"What'll you have?" asked Tom.

Joann removed a cigarette from the pack in her purse and tapped it on the table. She tried to read the label on the bottle, but it was turned away from her. "I don't especially like beer," she said. "What's that one with orange juice? Um, you know..."

"A screwdriver?"

"That's it."

"I'll have a beer," said Maureen.

The cigarette dangling from her mouth, Joann rummaged in her purse for matches. "Let me," said Tom, holding his lighter up, elbow on the table, hand steady, but a little far away. Joann leaned forward— still too far away. She put her hand up to bring the lighter toward her and felt his hand, dry and slightly hairy. Was it Ingrid Bergman in *Casablanca* who held Paul Henreid's hand when he lit her cigarette, and then lifted her eyes to his?

"I'm Ann Mariner," she said after blowing out the first puff of smoke. She leaned her right forearm along the edge of the table, held the elbow of her left arm with her hand, and let her left hand, holding the cigarette, sway gracefully. Turning her chin toward Maureen she said, "And this is Allie Cross."

The other soldier, a tall blond with very short hair and tiny blue eyes arrived back at the table, three beers in his huge right hand and a glass full of orange juice in his left. "Larry, this is Allie and that's Ann," said Tom. He poured a long drink into his mouth. Maureen sipped at hers, and Joann, thirsty, drained all but a mouthful of the screwdriver. It had a sharp, almost bitter taste, which she decided must be the vodka.

"That's the spirit," said Tom. "We'll get you another in a jiffy. How far are you going?"

"We're going to San Francisco," said Maureen.

Tom replied, "We get off there and catch the bus to Eureka. We're going to visit my folks for a few days, huh Larry?" Larry nodded. He was beating time on the table with the beer bottle and the fingers of one hand to music playing in his head. "You girls staying in the city long?" He took another long drink as Maureen answered, a bit uncertainly, "We're not sure."

Joann felt a rush of excitement. Her face flushed as she broke in, "We're going up to find a place to live in Berkeley."

"You go to Cal? What year are you in?" Tom asked. He leaned his head on his hand, tilting toward Joann, excluding Larry and Maureen from the question.

"Junior. Have you been in the army long?"

"Too long."

"Since the war?"

"End of '45."

Joann curved her lips in a half smile and inclined her head to look up into his narrow eyes. "Where were you from originally?"

"Western Wyoming, a small town in the middle of nowhere."

He shifted position, slumping back on the cocktail lounge bench and raising his arm to stretch along its back, just above her shoulders.

"I thought you said you were going to visit your folks in Eureka."

"Picking holes in my story already? Well, that's where they live."

Rather than scrabble in her purse for another cigarette, Joann pulled one of his from the pack he had left on the table and touched it to her lips.

"Hey, isn't that your cigarette burning in the ashtray?" he said. "Not that you can't have one of mine, but…"

He had dropped his hand to her shoulder and had shaken it, slightly, then left it there, the fingers splayed out. She refused to turn her face toward the red-and-gold ashtray embedded in the black tabletop to her right where she had indeed forgotten her cigarette. His hand would have been inches from her face if she had. She said, "Of course. I just wanted to taste one of these." She waited, the cigarette still touching her lips as he retrieved his lighter with his left hand and flicked it on. She leaned forward, her hand holding his, and pulled the smoke deep into her lungs. Then she blew softly and slowly, upward, wishing as the white molecules sped into the air for a ring, a puffy ring, just one. When the cloud had dispersed, she held the cigarette with its red-lipsticked tip to his lips. He moved closer, so his leg met hers, hip to knee.

"Ann," Maureen called. Joann gazed at her as if she had met her just that day. She sucked the last of the orange juice and vodka from around the ice in her glass. Tom signaled Larry for refills.

"I've never been to Wyoming," Maureen said to Tom across Larry's empty chair.

Tom explained the dry cold, the fierce winds, the arctic snows of a high plateau in the Rockies, spoke of his father's low income, the better opportunities in California, and his own intention of going to Cal when his time in the service was up. Larry returned with two beers and another screwdriver.

"Where do you come from, Ann?" Tom asked when they had settled down again to a foursome.

"Refugio, a little more than a hundred miles south of Salinas. My mother owns a restaurant there."

"I've been to Refugio. Larry, we've been to Refugio, haven't we?"

Back in time with his private music, Larry shook his head no.

Joann took a swallow of her drink, allowing it to cool her mouth. Her lips felt strangely numb.

"Sure, we were down there just last year. We had to pick up some guys from Camp Cook."

"That's at Lompoc." Larry had a surprisingly high-pitched voice for such a large man.

"I guess I haven't been to Refugio then. Why don't you tell me about it, Ann."

"Just a little town. Boring."

"Not much to do at night?"

"Just the usual." Her tongue also felt numb—she took another mouthful, just to see if she noticed the cold ice. Tom was laughing as if she had made a joke, and she smiled at him.

"I hear there was a lot of action down there during the war, especially at a place called Pismo."

"In Refugio too. We had a lot of action."

His hand tightened on her shoulder, pulling her closer. "Tell me about yourself," he said.

I want to create a whole new life for myself, away from Refugio, thought Joann. She closed her eyes, trying to think up a story to impress Tom, but this made her dizzy.

"I worked to catch a spy ring in Refugio during the war," she blurted out, then caught herself. "I mean, I was a telephone operator there at the camp. They had some Italian prisoners and a lieutenant who was in the secret service kind of thing…"

"The C.I.C.?"

"I think that's it. He asked me to listen in to their phone calls. He thought they were making too many calls to this Italian who lived in town and was suspicious they were giving information about the camp to the enemy. Or he was."

"And were they? What year was this, by the way?"

"I haven't finished the story yet." She paused to take a long drink

of the screwdriver and to poke about in her purse for a cigarette. She
had an intimation from the two creases between Tom's close-set eyes
that she may have gone too far with her story. How could she cover
her mistake, whatever it was? "It happened over a couple of years, one
thing leading to another, only there are blank spaces, like a chain
of islands."

Larry's voice scraped high over the rattle of the train and the noise
of the crowd surrounding them. He was telling Maureen something
about being transferred to work against the Communists, training
for special duty at Fort Belvoir, in Virginia. It wasn't hard to hate
anything to get away from Fort Ord and the fog; he hated fog so he
hated Communists.

"Where are you staying while you hunt for a place to live?"
Tom asked.

Joann lifted her shoulders. He let his hand slip down her arm and
grip it. "We don't know yet."

"Do you really not know, or are you maybe lying to me?"

"Of course I'm not lying."

"Well. So you're not lying. What if I had a secret lie detector right
here, right in my pocket, what would it tell me? Your secrets, huh? You
want me to know your secrets?"

"I don't have any."

Maureen was telling Larry about finding a grenade on the beach
"north of Santa Barbara," asking him whether they could explode by
themselves. "I'm not an ordnance expert," he was saying, "but sure,
yeah, I've heard..."

Tom was still looking directly at Joann's face. He said, "I hear they
got Alger Hiss to consent to a lie detector test. What do you think
of that?"

She had no idea who Alger Hiss was, though the name seemed
familiar. She shrugged her shoulders again.

"I have a secret. When I get out of the army, you know what I'd like
to do? I'd like to work for the House Un-American Activities Committee.
Have you heard of that?"

"Sure," she said, though she hadn't.

His lips brushed the side of her face. "How old are you anyway?
Don't you read the papers? Don't you know how to drink?"

She pushed him away and tried to rise to her feet.

"You know what, I think you're phony. Didn't your mommy teach you not to play games with strange men?"

She felt cold, saliva was filling her mouth. "Excuse me," she said. "Let me out."

Tom rose to let her pass, putting an arm out to steady her as she stumbled against him, but she pushed him off again and, bumping into a table, stumbled and swayed out of the club car to the women's rest room.

When Maureen found her there ten minutes later, she had vomited. "I'm okay, but I'm not going back to the chair car. I'm going to stay here the rest of the trip. I don't want to see them again," she said.

"What happened? I could have told you not to drink that stuff. Did he say something—funny?"

"I don't know. I mean it, I just don't know anything," Joann cried.

"Did he scare you then?"

"No, of course not."

Maureen never added to the story in her speech about abortion the incident of the soldiers on the train. At the 1989 meeting, she paused a moment while skipping over it, recalling her discomfort and embarrassment, and in the silence a fiftyish woman wearing a caftan spoke. The woman hadn't found a seat near the table, but had commandeered two chairs, one of which she used to hold her feet. She asked in a soft contralto: "You don't seem to blame the people who encouraged you to dream your life their way."

"Isn't that the best way to get through it? Follow a dream or something like that?" Maureen asked. Everyone laughed, even the questioner. "Really, though, blaming them didn't occur to me for about fifteen years, and then I couldn't figure out who the people were. Unless I blamed myself for not taking things seriously in the first place. When I was talking to my husband about the war—you know, *the* war, World War II—I found out that even though we're only two years apart, he knew every battle, suffered with the dropping of the atomic bomb, read about the Nuremberg trials, and I hadn't. I don't know, maybe it was living in the small town. I just really don't know. That trip to San Francisco, my friend and I, all dressed up, trying to look six years older. You know, we had to take a cab out to my Aunt Ida's. It was the first time I ever took a cab, and my mother had given me instructions.

It was as if I were going across Siberia. My friend wasn't feeling too well, and we both were kind of depressed I think. We were staring out the window at the streets, one on each side of the cab. It was the first time she had been to San Francisco, and I was thinking how awful for her to see the part down around Howard Street, where all the bars and flophouses were, and—since it was a nice day and still early in the evening—all the men in old army fatigues, some of them carrying bottles. At one stoplight on Howard Street a grey-haired woman wearing a knit cap and a long coat, open to show she had only a filthy underslip on, tried to climb into the cab on my friend's side. The driver yelled at her and she turned away, mumbling, as Joann pulled the door shut again. The driver said, 'Sorry girls, these things happen in the big city,' and gunned the cab through the intersection. We turned back to look—she'd fallen down to her knees and was just able to get up again. I think my friend started to cry. I always remember it that way, anyhow."

M A U R E E N

The table where the two old men were sitting is cleared; three young men—or younger men, they must be in their forties—take their place. They've come from an office somewhere, their pants are sober shades of grey and they wear dress shirts, undone at the neck, cuffs rolled up. They sprawl in their chairs gossiping about local development politics in a desultory way. Another table has a couple of young mothers with babies in high chairs and parcels from clothing stores scattered on the table and under. Back next to the building sits a table of men and women older than I; the women look like sisters and they seem familiar. I try to recall a family of three sisters who would have been contemporary with Marilyn or Rosemary or Bill, but draw a blank. Then the question occurs: will I recognize Joann when she comes in, will she recognize me? I start watching every movement at the door, certain that each new person must be she. But no, too young. No, a man. One tall stylish figure wearing dark glasses arrives, looks around, is this...no, she turns, finds the group at the back, and I am left with wondering what set of three sisters had a younger sister not much older than I.

But now I see her coming, Joann, and I know her immediately, without doubt. Though she's wearing white slacks and a cobalt blue scarf, the color of her eyes, and though her hair is still kept long, and the Mrs. Ridley I remember had short hair and wore aprons over cotton housedresses—she walks like her mother; there's a curve at the corner of her mouth like her mother's; and when she stares blankly as I rise to signal, I almost think it is Mrs. Ridley. I have this peculiar notion— it remains with me for the time I say, "Here I am," and she says, "Maureen," and I say, "The same," and we sit down and scrutinize each other—that Mrs. Ridley would have known me right off.

"How did you find me?" is the first thing she wants to know.

13

My thoughts while driving are like dreams: images in suspension rippling outward from one source. This is the center: the rustle of tires on an empty residential street blending with the swish of a sprinkler. The rolling circles follow: a hearse at the stop sign on its way south to the graveyard, then my dentist's office, then a street full of people all looking the other way. I rouse myself to interpret. I must be waiting for something to happen. A loved one—Michael?—to be buried and finally gone. A great physical pain that has to be borne. These are two of the most isolated moments of any life.

And then, most of my attention distracted from the appointment ahead of me, I drive into the downtown area and begin to search for a parking place. I find one, swing into it, get out, lock. No thoughts at all now, only the continuing apprehension and loneliness pinching my chest. Stage fright—that's a memory from a long time ago. Joann Ridley appearing in the role of Mrs. Joann Henderson.

I keep a fast pace, round the corner, stop at a light, and there coming toward me are David Blunt and Gene Manach. The curtain will come down for a brief intermission, the leading actress will perform in a comedy skit, and the haunts of my imagination will be replaced with the everyday, for Gene has stopped, leaning on his cane, looking for a chat, and David takes a position immediately in my path.

"You weren't with Gil last night at the city council meeting," David says pleasantly. He knows I disagree with my husband about most of the plans for development, and perhaps he had been hoping for a bit of family disapproval to sway the vote.

I smile with whatever charm I still have, "You know I don't go to meetings. I wouldn't be noticed anyway." Speaking publicly against Gil when he is present is yet beyond me.

David holds a clipboard on his forearm and steps to my side so I can see what his pencil is tapping. "I was hoping to be able to show you these figures on the traffic we'll have to handle, then you could talk to him privately. Maybe it might help."

I am obliging and push my hand into my purse to get reading glasses. Gene fills in the silence as David stands waiting. "It's really good to see you again, Joann. Been a long time, hasn't it?" He is trying to seduce me to rejoin the church group I used to belong to, reaffirm what I no longer believe, and I do not look at him. I find the case, way at the bottom of my purse, pull it out, replace the purse so it hangs from my shoulder, put the glasses on, bend my head to the clipboard.

"Two years," I agree, pretending to read David's figures.

"That long? I've been meaning to phone and ask you to make time for a talk."

I keep my head bent over the clipboard. For several years I attended a special weekly mass and private prayer gathering. To make life here possible? Plunge deeper, live in an underworld city? I don't know, I can't believe I did it, so how can I remember why?

"I told May I had to have some time to think. I told Father George, too."

Gene is a busybody. "We'd like to have you back; it hasn't been the same without you. We need a philosophical bent—you always seemed to take us a little deeper," he pleads.

I speak to David, stepping back from the clipboard, removing my glasses, turning my shoulder away from Gene. "Yes, I see what you mean."

"Then you'll talk to Gil tonight?"

"Oh, not tonight, I have an old friend in town, and well, you know how that is." I move past the two old men, feeling apologetic now that I have ignored Gene. "I'll call," I say insincerely to both.

The interlude has depressed my pace with its reminder that the stage I've been playing on is "everyday." I walk the half block to the restaurant slowly, noticing store windows—toys, jewelry, needlework, multicolored dresses—and people, the young woman pushing a stroller, the neckties and shirtsleeves of two men, and a middle-aged couple in striped matching shirts. Driving down Dana Street, this street, early in the morning I have seen two women dressed in the two dirty sweaters and coat that keep them warm outside overnight and men shambling with their backpacks, but all of them leave here by noon. The street is a facade of respectability, like me. I am homeless too, nights, early mornings. I do not know whether I can relax enough to be homeless before Maureen. What will she remember? The phrase "window of opportunity" pops into my head as I reach the restaurant doors.

She is not easy to find. Outside, yes of course, she would be outside. I feel foolish beside the fence surrounding the patio, checking each

table for a woman by herself. An older woman, she would have grey
hair, a long athletic body, and I cannot find her. But over there, by the
railing above the creek, a woman is staring at me, plump, unpowdered
face, carefully groomed short pale hair, her lipstick matching the loose,
flowered scarf she wears and the glass beads that hang in loops from
her neck. A firm jaw, firm posture, a woman sitting as if behind a desk.
I turn away, embarrassed, and then turn back. It is Maureen.

I am aware of my casual cotton pants and knit cotton shirt, my
dirty white walking shoes. My white hair still loose and long. My pale,
unmade-up face. How respectable she looks. I ice over. My resolve
gone. Is it envy? Is she coming here to show off how successful and
competent she is? She starts to stand, her arms up as if to hug me. I
ignore the face, the hands, and slide into a chair opposite her. We look
at each other, smiling. I say the first thing that comes into my head.
"How did you find me?"

There had always been reason for Joann to envy Maureen, but she
hadn't. Except twice, both times clearly remembered. The first: Maureen
had been chosen for a leading role in the sixth grade play. Joann was
convinced she had been slighted and spent an angry day re-creating
herself as a rock squeezing in upon itself until its core was hot lava.
The second: when still ambivalent about deceiving her parents, dizzy
from the drinks on the train, and nauseated from her horror at the plight
of the woman who had fallen against the cab, she saw Maureen
encompassed by love. When they arrived at Aunt Ida's house—a narrow,
two-story cottage on the bay side of Mt. Davidson—a pleasant and
slightly untidy woman resembling Judge Lewis took Maureen in her
arms at the door. As she hugged and hugged Maureen, saying at least
twice, "I'm so glad you've finally come to visit me this summer, and
you're all grown up," Joann could see that in the corners of Aunt Ida's
tightly closed eyes were two small tears.

Once they were in the house, their suitcases at the foot of the
stairs, Maureen introduced them. Aunt Ida reached out a hand to
Joann and, pretending to straighten a crown with the other hand, she
said, "We wish to welcome you to Munchkinland." Maureen, exploding

into laughter, hugged her aunt again, who tried not to laugh as she bowed toward the staircase, calling it the yellow brick road. Joann was left to stand awkwardly just inside the door until Aunt Ida put her arm around Maureen and said kindly, "Come on in anyway, dear girl. Don't pay any attention to us. We've been playing these games for, what is it now, eighteen years?"

Upstairs they were both silent as they opened their suitcases, hung up their blouses and skirts, and arranged their brushes and bobby pins on the dresser, Maureen hurrying because she wanted to go downstairs again, Joann fumbling, folding, rearranging and unfolding underwear so it could continue to cover the sanitary napkins padding the bottom of her suitcase.

"I'll go on down and see Uncle Al and help Aunt Ida get dinner on the table," Maureen said, her hand on the door.

Joann nodded without looking up from her suitcase. The house seemed very small. She had somehow imagined a house as big as Maureen's in Refugio, where the two of them could go off into rooms that seemed remote from the life of the rest of the house. If she were to vomit here, as she thought she might be going to, everyone would know. They would guess what was the matter with her.

"Are you all right?" Maureen was asking.

The light seemed to be buzzing, a static of black mixed into it. She closed her eyes and sat down on the bed. Maureen was far away, outside a wall of rock; Joann could barely hear her voice. She shook her head no.

"I've got to go downstairs. They'll suspect something's wrong if I don't."

She slipped her shoes off and lay down on the white chenille bedspread. "I can't."

"I'll tell them you're having your period and don't feel well; is that okay?"

After a while through the open door Joann could hear them talking at the dinner table, Maureen's voice falling and rising gaily and the two older voices, one male and one female, responding with laughter and words of praise. Later, after she had vomited and cleaned up the bathroom, rinsed the spots from her blouse, and changed into her pajamas, she was embarrassed to see Aunt Ida at the door carrying a tray with tea and toast. She had taken her apron off and Joann noticed that the ribs of her corsets showed under the torso of her light housedress. She sat down on the bed to watch while Joann sipped the tea.

"That should make you feel better. I've got some aspirin downstairs if you want some. Don't worry or feel embarrassed; Maureen has these little troubles too, and the aches will soon be gone. She always says that tea works better than anything, and the toast makes your tummy feel better."

"I'm sorry to be so much trouble," Joann said politely.

"There is nothing to trouble but trouble itself," Aunt Ida pronounced in a fairly good imitation of Roosevelt's radio voice. "Did I startle you? How about Truman?" She tilted her head watching for a reaction from Joann. "That's better, you have to smile for at least one impression before I stop. You must have thought we were crazy when you arrived, hardly settling to the stomach and all. But Al and I are so pleased to have Maureen here. She's such fun to take around; it gives us something to look forward to. This may not be the time to bring it up, but we have something really special planned for tomorrow, if you feel better of course. Maureen says you've never been to San Francisco before."

Much later when Maureen came up to bed, Joann was playing a game of solitaire, laid out all lopsided on the blankets. She was silent, waiting for Maureen to tell her about the plans for the next day. At last, just as Maureen, facing the dressing table mirror, had pinned up the last curl, Joann said as nonchalantly as she could, "How are we going to get out of here? We might as well have stayed at home."

"Shhh. They'll hear us," Maureen whispered.

"I'm serious. Didn't you tell them we had things to do?"

"How could I? They'd already planned all day tomorrow; Uncle Al took off work and everything. But it's all right; I said I wanted to take you round myself, and that's okay, that still leaves us four days, doesn't it? And we have to try to find Charlie Lapp's phone number and make phone calls anyway, don't we? We'll be able to do that tomorrow. Won't we?"

"I'm sorry I'm making so much trouble for you," Joann said, and regretted that she'd said it.

When Joann first met Winifred Farmer in 1971, they were both newly hired clerical assistants at the city library. Winifred reminded her in superficial ways of Maureen's Aunt Ida. At first an unfamiliar nostalgia stirred her when they were together, as if she were remembering the love she'd received as a child.

Winifred was grey, lined, and heavy. The ribs of her old-fashioned corset showed in outline through the torsos of her simple dresses. The second week of work she did an impression of the head librarian as she sorted books for mending—just a brief pursing of her lips and a long clearing of the throat, performed absentmindedly, without even a glance to see whether she had an audience. The other clerks present, even Joann, laughed.

Even Joann—for her son Michael had recently been killed in Vietnam and Joann had taken the job before she recovered from her first grief. She had locked herself in her bedroom for weeks, refusing to see anyone, not even Andy, still a child. To those who knocked at the door—Brenda, her daughter, come from Virginia, Gil, her mother—she said her life had been wasted. To Gil, personally, when he tried to bring her food, she said she had made a mistake letting him have so much influence on Michael, for Michael had loved him best and had gone into the Marines at his behest. To the priest Gil called after a week, she said she no longer believed in God. Then one quiet rainy day, with Andy in school, Brenda gone home, Gil at his office, her mother home with the flu, she emerged with the notion she would begin all over again. She would leave town, perhaps find Maureen, live one of the lives that long ago she had imagined. She began to think about driving her car north and had gone so far as to take a suitcase from the closet and begin to pack. Pale narrow houses on the slopes of San Francisco's hills sustained her for a few minutes, until the sight of a woman falling in the street behind a cab, a woman begging for money and a ride flashed into her consciousness. I don't have the courage, she told herself, I'd never make it without money. A few days later she saw the job at the library advertised.

"Nothing's ever wasted," said Winifred. "Every time you do anything you have to do it according to some rule. Anything, raising children, anything. It's the rules of the game that count. That's what life is, the rules."

She was at home in an apartment across from the library and just one block from the mission, serving Joann Earl Grey tea from a pot placed on a wooden tray. She was wearing a green print jersey dress that pulled tight against her breasts and torso, where the ribs from her corset showed.

"When I was in training for swimming the Channel, I had to fight thoughts about wasting all my efforts on nothing. I mean, look at it objectively (she was mispronouncing the words, deliberately affecting a middle-European accent, and she scowled as if to explain the theory of relativity to nonscientists): what's the purpose of swimming from England to France when you can always take a boat? The answer! If you don't keep things in, they fall out! I'm no one (she had switched to her earnest, almost diffident, ordinary self), just a bundle of chaotic impulses unless I have a set of rules to follow."

"You really swam the English Channel? That's amazing."

"Yes indeed. What else would prepare me for life in a library?" Winifred laughed, putting one hand on her cup to hold it steady in the saucer.

Joann thought Winifred particularly good at library work—always pleasant, knowledgeable, efficient even at tedious repetitive tasks, or, for that matter, tedious repetitive questions from the public.

"I don't believe in self-expression," Winifred would explain. "My personality is created by the rules I accept. If I didn't have discipline from outside, I'd start pretending I'm someone else."

Or, "Heaven is bound round by rules; it's hell that is all this way and that way." (Always spoken in an Irish brogue, Cork, she explained to Joann.)

Later, when she knew Joann was a Catholic, she said, "The trouble is, you let your faith change when the Pope John XXIII people started to take over. They had no idea that the old forms of the Church are necessary for us. We need them to project our own inner life into. No one ever gave you a medal, I'd guess, I mean something like this." She shoved her hand down the front of her dress, into the top of the corset, and brought out a chain from which hung a silver oval. She pulled the chain from around her neck, handing the medal to Joann. While Winifred rearranged her hair, Joann examined the tiny image of the Blessed Mother. "This medal, now. When I was in Hawaii during the war, my husband was killed. He was a Marine; they say it was a grenade. He was all there was in the world to me, and every day and all night long I kept seeing him, his beloved body, flying apart. The chaplain gave me this medal and told me to pray to Our Lady for help, and I did, for hours. One day I was sitting with the medal in my hands, when I saw red drops trickling from those tiny fingers onto my fingers. I wiped them from my hand, and discovered they were blood, and somehow I suddenly understood the meaning of both love and suffering. Now I'm not saying the blood was real, but it was real for me right then. The symbol had said something to me, what was inside me had actual expression. I learned that the Church gives you lots of symbols to pour yourself into, one for every occasion."

Joann was not certain whether to believe the story of the medal, deciding after a time it didn't make any difference whether she did or not. "What's in your own head is what's important, sweetheart," her dad used to say before she grew up. "If you think you're levitating, you're levitating."

Before long she had set aside all the doubts that had tormented her since Michael's death and was accompanying Winifred to daily mass at the mission and to a biweekly private mass held in the home of a retired Polish doctor. After mass they had discussions. Was the story of Adam and Eve and the serpent literal truth? They were supposed to believe it as literal truth, or at least as the sense intended by God, not in any personal sense. Was the body of Our Lady really taken into heaven? They were supposed to understand the meaning spiritually, not try to verify it in their minds. Winifred insisted one time that the mass was essentially a ritual of magic, that Catholicism was a magical religion, and Joann imagined as she forced herself into its age-old molds that she felt stirring in her some of the freedom and courage she'd had as a child.

Afterward, when Winifred had left town suddenly to join a commune of Catholics in Sonoma County, Joann continued her attendance at the private masses. But within a few months she had begun to wonder what it was that had enabled her to feel content, when, in her chaotic moments in the dark upon the hill or times she parked her car high above the sea and stared out to the horizon, she felt absorbed into whatever was unruly—wind, surf, the flowing and trembling earth. Then she knew her contentment was spurious. It came only from the constant imposition of insincerity. Still, she stayed, remembering her father's moves from one religion to the next. Following the narrow rules had become an obsession she rarely freed herself from, and when she looked back on this period later, she saw it as a kind of solitaire. I could think and not think, she described it to herself. Or more recently, she began to realize, she could ignore the needs of people: her mother dying without consolation, Andy left to Gil as much as Michael had been. Herself.

J O A N N

Our conversation is not going well. I keep staring at Maureen as if she were a painting, examining the brush strokes of flesh over bone, trying to recall the narrow pointed chin, the broad high cheekbones. One amusing point, our clothes must be more familiar to each of us than our faces: shirts shaped like the old sweatshirts—yes, she has her sleeves pushed up to half the forearm, just as I do—scarves, big ones with bright corners tied gracefully over neck and shoulder.

She stares at me, too, though she is sociably talking to fill up the time before the waitress brings us a bottle of wine. She has told me how like my mother I am, and I cringe momentarily at an unexpected vision of my mother's face, set in death as I saw her last, rigid and black on the floor of her house. She notices the—what is it?—twist of my lip that gives me away and after asking if my mother is living continues with the information that her mother is still alive, active at ninety, and living with Bill in Seattle. I listen until the waitress brings the wine, when she shifts her attention to the children playing in the creek. They remind her of her own when they were little.

"I have two daughters," she says. "One lives in the East. The other, well, I've just come from there. She's just moved, in San Diego, and I was down there helping out."

I cannot find a reply right this minute. I sip my wine, to hide the twist of my lip, the need to respond. I cannot decide what to say. Again, she notices. She lifts her wine to her lips, saying, "Let's drink to this reunion. I am so terribly pleased to be here."

Their first day in San Francisco they had felt as closely guarded as kindergarten children on a field trip. In a rest room at Coit Tower on

Telegraph Hill, one that Ida had not accompanied them into, Joann said she would sneak into a phone booth and check the book for the name Bobby had given them. Outside, while Maureen entertained Ida and Al, she found the number and rang it. But the operator came on the line to tell her to deposit money for the call. She discovered she had no change smaller than fifty cent pieces and when she went back to Aunt Ida, Uncle Al, and Maureen, they were ready to drive on to Golden Gate Park. That evening when they were supposed to have gone to bed, Joann climbed out the window, using a tree as a ladder, and ran up the street to a small grocery store. There was a pay phone in the front, and she tried the number. After several rings a man's voice answered.

"Is this Mr. Lapp?"

"Who?"

"I'm looking for someone called Charles Lapp."

"Don't know him. Anyone here know Charles Lapp?" he shouted out into a void.

A faint voice answered. "Who wants him?"

"Some little girl."

Laughter.

"Well, he's not here. They say he left here about a month ago."

Desperately, Joann asked whether anyone knew where he was now.

After a moment away from the phone, the man rattled off a number and the name of a street. She wasn't sure she had it right, and asked him to repeat it. All the way back to the house, down the street made dark by fog, she repeated the number in time to her running feet.

The next morning they told Aunt Ida they were going over to see the campus at Berkeley. She kept them long enough to give complicated instructions about how to take the streetcar to the train station and where to get off the train in Berkeley. It was after twelve when they climbed off the train at the stop below the campus.

14

This is not working. Joann and I might as well be strangers meeting at a convention. We sip wine. I comment on the weather, she mentions local wineries, I compare with Napa. Move in closer, I tell myself, and ask after her mother and tell her about my daughters.

In an uncomfortable silence, I catch a glimpse of us, eleven years old or so, kneeling on my bed, bending over looms that hold the beaded headbands we were making for Camp Fire. The designs we were working on were supposed to represent what we hoped for from life. Suddenly Joann emptied all the little bottles full of colored beads onto my white chenille bedspread, where they clustered, rolling back and forth in patterns under her fingers. "Hey!" I said, shocked. "Mine was wrong; it wasn't working," she said.

I try to phrase this recollection for us. "Remember," I'm about to say, then notice the deep double grooves between her eyebrows, a left-sided twist to her mouth I can't recall. I lift my glass, saying, "Let's drink to this reunion. I am so terribly pleased to be here." As I taste the wine, slightly sun-warmed, I become aware how happy I am, after all.

The waitress serves my salad, Joann's sandwich, and I begin to eat, listening to the murmur of conversations around us, the occasional sharp call of one of the children down in the creek. My friend has taken one bite and is watching me pick through the salad with a fork. After a while she asks, "How do you find Refugio after all these years?"

I put my fork down and reach for a piece of bread. "Different. But everything's changed, hasn't it? Have you been to the Bay Area recently?"

She shakes her head, no.

"You wouldn't recognize it—too many people, too many cars, too many houses—but I suppose that's part of growing older in the same place." Joann is waiting for more, but I must try not to chatter.

"How would you say Refugio has changed? Is it just bigger, or is there a change in essence, soul, the way you see the soul, anyway?" she asks.

I smile, catch her eye. The question is a remnant of the child I knew. I can still hear her saying, "Just what do you think the very soul of hopscotch is?" The child I thought I was, the sincere and earnest— maybe even helpful—person willing to collaborate in a hundred schemes, rises, a burst of warmth in my chest, but I clench the hand held in my lap. Whether from joy, or caution, I don't know. I say, "Right here my guess is that it's not happy with itself. It's trying to look woodsy, like Marin County, and it isn't. I always think of it, thought of it, as barren." I see a chance, take it. "I still get the feeling I got that day we went to San Francisco on the train. The hills, all grazed bare, and when we looked back, it was like a little desert town. Remember?"

"Vaguely," she says. "I remember the train trip, but not the details."

"There was a soldier on the train. He kept pretending he had a frog in his pocket, and you got sick."

"Not on the train," Joann says. "That man wasn't on the train."

Joann would rather not remember the man obsessed by an imaginary frog. Now and then she has nightmares about plagues of frogs, and she always wakes panicky and helpless. The dreams vary—sometimes there are great mounds of frogs, like mountains, falling down on her; sometimes they are in a well with her, filling it, she feels their delicate webbed paws and knows she cannot breathe; sometimes she finds one under a rock and it explodes all around her, just when she thinks she has it conquered. When she wakes, she remembers the face of the man. She calms herself by driving the memory away.

They had taken the electric train all the way to the stop just below the university in Berkeley, then trudged up through the green lawns and woods of the lower campus into the maze of massive grey buildings at its center. Maureen, unable to stop herself, gaped greedily at the arched windows glittering with the gold of the afternoon sun; turned her head to look after young men in khaki pants and white shirts hurrying past them, carrying briefcases; and wondered whether she would ever meet any of the women she saw, dressed like her and Joann in flowered cotton skirts, blouses, and white socks rolled down below the ankles. After they left the campus, they had to walk on to a street leading down toward the bay, almost a mile past bookstores and cafes and then a set of small grimy shops and dirty apartment buildings. By that time it was midafternoon, and the sun was shining into their eyes. Maureen, noticing the shabbiness of the neighborhood and connecting it to the two novels she had just read where someone had an abortion—"She made her way down the dirty alley to a green door, where…"—thought nervously about whether they should have brought the sanitary napkins with them, just in case.

The address they had been given brought them to a tall, wooden house whose front stairs sagged and whose windows looked as if they were never opened. A set of battered tin mailboxes hung near the door, which was propped open by a smiling cast iron fish. They entered, hesitated, then continued to the end of the hall where a grey door smudged with fingerprints had tacked to it a card bearing the number 16. The card had been torn down and retacked more than once, for holes and rips mottled its top edge.

When Joann knocked, the panels clattered, echoing through the building. She waited, turned to Maureen, who shrugged. She tried again, drawing this time a response, a bass, throaty gargle repeated twice. Encouraged, she knocked once more, and the immense croaks sounded, immediately drowning the echo.

"Open it," Maureen urged.

Joann hesitated, thinking, this must be a mistake, I don't want to do this, I want to be at home, I can't be afraid, I can't be afraid. "Just a minute," she said, then immediately regretted it. Maureen can't know I'm afraid.

"Enter," a theatrical, echoing bass shout. "'Whence is that knocking? How is't with me, when every noise appalls?'" Then high-pitched and mincing, "'I hear a knocking. Retire we to our chamber: a little water will cleanse us of this deed.'"

They pushed open the door, each with a hand on its scratched panel, and stepped into a small room, first Joann, then a moment later, Maureen. The room was darkened by the shade over its one window. A table shoved up beside the window held piles of paper, several stained crockery mugs, a plate with dried-up food soiling it, and some books propped open with the covers and wadded pages of other books. An old-fashioned dresser stood next to the table, its marble top holding more cups and books, two empty wine bottles with candles stuck in them, and dirty underwear. Jeans and a sweater hung over an opened drawer. In the corner right next to the dresser rested a low mattress on a set of squat springs. A bony redheaded man lay on the mattress, dirty grey sheets covering just the middle of his body. His head was leaning on one hand, the long fingers of the other crouched on the edge of the bed as if covering a small animal, keeping it railed within the fingers like bars in a prison. He glanced at Joann when she walked through the door, but otherwise he did not move. The room smelled of wine and tobacco.

Suddenly as they stared at him, uncertain what to do or say, he made his crouched hand leap up onto his chest. "It's only two little girls who don't understand frog talk," he murmured down at his hand. "Croak. Croooaaaaak." Turning onto his back, he held the hand against his heart allowing all his left side, including grimy undershorts, to remain exposed by the inefficient cover. He looked up, curling his lips back in a wide simian grimace, "We are not accustomed to having ladies present, so you will excuse our not getting up."

The moment he smiled Maureen tugged at Joann's jacket. The man had not brushed his teeth for so long the scum on them looked green. "Come on," she said. "This isn't the right place."

"I can't," Joann said. Her face felt cold, but moist with sweat. "Are you Charlie Lapp?" she asked in child's pitch, her voice rising as it always did when she was frightened.

At first he wouldn't answer, just lay there with his lips pulled back from his teeth, staring up at the ceiling.

Joann moved closer to the bed, leaning her hip against the dresser, staring down at him. "I have to know. Please."

He allowed a moment to pass before he said, slowly stretching his lips back across his teeth in a croak, "Why?"

"Because I have to."

With the same exaggerated motion and a pause between each word he said, "Suppose I'm not?"

"Then maybe you can tell me where I can find him."

He sat up suddenly, his torso rising from his hips like a jackknife, his left arm at his side, his right hand suddenly tight around Joann's wrist. Maureen jumped back toward the door. "Come on," she said. "Let's go."

The man, without moving his head, opened his mouth and laughed.

Her heart pounding wildly, Joann kept her wrist motionless. "You can go, but I can't," she said.

"That's right," he said. Slowly he pulled her down toward the mattress.

Acquiescing, kneeling beside it, she looked into his eyes, widening hers as she saw his were moist with tears. Suddenly he released her, his whole body going limp at the same time. "If I knew where to find him, you'd be the first to know," he said. With his knees pulled up, his head resting on them, his arms shielding his face, he said, "Now get out of here." His dark red greasy hair splayed out over the faint sprinkling of freckles on his forearms.

"But you do know Charlie Lapp," Joann persisted. This is the worst moment of all, she said to herself. I feel cold and it's as if I can't hear.

The man was paying no attention to her. She shook his naked shoulder. "Look, I've got to find him."

"Me too."

"Then you must know him. You do know him, don't you?"

"What difference does it make to you?"

"I'm pregnant."

Suddenly he was up on his knees, screwing his face into an imitation of a girl receiving a compliment. His cheeks were dead white. "That's the sweetest thing anyone's ever said to me. I've been waiting all my life to hear it." He twisted his mouth down, frowned, and snarled, "I don't believe you, you goddamn princess bitch."

Afraid he was going to strike her, she pulled back up on her knees, then stood up. Puzzled, she narrowed her eyes, staring. But driven by her need to end the cold on her face, the buzzing in her ears, she said, "I have to find him, he's the only name I have. Charlie Lapp is supposed to know how to help people in trouble. And you don't have to call me names, you goddamn son of a bitch."

"So you're in trouble?" he sneered. "Well you want to know something? So am I, so am I. And Charlie Lapp won't do a thing about it."

She stood quite still, staring down into his eyes, her hair curling down around her ears, one lock hanging over her shoulder, her hands stiff against the folds of her flowered dirndl skirt, her thin legs trembling a bit. After a moment he said, "He's more likely to get you into trouble than out of it, if I know him."

"So you do know him. All I want is some way to find him."

"I did. A month ago. He promised. He made all kinds of promises." He stood up, balancing himself on the mattress. His grimy underpants slipped down to hang on his hip bones and he made no move to pull them up. The hair on his belly was the same color as the hair on his head.

Maureen refused to look, staring out the door instead. "He's, uh, gone to San Francisco, got a job with a night club, left everyone in the lurch."

"Do you know his phone number?"

"Somebody's taken my last pair of pants." He stepped off the mattress and began to poke into piles stashed here and there around the room.

"What are these on the dresser then?" Joann asked.

"Some guy's. He left here with mine. I've already tried them on, when I got up to take a piss. They're too short." He gave a croak, closed his eyes, and jumped his hand down to the exposed hip, where he thrust it under the elastic band to scratch vigorously. "I take it you know what a boy looks like," he giggled. He directed a stage glare at Maureen, who still stood in the doorway with her back to the room. "At least one of you."

Joann said nothing. Until the day Mr. Genley, the biology teacher, had brought out the plaster human torso, all pink and liver, with red and blue lines showing arteries and veins, Joann had never seen a human penis, not on babies, not on statues, and had always been told by her mother not to stare at pictures in books. She had, nevertheless, neither blushed nor tried to see who was giggling, but had kept her eyes steadily on Mr. Genley's ruler, willing herself not to have an emotional reaction. It had been much the same when they had cut up cats in the classroom, though several girls had been overcome with the first cut.

Unlike Maureen, as the man scratched and arranged his testicles, Joann simply continued to stare earnestly into his face, her eyes grave, her chin slightly tilted, and said, "I really need that phone number. You've got a pair of jeans over there on the floor. I really need it, I mean the phone number." Then she picked the jeans up and handed them to him.

He pulled them up, buttoned them, and rummaged soberly in a drawer for a sweatshirt. "And when the princess handed the frog his jeans, the frog disappeared and a beautiful prince appeared," he said. He stood in front of the mirror, dug a comb from his pocket, slicked back the sides of his hair with the help of oil from a bottle, arranging at the same time a large, full pompadour.

"That is," he added, "if you tell me who gave you this address. The prince of frogs has to know how you found him, after all."

"Phil Moss," said Maureen. "He used to know Charlie during the war. He said Charlie could help."

"That rascal Phil. I'm sorry I didn't know him," he said, turning around and smiling—a pleasantly natural smile—at Joann. "Suddenly I feel like a prince. I'm hungry; are you going to feed me? I'll take you to see him if you do."

"You haven't told us your name yet," Maureen said.

"Collie. And my frog's name is Friendenstein."

M A U R E E N

"There are some strangely disconnected scenes." Joann is cupping her wine glass in two hands, looking down into it. "Dreamlike. They don't have any story to them. Do you know what I mean, that unless you can connect something going on they are just scenes? I'm sitting in the train, I have that grey suit on, you know the one I was supposed to wear going away to college, and I'm thinking the biggest risk I can take, really, is to stay, and it's like that quotation Tynan gave us, the one from Ruskin. You remember how she loved Ruskin?"

Of course I do, but I simply nod, my two hands also holding my wine glass.

"Ruskin, the one about if you're a coward once then the next time you have to confront something, you find it even easier to be a coward, to step back from what you have to do, and I was thinking, maybe this is a mistake, maybe I'm really being a coward."

"Oh, no," I say, "I don't think so. I've always thought having an abortion was one of the bravest things anyone could do, right then. You risked your life."

Joann does not respond. I want to go on about a woman I heard call abortion the guerrilla part of the war to reclaim our lives, but I'm not sure how she will take the analogy. I veer away. "Is it all right to smoke out here?" I ask, reaching in my purse for a cigarette.

"I think so." She has not eaten her sandwich.

"The funny thing is, about the soul of Refugio I mean, I always think of it with two responses, as if it's got two faces for me..." She nods, yes, yes go on. "All right, it's barren, but the other face, I don't know, I can't quite give it a name. This morning I took a walk up toward Murray Elementary School, over Pacheco Street, you know where the camphor trees are and the houses where I used to wish I could live, and I still have that feeling. I wonder what it would be like to wake up in one of the paneled rooms and have breakfast looking out at the old-fashioned flower garden, and I want to do it."

"The secret garden, the imaginary world," Joann says, smiling with her eyes down. "I sometimes do that too. But then I remind myself, I live there, here. Where even the dangers are imaginary."

Occasionally when she thinks about poverty and helplessness, Maureen chooses a scene from an old hotel on Mission Street in San Francisco as an icon deserving of meditation. Though she can remember only one vision, like a tableaux, from the experience, she relives the shock and anger and believes the rising adrenaline in her blood helps her persist in a course of action, no matter how trivial or futile or difficult it seems. She used it to impel her in the '50s to stay after school to tutor the black students who came to San Francisco from the South, where they had not learned to read; she needed the energy to keep her going while she taught more family living classes than history, supported Chet in graduate school, and gave birth to her eldest daughter Nancy. She used it for the courage she needed to leave Nancy with Marilyn and join the Freedom Riders in Alabama in the summer of 1963, and to organize a drop-in center for welfare mothers in San Francisco in 1970. It stirred in her mind when she campaigned for Hubert Humphrey in 1968, and it was her strength when she went to jail for Vietnam protests twice. It sent her off several times to march with the farm workers, and it was the inspiration for her scholarly studies of the working women's movements in the early twentieth century. When her graduate students ask her how she maintains objectivity, she says, simply, "I don't."

By the time Collie got them to the cafe where he wanted to eat, it was already four in the afternoon. Joann kept her eye on the clock at the back of the room while Maureen watched him eat a plate full of eggs, ham, greasy potatoes, and the catsup he poured all over them. "Vegetables for Friendly," he said as he shook the bottle, then croaked three times. After he had wiped the runny egg from his plate with a piece of toast, he picked up the check, said, "Twenty dollars will do it." It was almost five o'clock. Maureen handed him the money, picked carefully from the wad in her purse.

"Let's go," he said.

"But you promised us an address, or at least a phone number," she said.

Grinning, a bit of jam still adhering to a front tooth, he croaked in a singsong, "We're going to take you there, aren't we Friendly?" He pulled his jaw down into a mournful sneer and looked into his pocket. "What, no giggles from the sweet little girls?"

"We have to go home now," said Maureen. "We can't do anything until tomorrow."

"We have a previous engagement tomorrow, don't we Friendly? But they can suit themselves. Maybe they don't trust Collie. Maybe they don't think he really is a prince of a fellow."

On the way out of the restaurant he paid the bill and pocketed the change from the twenty. "Car fare," he said, and neither felt she could object. Though they tried to set a fast pace back to the train stop, he ambled along, peering into the windows of the bookstores as they went. At the university gates he burst into song, high-pitched lilting melodies, most with bawdy verses. Embarrassed at first, Maureen examined the faces of women in heels and sober skirts who passed them, dashing down the asphalt paths away from offices. None gave her a second glance, and she was comforted. Joann strode along in a daze, outpacing Collie and Maureen, who lingered out of politeness. When Joann was too far ahead she turned to face them, waiting for them to catch up.

It was almost six when they reached the corner of the wide street where the tracks ran. Maureen took fifteen cents from her purse to telephone Aunt Ida, hoping that Uncle Al would answer because he would ask fewer questions.

"I'm sorry we're so late; we haven't left Berkeley yet. You go ahead with dinner. We'll get a hamburger and maybe we'll go to a show on Market Street." She knew this excuse was possible from times she had stayed at Ida's with her sisters, when they would call, just before dinner, and Ida would tell them it was all right, go ahead, enjoy the show. "Yes, I've got a key. No need to wait up."

"Necessity makes liars of us all," Collie chanted not two feet from the receiver.

"What's that?" said Ida.

"What's what?" said Maureen, pretending to be unaware. But as she put the phone down, she felt exactly the way she had when, as a child of five, she had become separated from her mother in a large department store crowded with people who neither knew nor cared about her. "I'm starting to hate lying," she said to Joann.

"It's a survival tactic," sneered Collie.

On the trip back across the Bay Bridge, they sat together, silently, while Collie whispered into his cupped hands, now and then leering at them from across the aisle.

"Do you think he's crazy?" Maureen asked while the train stopped at Treasure Island to pick up a handful of sailors. One of them took the seat next to Collie, who ostentatiously put his hand deep into his pocket, pulled it out again, and raised his voice above the roar of the starting train to tell them, in mincing tones, "I put Friendly away. Some people just don't understand."

"No," said Joann. Her voice quavered and she paused, seeking control. "But I think we're going to have to believe in the frog if we don't. Think he's crazy, I mean."

Neon lights on enormous billboards announced their arrival back in San Francisco. Even though the sun had not yet set, the lights radiated from the windows and up the sides of the bars, pawn shops, and liquor stores the three passed after they left the Key Station on First Street. Maureen and Joann went arm in arm with Collie, so they would not get lost, he insisted. "If you're good little girls I'll tell you the story of Friendenstein's life. It's a sad life, which is why he's a sad frog and needs lots of comforting."

"That's better than singing," said Joann.

"Where are we going?" asked Maureen.

"Don't be bad," he said, strolling along, pinching her hand in his. "Friendly wants you to be good and listen. He's preparing a lecture for the anthropology department. It all starts when his mother left him in a pond."

Half an hour later, a block past the Greyhound bus depot, Friendly was being jumped upon by all the bigger frogs in a military academy. "To be continued," Collie said, stopped, and turned them into the lobby of a small hotel. It smelled of disinfectant mixed with cigar smoke. The floor covering was linoleum, and the chairs, sagging and sprung, in rows along the walls, were dirty, dark green, and spotted with burns. Once they had pushed in through the greasy glass doors, a woman in heavy makeup, cheeks bright as a doll's, lifted her pencil-thin eyebrows at the man behind the desk. "You kids sure this is where you want to be?" she asked as they passed her chair.

"Pardon me?" asked Maureen, pausing and leaning her blond head down toward the woman.

"I said, girls like you don't belong here."

Collie, holding tight to their hands, leaned his face close to the woman's, spread his lips to show the full green grin, and let out a croak as loud and resounding as a burp. Then he tugged them over to the desk.

"We have business with Charlie Lapp," he said to the man behind the desk. The man rolled exophthalmic eyes toward Collie, then at Maureen, then at Joann. He had a mottled red nose, jagged broken teeth, and sores in the corners of his mouth.

"I know you, I guess. Room 350. You'll have to take the stairs, elevator boy's out for his supper," he rasped, pointing down a long corridor. "Or would be if it worked. And only you. You leave them girls out here; I'll watch 'em for you."

They stood near the desk, waiting. Maureen watched the desk clerk sit at a table, unfold a newspaper, light a cigar, read. Whenever he glanced up at her, she transferred her stare to the window where in the dirty light of early evening three men leaned, sharing a bottle of wine wrapped in a paper bag. Their faces were grimy and yellow even in the occasional flash of the hotel's red neon light.

"I have to go to the bathroom," Joann whispered after a while.

"Can you wait?"

"Maybe."

An old man in a business suit and hat pushed through the door and came up to the desk. His face had so little flesh his teeth held his lips open, and the sleeve of his suit was torn and dirty. Slowly, his hands shaking, he counted out seven one dollar bills and two fifty cent pieces for the desk clerk, who took the money and handed him an envelope. "Got some mail today, Eddy."

"Thanks." The old man began to cough as he walked down the hallway to the stairs holding a postcard in his hand.

"You girls can sit down," the desk clerk pointed to two chairs facing the windows. "Anyway, get away from the desk, will you?"

Obedient, they settled gingerly into the chairs, flattening their skirts from behind and tucking them in at the sides to make sure no part of their flesh touched the dirty green cloth. Maureen kept her purse in her lap, reaching into it for her cigarettes. She offered one to Joann, and they both lit up. The woman with the heavy makeup watched them with her eyes half closed.

"At least the smoke kills the smell," said Maureen.

"I hadn't really noticed."

"He's been gone a long time."

"Only ten minutes. I think I'm going to ask where the bathroom is."

"But it will be filthy."

"I suppose."

A black woman wearing a long brown coat and carrying a wan child with dark scabs disfiguring the skin around her mouth leaned against the door to the lobby until it opened. Breathing heavily, as if she had walked up a steep hill, she made her way to the desk. Her left arm still around the child, she struggled one-handed to open the clasp to her purse. Pieces of change rattled on the counter. "I've only got six dollars left," she said. "Somebody over on Third Street said he'd maybe have something for me tomorrow, though, and I can get you the rest then."

"Sorry, Milly, you know the price is eight. There's other places that takes colored."

"But I can't get there tonight; I don't have the carfare, and I'm awful tired. I ain't had nothing to eat all day."

"That's not my affair."

Tears began to roll down her cheeks. The child put a hand up and with one finger gently touched the wet.

"Can I get my stuff out then?"

"Don't take too long. I ought to charge you for keeping the room full all day. But I don't want to take your carfare. And for god's sake get something to eat with the six."

She turned and walked heavily down the corridor to the right, Maureen staring after, observing the thick weight of the coat, the thin legs, the worn heels of the shoes. This was the first time she had ever seen a black woman or child outside of the movies, though she had passed men on the street or noticed an occasional serviceman at the bus depot in Refugio during the war.

It was dark outside when Collie appeared looking pleased with himself and knelt down before them, pushing his head close to theirs, whispering. "Friendly had to beg and beg old Charlie before he'd see you. Charlie told Friendly he didn't like to see girls in trouble, too much trouble he said, but Friendly said he'd do nice things for Charlie and get him lots of money. Just one, though. Just one at a time, that's all he can handle."

Joann turned white. "He's not going to do it now?"

"Oh, Charlie doesn't do anything; he just makes arrangements and gives places to meet, things like that. But just to one, not two." He took Joann's hand. "You're the one. Aren't you? He won't tell me; he doesn't trust Friendly." He pulled her up and led her to the corridor. Maureen listened, trying to hear their footsteps on the stairs.

Collie first, Joann behind, they climbed up four flights of stairs with rubber treads, the walls grimy where people put their hands for support, dust and cigarette butts and crushed pieces of french fries and an occasional orange peel underfoot. Down a dingy hall lit by bare bulbs in wall sockets, past high doors with transoms at the top and an occasional sound of humans moving about or talking within: Joann thinking of the path through the willows along the creek, the alley behind her parents' cafe, the dark cool basement of the library.

"So how is old Phil?"

Collie had opened the door and crossed the room to stand at the window. She was left in the entrance, frozen. She had for several hours been trying to close herself off from what she was experiencing, remain conscious only of her need, a pair of ears to hear the answer to her request and eyes to find her way with. At the sound of that voice she was suddenly completely successful.

The man was perched on the bed in his stocking feet, smirking. He was thin and angular, a knobby face, a shock of black hair hanging down over one eye. "Come in," he said. "Shut the door. Now tell me, how is old Phil?"

Joann obeyed, closing the door, taking one step forward, standing still, her arms straight at her sides, one hand clutching the cloth of her flowered skirt. "Phil Moss...he's fine," said Joann. Her voice sounded weak to her, and she raised the volume and tried again, "Fine."

He patted the bed next to him. "I've only got one chair in here. Sit down. What's he up to these days? Still in school?" He had a tenor voice, smooth, the words run together in a kind of constant whine.

"He's in veterinary college, up in Washington, I think."

He laughed, slapping his knee, then told a joke about a farmer having sexual intercourse with a cow. Though she did not understand the joke, she smiled obligingly. She could smell the stale tobacco on his breath.

In the lobby, in a momentary stillness, the heavily made-up woman began to hum a melody familiar to Maureen. She kept her eyes closed while she hummed and her mouth sagged as if she was putting herself to sleep. The tune was simple, high, lilting, and Maureen was sure she'd heard it a thousand times—it was a favorite of Rosemary's—it went round and round like a music box. Yes, she suddenly remembered, it was something about a paper doll, buying a paper doll. The words took shape and wedged themselves into consciousness. She began to sing them silently in tune to the woman's accompaniment, unable to concentrate on anything else. Meanwhile, the troubled feeling that she should be doing something increased, though she couldn't decide exactly what it was she should be doing. The rules of the game said she was supposed to sit here and wait; she might lose Joann's chance to win if she left, if she went in search, if she interfered, if she didn't believe the magic, if she tried to tag along with the older kids, if little sister tried to take responsibility.

When the woman stopped, stirred, shifted her legs about in the chair, Maureen looked at her watch. Joann had been gone almost fifteen minutes, and her troubled feeling had become tension. She really should climb those stairs and find Joann, but she really should stay where she was too. What is the most responsible thing to do? she asked herself. But she had made no decision when she stood up, brushed her skirt off, and entered the corridor to the right of the desk.

She realized she was angry with herself for wanting to shirk responsibility and at Collie for taking over her position and angry with Joann for letting herself dive so deeply into the unknown without a protest. When she reached the stairs she began to run, taking two steps at a time, holding to the wooden banister to try to keep her feet from drumming out too much noise. At the top of the third flight she burst, short of breath, into a dimly lit corridor paneled in wood that had been painted pale green so long ago the chips had coalesced into large dark spots. A door stood open before her and without thinking, not even looking at the number, she knocked and entered. Then, right at the entrance she stopped, to catch her breath. Over the heaving of her own lungs, she heard deep but stifled sobbing. Alarmed—Joann?—she took a step into the room and saw in the dim light, the thin child lying on an unmade bed and the woman in the brown coat leaning over a battered suitcase on the floor, head almost between her knees, hands over her eyes, wiping at them, wiping at her nose, wiping. Horrified at the despair, truly frightened by her intrusion, Maureen stepped back, hoping she would not be seen, but the child looked up, began to wail, and the woman saw her. "What you want?" The woman forced a smile, a humiliated, ingratiating smile. She had a wide gap between her two front teeth, her face was shiny with tears, the wet eyes red and hostile.

Inside her white skin, underneath her long blond hair, Maureen felt ashamed of her full stomach, her clean clothes, the deeper, unerasable knowledge that she would always, one way or another, be taken care of, by parents, teachers, police, even, in some way, by women like this. She couldn't move for a moment, burdened by this shame, and when she spoke, she heard her voice from far off, insincere, disdainful, "I'm sorry. I didn't mean to. I'm looking for my friend."

"She's not hiding in here." Still that smile, as if she were staving off a blow, keeping her eyes on Maureen while slowly taking the waxed paper wrapping from a thin, half eaten sandwich, handing it to the child, who did not eat and kept on wailing. "Go on now, don't like no white girls seeing my troubles." She turned away then and spoke to the child. "Come on honey, eat it, just a little piece."

"I'm sorry," said Maureen, remembering the scene downstairs. "What are you going to do?"

"I got to close the door now," the woman started to rise, but the child's wails turned into hoarse wrenching screams, and the sandwich dropped on the floor as the child threw her arms around her mother's neck.

"I'm sorry," Maureen said again, backing toward the door, "I just..." and in a gesture she squirmed over for the next forty years, thinking how patronizing, how awful, what possessed me, she unzipped her purse, snatched several bills from the wad of money and tried to hand them to the woman. But she would not take them, allowing them to drop all crumpled up, into the suitcase open on the floor.

As soon as Maureen put her hand out with the money in it, she wanted to take it back. She didn't even know how much it was. She would have to count as soon as she got downstairs.

"I said I didn't want no white girls seeing my troubles," the woman said. She had not picked the bills up from the open suitcase when Maureen closed the door.

At the end of the long corridor Maureen saw Joann, a grey figure floating forward through the muted light. Silently they came together, silently they slipped down the stairs, through the lobby, out into the street. They walked back the way they had come because they had no idea how to find their way home yet. "Is it all right?" Maureen finally asked.

"I guess so. I don't know."

"You were gone an awfully long time."

"He kept talking about Phil, Bobby's brother."

"What about the operation?"

"It's Thursday night."

"Where?"

"I don't know. He said he wouldn't...couldn't do anything for me, I'm too young; he thought it was funny. He said Phil or whoever it was should marry me. Then he said he knew it wasn't Phil, because he didn't molest children."

"I thought you said Thursday night."

"Collie came out in the hall. He said he'd find someone for me."

"Thursday night's the night we're supposed to go to the play."

"He'll meet me then. Just me, though. You can't go."

"I don't care, I'm going."

They were in sight of the Key Station where they could find the same bus they had taken down from Ida's house, when Joann said, "You can't." While they waited for the bus she said, "It's going to cost five hundred."

"What are we going to do?"

M A U R E E N

Joann has broken a piece of bread from her sandwich. A jay struts under a table a few feet away. "I mean," she is saying, "You make up the dangers in the garden and pretend that real ones don't exist."

I order coffee, though Joann is still sipping the wine. "Have you been here the whole time? I mean here in Refugio?" I ask.

"Yes, except for a short period in Redding, but Gil always wanted to come back. He liked it here."

"That's how I found you," I say. "I remembered Gil, and I just guessed he'd stay here forever, if he could."

She laughs, the first time she has laughed at all. "It's funny you should come today then."

"Why?"

"I'll tell you later. After you tell me about you."

It's taken us all of lunch, and a full bottle of wine, but at last we are beginning our reunion. She is animated, asking questions, responding. I am telling her about how I might be running for city council. She says, "Just like your mother." I say, "No, I'm not."

15

Now and then the shadow of one small sycamore leaf flutters against
Maureen's right shoulder, a small flickering hand, like a ghost baby
patting its mother. Since Maureen does not want to be like her mother,
she must pretend to herself she is too eccentric or difficult to be admired.
Still, she does resemble her, mostly in expressions, and, now that she
is smoking, in the way she leans back, crossing her legs and gripping
the elbow of her left arm with her right hand. Also the hands, big
bony-knuckled hands.

Pleasing my friend, I say, truthfully, "I liked your mother." For an
instant as she responds, I see the girl's face I was trying to recall last
night, the face peering down at me from the mouth of the well, deep
set and narrow blue eyes alert with curiosity, full lips slightly open, as
if about to ask a question. "She telephoned me once, you know, when
you were away at school."

Maureen responds in the amused, apologetic tone women use for
the foibles of their children or their elderly parents. "I hope she was-
n't meddling in your affairs!"

"I don't remember, only my surprise at hearing her. Maybe it was
one of the early atom bomb crusades, I mean anti-atom bomb. I don't
know what either of us said." She is about to ask another question,
but presses her lips together instead. Why is she being careful? "She
probably just had me on her election list. Anyway I'd forgotten about
it until just now."

"I really liked your dad," she says. "There've been some times
over the years I thought I was more like him, really, than I was like
my own parents, my mother. I can still remember him getting terribly
excited about the war and how awful it was, trying to tell us it was
wrong. That desperate excitement, trying to get someone else to
believe and really, I couldn't understand what he was saying."

"When I was young I always thought that was his biggest mistake,
the way he used to talk to everyone." I still think so, but I hold that
back. How can I explain my pity and fear for anyone foolish enough to
try to change events, especially if the person is trying to do battle with
the contents of other people's minds?

"Oh, but it wasn't a mistake. There are times I've thought of him
as a kind of hero. I used to imagine what he would be like if he hadn't

just stayed here, what some of the people I knew would think of him. In some ways Chet, my husband, reminded me of what your father might have been."

My father as a hero? Yes, I suppose he had courage—more than I had. He made his secret gardens public, but then they were, after all, gardens. Not like mine, exploding with weeds. Needs. I smile inwardly—Michael as a weed, he's small, carrying a flower across the lawn to me; I hope I have my arms out, but I can't remember.

"What is your husband like?" I ask her.

Maureen thinks for a while, her eyes set vacantly beyond my shoulder. "I've been a widow several years," she says. "He wasn't handsome, he was bookish, he always wore tweed jackets," she smiles. "A uniform for men of our generation who worked in schools, I guess. He worried about himself a lot, whether he was doing the right thing, the ethical thing. I was the decisive one. We did a lot together—a weekly radio program." Moisture brightens her eyes. "He even wore his tweed jackets at the protests we knew were going to land us in jail. That always used to worry me somehow. Once he had his teeth knocked out." She is unable to say more, and I too am silent.

There have been no jails in my unweeded garden, which is full of stones—are they headstones, really? I remember an old family graveyard outside Las Virgenes where they'd used flat pieces of sandstone set on end, yellow and tan pieces like the kind I've found in the hills around here with fossils embedded in them. The shadows of a dozen leaves, a dozen souls, imprinted on the yellow stones.

Suddenly I remember a bed, lying curled on my side in a bed, my back to Maureen, my eyes open on the dark outlines of houses against a city skyline. I wonder whether I should try to talk with her, whether I should try to tell her how frightened I am, but she is too sleepy or I imagine she is, then I feel her stir and reach out for a handkerchief and blow her nose.

"You're not asleep," I say.

She blows her nose again. It sounds as if she's been crying. I turn over and sit up, pushing my pillow against the tall headboard, drawing my knees up. "Are you worried?" I ask. "Don't be worried." She tells me she is sorry about the money, and I say it's all right. But it really isn't. Wasn't.

The morning after they found Charlie Lapp, Maureen woke with the first light, her head jammed against the edge of the pillow, her long hair—which she had neglected to roll up the night before—tangled over her ear, her arms cramped beneath her belly. Eyes opened on the hazy eastern glow, she tensed immediately: three dollars for the taxi the first day, two dollars for stuff the next, twenty dollars to Collie, sixty to the woman and child, five for carfare; they had three hundred and ninety-five left; they had to have fifteen at least to get them through the next two days. She could borrow that from Aunt Ida, if she had to, but still they were short a hundred and five dollars. It wasn't completely her fault, Joann had pointed that out, even with the sixty dollars they would have been short, but they might have been able to get an extra fifty, she could have called home, she could have asked one of her sisters for a loan of fifty, but not a hundred and five.

Pressing in from the brim of consciousness, bits and pieces from the scene the day before in the hotel took on color and expanded whenever she stopped adding the figures: the obsequious and frightened smile, the black spaces where teeth were gone, the sound of a man shouting up from the street, a stain on the bedsheet, the child's sunken brown eyes, the crumpled rags in the suitcase, the smell of dirty diapers, the small pan on the radiator, the clang of streetcars, and somewhere in the distance a siren. She did not understand herself, why she had reacted so swiftly, had not thought through the plan, had not considered that the woman might have been okay in a day or two, but this meant Joann's whole life. She had acted as if she had been specially sent to save the world, her sense of helplessness replaced by a great flow of power as she held the bills out in her hand, as if they were all hers to give. But the helplessness was back. Now what would she do?

She scrambled up, as quietly as possible, and sitting on the edge of her bed looked over at Joann. But her friend was already awake, lying on her back, hands at her sides. "I'm going anyway," she said, not moving. "Maybe they'll take what I have; it's still a lot of money. I'll just say that's all, take it or leave it."

"Listen, we haven't tried the drugstores yet, I mean for the pills that make periods start. I know the book said they didn't work, but maybe that was just to discourage people. We'll spend the whole day, if we have to." Maureen waited for a reaction.

Joann closed her eyes. The lids were blue, the skin under them grey. She looked terribly thin, as if she had been ill for weeks. "The book is right, or you have to get the pills from a doctor, or anyway you have to know the name of them. Besides, my period isn't just late—it's two months late." She spoke in a husky whisper, as if arguing with herself.

"I wish you wouldn't act this way," Maureen complained.

"What way?"

"Arguing. It's the way you always are when a game's over."

"Maybe it is."

"You just say it is."

"Well, what do you say?"

"Will you try the drugstores with me?"

When they were dressed, school skirts and sweaters because of the fog outside, they went downstairs to the kitchen where Ida was waiting to serve them French toast. She had asked them about the movie the night before, and they had said they'd gone to see Vivien Leigh in *Anna Karenina*, because Joann had read the book and would be able to answer questions. This morning Ida was imitating Leigh's imitation of a Southern accent in *Gone with the Wind*, trying to make them giggle about having grown the oranges for the orange juice on her very own plantation down in Hollywood. They sat in the breakfast room, Joann staring out into the garden below, filled with pink blooms of roses and geraniums, almost garish in the grey fog. Maureen laughed, keeping Ida entertained.

Ida made several pieces of French toast, sprinkled them with lemon and powdered sugar, talking nonsense about the south of France, then brought the plates to the table and seated herself at the end. She moved her eyes from one face to the other as she forked up pieces of crisp bread, chatting about how she had spent yesterday and asking polite questions about their visit to Berkeley. What did they think of the campus? Was the university still working on the addition to the library? She had heard of a new administration building outside Sather Gate, was it finished yet? As Maureen answered the questions and praised the campus, Joann tried to eat the French toast. In spite of frequent sips of the orange juice, her mouth remained dry and she had trouble swallowing. After one almost disastrous gag, she turned to the window again, pretending serious interest in the roses. Maureen nudged her foot under the table, made an excuse for her inattention: "Joann's going to Mount St. Mary's, in Los Angeles. Only I am going to Berkeley."

While they were helping with the dishes, Ida asked what they planned for the day. "Just for form's sake you understand. You'll be surprised how much you can get away with if you just fill out the proper forms," she said, then waited for them to laugh.

Maureen glanced swiftly at Joann, who was polishing and repolishing a tumbler, head bent. It's all right, she wanted to say, she's saying we don't have to tell her. "We're thinking of going downtown and looking around the department stores," she said.

Ida nodded approval. Until Joann had finished the glasses and excused herself to go upstairs, she listed stores they must go into and suggested they walk up the tourist blocks of Chinatown. Before Maureen, too, could leave the room she said, "Wait," and pulled a brown paper lunch sack from a drawer. Then lowering her voice she said, "I noticed your friend didn't leave anything in the wastebasket yesterday. Tell her not to be embarrassed. If she wants to get rid of her used napkins, she can wrap them in this bag."

Maureen, terribly embarrassed herself, blushed, and fled upstairs, carrying the paper bags. She and Joann filled them with rolled up clean napkins from the suitcase and stuffed them deep into the bathroom wastebasket.

J O A N N

Maureen leans back in her chair and tilts her head to the side. "Do you remember when we almost went to jail?" she asks. I shake my head, scanning the possibilities, times when I knew I was doing wrong. Were there police in the neighborhood when we saw that boy beaten and I knew we should have reported it, or when I attacked the Rendez sisters that day? Can I have forgotten a reprimand for that?

"We were such babies, it's almost funny, if it weren't so awful," she says, waiting for me to catch a glimpse of what she means.

"I was always so afraid of disgracing my parents, so certain my mother would suffer from the kinds of things I wanted to do that I can't imagine I'd forget. It would haunt me, I'm sure." Though, to be truthful, there are blank places in my memory, I mean places I know are blank because my memory runs up to them and stops. A dark winter flood of silt laid down over a still living twig of oak, pressing it firmly, inexorably, downward in stone.

"It was in a drugstore in San Francisco."

"That summer trip."

"That one."

"Yes." She checks to see if I'm alarmed, and then continues. "We were so young-looking, we were even wearing bobby socks. I remember you, it was a pleated skirt and a white blouse, a pale blue cardigan, and you were wearing a scarf over your head, because of the fog."

"Everyone wore scarves when it was foggy. Tell me, was it white, a dishcloth style? Were we still wearing that in '48?" I ask.

"I don't know—I just remember the frizzy curls sticking out at the front and you on a streetcar furiously shoving them back in."

The strangest thing of all is that I would be thinking at all about my hair at a time like that.

She insists on telling the story. "I remember we were very tired and upset; my stomach was upset, as if I hadn't had anything to eat all day, and maybe we hadn't, maybe we hadn't bothered to stop for breakfast. We were standing next to a lipstick counter, there was a pile of papers, it was a really dirty store, there was dust all over the lipsticks, and this awfully old, frail man came out."

"Was he bald and kind of shaky?" I try to remember.

"Not so old as to be shaky, maybe he was really only our age now, and I remember a thick head of grey hair."

"What happened? I just can't get it."

"Sometimes I think I imagined it, but then I know I couldn't have. Anyway this old man said, 'Can I help you,' and you asked him if he had any cough drops, then I got the giggles."

I can imagine Maureen giggling just then, but I cannot remember. She continues the story, I smiling and nodding her on as she describes a person I never knew I was. She tells me I seemed enraged by her giggles or prodded by them and that I stood up very straight and looked the man in the eye. "You said, 'Would you please excuse my friend. She knows I don't want cough drops. I want something to start my periods.' Then he said, 'What was it you said? I'm a little deaf,' and you said loudly and plainly, 'I need something for missing menstrual periods,' and he said, 'You missed your period did you, how many days?' and you said, 'Two periods.' Then he got all red in the face and said, 'You're asking me to do something illegal. You should go home to your mother.' Or something like that, and then you said as loudly as you could, 'I need an abortion and they said I could get some help from here.'"

"I did?" I ask her. Is it possible she could have dreamed this scene, invented it from some game we played?

She is laughing now, telling me, "And he said to get out of there or he would call the police. It was just an ordinary voice, not very loud, maybe he was afraid of antagonizing you. You wouldn't move." She stops laughing, becomes serious, wipes her eyes, goes on, "He went to his telephone and picked up the receiver. You said, 'You don't know how desperate we are.' Then I took your arm and pulled, and I guess we got out of there because that's all I recollect."

Still amazed at this version of a foolish and foolhardy child, I try to unearth her in myself. I see a linoleum floor covering, an old man, bald and shaky, handing me a package wrapped in green paper, tied in a bow with thin red string. "There must have been another drugstore, because I think I went in one and there was an old man wearing a white coat, he was handing me something in a package, a douche, and I didn't know what it was." But Maureen remembers no other drugstore. Maybe this was in Redding, after I'd married Gil, and I couldn't stand the smell after sex. "There's an old woman, too. Did we go to a palmist or a medium looking for help?"

"That must have been Tynan," Maureen laughed.

"Why were we going to drugstores, anyway?" I recall sitting in an old-fashioned telephone booth, the kind made of wood, with a wooden stool, and a phone with a mouthpiece and a tube-shaped hearing device. I think I am in the lobby of a hotel or a movie theater, for there are red carpets and velvet curtains at the end of the hall. The voice I'm hearing is a man's, telling me he was sorry there was nothing he could do and why was I bothering him. I cannot remember his words, of course, I only believe that is what he was saying. I do not, to tell the truth, feel the desolation I must have felt, though now I feel—unutterably—sorry for the girl I was. Was it that soldier we had met on the train? Had I tried to reach him? Was he the person I was saying please to, trying to hide my tears from Maureen, who was standing outside, leaning on the door?

"The drugstores were my fault. I'd given the money away, or part of it. We were trying to find another way," she reminds me.

For years after that phone call I almost never said "please," the word choked me. "That was so long ago, so long ago, it's like something I read in a book," I say, and hold back the observation that the more remote I can keep some of the past the better. The leaf silted over. Other times it's a midden, the soil piled up on it, mounding, a small scar in the surface of the earth. Not bruising, just a warning of how one may be bruised.

"Me too," she says. "But I'm afraid I don't remember the book very well, and I write new chapters the way I want them to be. Or rather, to have been."

Why did you telephone me last night then? Surely the Joann I was has been replaced. "I remember the first time I noticed you, in the old kindergarten room," I say. "Miss McNeil—that was her name, wasn't it?—had you passing out the milk, and there weren't enough straws, so you gave yours to that little blond boy with the curly hair and then you just lifted the bottle and drank out of it without a straw, and it spilled all over your dress. Miss McNeil scolded you for not coming back for more."

You chuckle. "I remember that. I was so puzzled; I didn't know what I should do. I was trying so hard to do it right."

You wanted to regain the past, is that it? I spin out more of my images for you; you seize them and embellish them and send the thread back to me. You seem content with sketchy and childish designs until the leaves upon your shoulder are all one solid shadow and the waitresses have gone, leaving us with cold coffee and your ashtray full of cigarettes. But I am troubled, I have not freed myself from the ordinary; I might as well be talking to Josie Rendez. Or Miss Tynan. I try once again to escape from my hiding place.

"You know, I hardly remember the person you describe, Captain Terror. It really sounds like my inner state. Even then. Fear. Terror. Always afraid of doing something wrong myself. That's why I remember that quotation from Ruskin," I say.

I'm not sure you understand, not from what you say next: "I think the war made us all afraid in ways we wouldn't know because no one talked to us about it, people just kept coming, all those soldiers. And going. But no, I always thought of you as taking chances I didn't know enough or wasn't brave enough to try."

"I never take chances anymore." I mitigate the truth with an ironic smile and a shake of my head. "Miss Tynan says I turned out remarkably well."

It is then you begin to search again, Maureen probing for the bottom, and I will let you. You had walked past Miss Tynan's house this morning, you tell me, and you could see her in her kitchen sipping coffee. "She still does her hair in the same old way," you marvel, then you add, "I sometimes try to rework my life so that she'd say that about me. Why does she think that about you?"

"She doesn't, really. I'm just saying that."

You stare at me, avoiding the irony, whichever way I mean it to cut. "What has your life been like here, anyway?"

"What would you expect?" I mean it as a lure, and you accept the challenge.

"No matter what, I'd expect you to be fiercely passionate, a fiercely passionate lover of Gil, a fiercely passionate mother, something like the nature poets, climbing mountains, swimming, making up stories, shouting out the joy of living."

I laugh, "In this barren town?"

"I'd hoped it wasn't barren for you."

"Let me tell you the story of my life."

"All right."

"It's quick. Let me see, remember that old pirate you used to know? She left her ship and rowed in to an island one day, I'm not sure why, maybe because she needed water, maybe because it looked green and full of life from the sea, and when she decided, well, I've seen this island and now it's time to go on to others, maybe to the mainland, she found her dinghy was gone and the ship was out of sight, and everyone who lived on the island expected her to stay. She considered swimming out, but it was too far and too deep, so she didn't and she married and had three children. Sometimes, during the time the children were growing up, she thought, maybe I can build a boat, and get back to my old trade. And I really think she would have, but she found a cave leading down under the surface of the island and she went into it, looking for treasure, I suppose. When she discovered there wasn't any treasure and tried to get back to the surface, her ladder was gone and she was in the dark, and I'm sorry to say she was afraid of climbing rocks. Eventually the tide pushed her from the cave into a tunnel, from a tunnel into a hole. All the time she kept thinking, one of these days I'll find a way to be a pirate, out on the ocean again. But she knew the truth: it was too much for her courage."

You have not heard one of my stories for forty-five years, and you are puzzled. I do my best to explain, but I'm not good at that any longer. "The pirate may have been fiercely passionate, but passion didn't get her very far."

"It's strange," you say, pausing for another cigarette. Sometimes I wish I could join you. My hand almost moves with yours, flicks the lighter, and holds the flame against the cigarette as I draw my own breath in when you take the first long pull. "Strange. I've spent a lot of time thinking about you, what I learned from you, that core-of-yourself story you told me. It was just before you went off by yourself for the abortion. I...to be honest, I was just mad about you, you were so damn brave. I've always wanted to be that way."

What can I say? "I don't remember it." And I don't.

"It was the night of the play, I mean the play that I went to and you were supposed to go to, the night when you took the money we did have and went to the address you had. We had to go home in the morning, and this was the only chance. I was insisting I go with you, and you said no I couldn't because it would ruin everything."

It's time. For half a second I'm a child again, it's winter, and I'm leading the way across the rising, muddy creek on a narrow cement dam. "I remember that; it's just the story I don't recall. I don't recall talking to you at all, just leaving you at the door to the theater, it was on Geary Street, and walking through a tunnel."

"The story...we were arguing about you going off alone, and you told me a story about a soldier who had come into the cafe during the war, who talked to your father, there in the back booth. He said he'd been on a troopship in the Pacific and got into a fight one night and fell overboard, or was pushed, or thrown. You said he didn't remember falling into the water, but he remembered the water, how black and noisy; he said he thought he'd never stop going down, then, when he did stop and started to kick himself up, everything was quiet, or it got quieter and quieter the longer it took him to go up. He said it must have been just the passing of the ship—the ship getting farther and farther away—but he didn't think about that at the time. He thought maybe he'd died or was dying. Then when he finally did come to the surface, the only way he could tell was that he could breathe. He couldn't see the ship because of blackout and it was overcast. No light at all. No voices, no one calling 'Man overboard,' and he knew he was just left there, that the man who had pushed him overboard had been afraid to call the alarm. He had to float in darkness all by himself for five hours, until dawn. You stopped telling the story then, and I said, 'Then what?' and you said, 'That's all, except he said he saw down to the very core of himself that night.'"

The only place this story has in my memory is the way my father used it over and over again to illustrate meditation and the way people come to understand themselves. I always think of it, when I do, as that story my father always bored everyone with. How very like me to bring up some story of his to win a point, especially a religious one. Shall I tell you Maureen, that for an instant last night I saw you all clothed in white, a halo round your head, the angel who always arrives in a crisis? No, or anyway, not yet, not until you understand I'm—fairly—serious.

They had spent the afternoon with their hair up in curlers, ironing their blouses and pressing the wrinkles out of their suits. Maureen avoided Aunt Ida, staying upstairs as much as possible, but she couldn't escape from one long and intimate conversation in the kitchen about how her parents were and what she planned to study next year and how the bedroom was available any weekend she wanted to come over from Berkeley. Ida herself had been sent East to school, and she remembered the loneliness she experienced weekends until she had begun to try out for the school plays.

In the bedroom with Joann, the long silences rose like sand dunes.

"Is your hair dry yet?" A small handprint.

"What time did Collie say he'd meet us?" A broken bottle.

"I really think I should go with you." Panic at the thought of something happening to Joann creeping like ice plant. What if she never came back? And silence again.

Joann played solitaire on the bedspread, game after game, the ends of the rag curlers that held locks of her long hair rolling and flopping down over her shoulders.

"Why are you playing solitaire?" Maureen ventured once when the clock said three-thirty.

"Because I can think and not think. Because I keep thinking I might just win. But I don't." The room is blue, a large square of bay and the Bay Bridge filling the window. The voice was almost singsong, as if reciting a lullaby.

"Don't say that," Maureen said. "It scares me."

They had sandwiches while dressed in their robes, Joann stuffing hers into her pocket while Ida was absorbed, presenting what seemed like one whole scene from the play for their entertainment. When they were dressed, Uncle Al led them down the stairs to the car and drove them to the entrance of the theater. It was in the central part of the city, near the big hotels and the department stores, only a fifteen-minute drive from the house, and he told them, just as they climbed from the car to the sidewalk, to give him a ring and he'd be down to pick them up when the play was over.

"No, that's all right," Maureen said. "We'll take a taxi. No need for you to stay up."

"Just see that you call me," he said.

"No, we'll take a taxi." She was leaning over the open door, trying to make herself heard over the clang of a streetcar and the horns of two taxis waiting behind.

"Shut the door. And call," he ordered, moving his car forward slightly.

"We might get a milkshake or a soda," she shouted as the door swung closed. The car moved slowly out into the traffic, and a taxi pulled up next to where she was standing, releasing two middle-aged women in dark suits.

"Collie's not here," Joann said as they pushed through the throng waiting to file into the theater, making their way to a small open space near a glassed-in poster ad.

"What time is it? We don't have any time; Uncle Al is going to pick us up." Maureen gripped Joann by the arm, following her. Though she was trying to control herself, she was wailing.

"You can just tell him I've gone off with someone; you'll have to."

"But I'm going with you."

"No. You can't."

"You don't know the city. You could get lost; I have to go with you."

"I told you I have to do it myself. And stop talking so loudly. People are staring."

They stood next to the ad and argued, two girls with long hair in light-colored wool suits, a bit unbalanced in their high heels, clutching their purses under their arms, facing each other. Joann, her eyes a little wild, her face pale, said at last, calmly, "I don't want you with me. I really don't. I want to meet you here when it's over. Period." As Joann recited the story about the soldier in the water, Maureen felt her shoulders and throat relax; it was going to be all right, it would work out, this was the way it should be.

J O A N N

The children and the strollers have left the creek, the breeze is brisker, and I feel a slight chill. One or two shoppers carrying bags hurry up the shadowy paths. Two young men with beers in their hands have seated themselves at another table, two down from us. They've pulled up chairs to hang their legs over. I would have more wine, if a waitress could find us, if there were any waitresses at this hour. I look around for one.

Maureen speaks. "All this time I've soothed myself with the idea that this story about having to find yourself in the darkness of solitude was the reason, or I mean was part of the reason we weren't supposed to see each other any more, and here you don't even remember it."

"I'm sorry."

"Why did you say that as soon as we got home? You called me up the day after, or maybe two days after, we came home and said something about the worst thing for you was to have me around watching your life, that it would be a form of betrayal. I didn't know what you meant, but all you would say is you didn't want to see me again. And I haven't."

"Something happened that night when I went off by myself."

"You never told me." A soft and gentle accusation.

"I never told anyone." I see your image fading into the theater, Collie comes up. Then we are in the train, and I know I can't bear to tell you. "I think I really did get down to the core of myself, or believed I did," I venture. But when I arrived, there was just a darkness, an empty circle.

It always happens this way when I flash onto that night: crowds of memories swarm like clouds of starlings and sparrows rising noisily from a corral when someone walks past. "Alone" screeches at me, trying to drown out the rest. I evade it and find myself kneeling in church, early, a Lenten morning, any morning, waiting for communion, community. "Core of the self" chants at me, "the community is a hollow box" flutters bravely down, a tiny thing, hopping, chirping. At last, "I had never wanted you with me so much" breaks through the surging flock. I speak the words aloud, and I am standing in the golden circle of light on the sidewalk outside the theater, following your progress as you hand your ticket to the man at the door and disappear from my sight.

I cannot hold the memory back. It overwhelms me while I sit staring past your shoulder. Then I'm hearing the roar of automobiles, the distant clang of the cars on Powell, chattering voices, and I am there in front of the theater exposed, waiting, hoping, pretending it's all over, counseling myself on what I will do next week, fearful, praying for Collie to appear and take your place. The moments pass in waves, I count to five hundred staring up the sidewalk, then five hundred staring down. For the last time, ever, in my life, I try the magic thinking we used to change things with—one part at a time I tell myself. I become aware of theater latecomers puzzling about me, and I turn to the marquee, determined to read every word. A man speaks at my ear, his body touches mine, he says, "Someone stand you up honey?" I startle, glance at someone short and middle-aged, dressed like the gamblers and race track touts I've seen in the movies, a light-colored suit and a flowered shirt open at the neck. He is leering at me and moving closer. I step back, my insides crawling, hoping no one has heard or seen him, trying to look cool and unhurried as I take myself to the other side of the theater doors. My skirt is too tight, my jacket not long enough, my breasts too prominent; I'm sure he can see my fear, he knows I'm not grown up; he knows he can dominate me; I feel soiled.

I am standing at the curb, trying not to cry when Collie comes at last, strolling down the street, hands in the pockets of his stained and loose pants. He is mumbling to Friendly when I hurry up to him, and for a time he will not look at me.

"We don't have much time," I say.

"She doesn't have much time," he tells his closed fist. Then, finally, to me, "That bastard didn't have a job for us after all. We haven't had any dinner, and Friendly is getting hungry."

"I have to be back here by eleven o'clock."

"Ah, it's Cinderella tonight. She's going to turn into a pumpkin." He giggles, making a curving gesture over his belly.

"I have the money."

"Fifty dollars for me and Friendly."

"But I won't have enough."

"This one's cheap."

"Is it safe?" But I am already struggling with my wallet.

When I bring myself to look into your face again, you are no longer regarding me, but have your eyes set on a stiff brown leaf, broken, two-fingered, that you are tearing apart bit by bit on the table. You say, "Then tell me now."

"Remember, Collie was supposed to take me to the place."

"And he didn't, I remember you said that when you got back. You had to find it by yourself."

I see the dull black of Collie's jacket and his loosely flopping red hair as he disappears into a stream of pedestrians across the street. The lights of the cars glare.

"When he left I tried to get into the theater to find you, get you to come, but they wouldn't let me in. I didn't have a ticket; you'd kept both of them, in the little envelope in your purse. Then I asked a policeman how to get to California Street, and he sent me the wrong way."

I am walking through a yellow tunnel toward a dark residential street, so frightened my knees are shaking. I have no idea, even now, where I was. Go back, go back, go back, I tell myself.

"I got into a dark neighborhood, it must have been where there were houses, and I found a little store, there were oranges outside in boxes, and the man in there told me to take a taxi," I say aloud.

He is Chinese and does not speak English well. He tells me several times to take the taxi and go home. When I am in the taxi, in the dark on the leather seat, I try to relax, try to feel sure it's going to work, that I can win anything, and if I don't, it won't really matter, the way I sometimes feel when I'm playing a game.

"The taxi seemed to take forever, uphill, downhill, then out a long street, then I got there."

You are biting your lip, frowning.

But as soon as the taxi stops I know I can't make it a game and instead of feeling calm, I feel frozen, as if I'm dead, or as if it's not me. This is just some shadow of me and I am really seeing the play with Maureen. My hands are cold as I count out the money, most of it in change, into the taxi driver's hand. It is like the time I made the speech for graduation; I am acting automatically, only instead of a blur of lights and faces, it is a blur of darkness. Stairs, corridors, electric globes, I am wondering if I can climb all the way to the third floor.

I say to you: "I was terribly frightened. I kept thinking, shall I tell them I'll bring the rest of the money tomorrow? Then something would catch in the pit of my stomach, and I'd wonder whether I would still be alive tomorrow. A woman answered the door. I said, 'Collie sent me.' I could hardly get the words out; my mouth was numb."

She is young, I wasn't prepared for someone so young, and I've never seen anyone young look so terrible. A loose cotton dress hangs around her, her arms are grotesquely thin, narrow as the bottle of beer she is carrying. Her hair hangs in greasy strands, partially hiding a red discoloration on her face, and when she speaks, I can see she is missing several teeth at the front. She is saying, "What do you want?" and I can't get an answer out. She is repeating it, louder, because she thinks I can't make out the words, and angrily, because I'm intruding. "What the hell do you want?" I keep my eyes away from her, I don't want to look; I am staring at the piles of newspapers and magazines on the floor of the hallway, trying to answer. "Collie, do you know Collie?" With her eyes still on me, her tongue licks once through the gap in her teeth, and she shouts, "Hey Junior, she's here." A man's nasal voice is answering from another room, "You sure she's the one?" "How should I know?" No one is answering. I look past the woman to the right, where there's a room shrouded by dusty venetian blinds, filled with heavy furniture and glassed-in bookcases, books piled helter-skelter within the cases and on the floor beside them, clothes all over, plates and empty bottles everywhere, and ashtrays. I am sure I've come to the wrong place, that Collie has just conned me out of the money, and I am overwhelmed with relief. It's over, it's over, it's over echoes in my head.

"There was a man, too. He was young, just like the woman. I think they'd both been drinking. Everything was terribly dirty and smelly." I am speaking to you slowly because I do not want my voice to break.

"Well I'm not going to stand here all day waiting for you," the woman is calling. She is stepping forward; I am shrinking to the side, afraid she will touch me, but she just keeps on going, past me and down the stairs, and I hear a door slam somewhere. I begin to think about following her, when I feel a touch on my arm; someone is holding me, a young man in a white shirt and jeans. "Is your name Joann?"

"After she left, at first he seemed, well, all right. I calmed down a little."

I am nodding, I am following him into the hallway, I am watching him shut the door. He speaks very quietly, very carefully, "And you know Friendly? Sure you do. And you brought the money?" He has been holding my hand, and now he lets it go, waiting for me to open my purse; he is staring at me opening my purse, and I pull the money out, and I say, it's almost a whisper: "I'm sorry, it's not as much as…Collie took fifty, but I've got three hundred twenty-five." He is sighing, he is saying, so gently, "I don't know, we'll see, maybe we can do something about that." Then he is turning the bolt on the door. "Just so we won't be interrupted; this is against the law you know." I am nodding; I am beginning to think, maybe it's all right, because he is so quiet and seems so clean. Then he is moving me along, his arm around my shoulders, and I smell alcohol, and I am telling myself, they say that boys in medical schools do this, and it's probably okay, and anyway I don't care if I do die, but still I'm shaking as he leads me into a room where there is a bed pulled out from the wall. "You girls who get into trouble are so naughty," he is saying. "So naughty, are you a naughty girl, Joann? Answer me now; I won't hold it against you. It's such a temptation, you never think of the punishment, and I guess this is the punishment. But I don't want you to be afraid; you're not supposed to be afraid of punishment after you've done something wrong." He is backing me up to the bed and sitting me down on it; his arms are strong, and though I resent his touching me that way, I don't even shake them off. "You'll have to take your skirt off and your underpants," he is saying. "It's kind of funny isn't it, things ending the way they began; you could have quite a philosophy based on that." His voice is rambling on as I undress, but I cannot listen; I am trying to keep the skirt in front of me, but he is taking it away, folding it, putting it on a chair with my underpants.

I keep all this from you. I say only, "He took me into a back room, where there was a kind of couch made into a bed. The sheets were clean, and I thought it was okay, then he started to explain what he was going to do."

He is holding a long thin instrument in his hand, and he keeps talking about punishment and asking if I liked punishment, and then he is saying there is a little extra punishment for not having all the money, just a little extra.

"Then he said to lie back and put my legs up, and when I started to do it, he kept talking about how I'd be making up the money. I think that was his way, he was trying to be kind by teasing, at least that's what I thought later, afterwards, but then, then, I think it was a noise, the noise of a door slamming, but it sounded, somehow, like a terrible explosion and, well, anyway…I pushed him away and I put on my clothes and I left. It was later before I thought that if he'd meant seriously to harm me, he'd have stopped me."

I am here with you, beside Refugio Creek, and you are swallowing, unable to speak. "I don't know how I got out. Or how I got back to the theater. I blank out on everything else." I give you a little smile, "So all these years I've owed you, let's see, one hundred was yours, and there should be interest, shouldn't there? I mean, I couldn't take it, I ran, I never had that abortion. I thought about it and thought about it, and there was no real reason for my running, except I panicked. I was scared of the noise, scared of him. I went over and over it in my mind, and everything was so ambiguous, I probably just interpreted him incorrectly. I was a coward, plain and simple. How could I tell you or anyone else what a coward I was? I figured, after that, I didn't deserve any more help. I came home and I dated Gil and after a while, a very short while, I said I'd marry him."

I am staring at the thin brown ribs of the leaf, still between your fingers. "He knew that Michael wasn't his." I smile. "And here I am."

"Oh no, Joann," you are saying. It's like a groan, and for as long as it takes a voice to echo across the creek I remember your face as it was at eighteen, the night I began to hide my humiliation from you: you had one arm under my head, the other holding me close, your eyes cast down, and that rare smile combining pleasure and tenderness, as if happiness was the fruit of caring. Then I see tears in your eyes, and though it's against the rules in Refugio, I reach out and take your hand.

16

Yet what would I have done, what would I have said if she had told me that night she had run away from the abortion? She must have known or somehow sensed how I yearned for my share of the burden to end, and so appeased me with another lie—for my sake, not her own.

I am beginning to cry (am I getting to the age when this happens every other hour?), and I fumble with my words: "Look at it this way, will you? Any sensible person would have run, what else could you have done? You may have saved your life."

She slips me a glance like an arrow to show me how foolish she thinks me, but her hand, dry and comforting, remains on mine.

There is an image I used to carry like a banner, especially when asked to give my views on women's right to choose abortion: Joann hurrying across the sidewalk in front of the Geary Theater, hair neat, eyes bright. She's smiling, and I used to interpret the smile as the end of an adventure, the sense of relief and freedom you feel in spite of pain when everything's over.

This afternoon everything refocuses, and I am so overwhelmed all I can say is, "Oh, Joann," and then tell you that after all, you did the sensible thing to run from danger.

But your pain is running through me as if what happened was ten minutes ago, not forty-five years. I am trying to think, what could I have done, how could I have helped? You have taken my hand as simply as you put your arms around me the night before we were to leave the city, and as before I am overwhelmed by the desire to lift you up the way you lift a child to touch something just out of her reach—not because she needs it, but because she wants it so.

Then what it was I must have really seen unfolds for me like crumpled and discarded messages. I shake my head to show how ashamed I am and pass the messages to you.

As soon as the last curtain was down, I left my seat and dashed out into the corridors, down the stairs, outside, hoping you'd have made it back by then, scared you hadn't. Nowadays I'd worry about whether you'd have had time to recover, but then I didn't know—how could I?—what would actually happen in a real abortion. But you weren't there, and the awful thing was, Uncle Al had the car in a parking place across the street. He'd come down a half an hour early, he said, and gone around the block five times just to get the space, and then he said, "Where's Joann?"

"We'll have to wait for her a bit," I said.

"Has she gone to the rest room then?" he asked after a while.

"She met a friend," I said, wishing you'd get back early.

"Doesn't she know she's keeping us waiting?" And so forth, until I finally had to tell him you'd gone off with the friend and expected to be back an hour after the play was over. He was terribly upset, went on about what kind of girl you were to leave me like that and whether my mother knew you did that kind of thing. I defended you for a long time, until he began to get worried that you wouldn't come and asked where you might have gone with this friend. By this time it was more than an hour and a half we'd waited, the whole time my head full of all the things that must have gone wrong. The streets had pretty well cleared by that time, so Uncle Al went checking into the nearby coffee shops, making me wait in the car with the doors all locked. I was so scared I was shaking, and I kept thinking I'll close my eyes and then I'll see her, she'll be walking up the street, and then every woman who passed by became you for as long as I could manage to believe it. Once I could hear high heels clicking on the sidewalk, coming from behind, and I didn't turn around to look, just tried to work that old magic trick we used to use when we were little until she passed the car and I could see she wasn't you. Then I saw you from some distance away, unmistakably you. I jumped out of the car, ran across the street, all excited, bent on telling you about Uncle Al and the story I'd made up for him. Even now I'm embarrassed to think of myself, the busy-body, hobbled by my long skirt, limping across the street, not thinking about how you felt, just assuming that because you had arrived you must be all right. I remember your face as a blur—but you weren't smiling, I'm sure of that now—and I think you said the story I told Uncle Al was okay. You actually reassured me, now I think about it; you said it didn't matter what he thought. We crossed the street. I was trying to walk slowly, to give you a chance to get ready for Uncle Al, but you moved ahead of me, climbed into the backseat, and when I tried to get in after you, you had locked the door. I slid in next to

Uncle Al, then, and he said nothing and we said nothing all the way home. When I turned around to look at you, whenever we passed through some lights, you had your eyes closed. Once I even thought you might be sleeping, and I did think you might have relaxed, finally, the ordeal over. What an idiot I was!

When we got to the house you went right upstairs, and it was okay, I was glad to be the one who had to talk to Ida and make apologies and explain some more. She spent a lot of time telling me that I should be more careful of who my friends were. Even if my mother didn't look into their backgrounds, I should on my own, and she didn't really think you'd be welcome in her house again, and she repeated several times how dangerous it was for young girls to go out in San Francisco at night. By the time I got upstairs you had gone into the bathroom, and I could hear the bathtub running. I waited for a long time, even knocking on the door once to ask was it all right. You answered, "Fine." Then while I was waiting for you, I fell asleep. When I woke, it seemed just a few minutes later, you were lying beside me, and I thought I heard you crying. So I put my arms around you, and when you hugged me, crying and crying, I held you with all my strength, your whole body with mine, as if I thought I could keep you forever. And maybe that would have been all right, I thought. You might want to stay with me. It was the end of our personal war—those weeks of wandering, searching for a way out of danger. We had thought all we wanted was to go home—that place where our imaginations worked magic as long as we followed the rules, and nothing, especially not the land mines in our bodies, could stop us. But now, I thought, though we might go back to Refugio for a time, this wouldn't be the path home for us. We'd choose another way. Together.

In the morning we had to get ready and go down to the train station before seven-thirty. If I had any sense at all, even paid attention to the reading I'd done, I should have known you hadn't had an abortion, but I suppose I was so excited about the future—just the peace I felt that morning was so glorious—I probably didn't ask anything more than, "Is it all right?" and you probably said, "Yes, but I don't want to talk about it." I may have said then that I was really frightened last night that you wouldn't get back, I don't remember, but I remember one look you gave me; it was like the look you had when I argued about smoking when we were thirteen, so I thought you just wanted privacy. No matter how I tried, all the way home in the train you wouldn't talk to me, just stared out the window or seemed to sleep. At first I thought you were just tired or in pain. Later, I wondered if you'd been upset by the story I'd told Uncle Al or distressed in some way because of the money I'd given away. I was certain you were blaming something on me, and I couldn't understand—we'd been so close the night before. Then before we pulled into the station, you said you were probably going to sleep for a week, so I wasn't to call or come over, that you'd call me. I remember having to hide my tears from my mother on the drive home from the station.

"I didn't want your pity," you explain to me this late afternoon beside Refugio Creek. "I was terribly ashamed. It happened because there was something wrong about me, something destructive, something dirty, and I was afraid, and afraid to admit I'd been afraid."

Her words are a warning to me. I must be careful how I respond.

"What could you have done to help?" you say. "What could anyone have done? As a matter of fact, I was so angry with myself, so horrified, so at the bottom, I was about to commit suicide. I thought it through, I thought about it for five days, and then I realized I wasn't brave enough to do that either. I mean kill myself."

At home, waiting through the days until Joann was well enough to call, Maureen stayed in bed until late in the morning, curling up into a ball as soon as she was conscious and using every daydream she had ever comforted herself with to smooth the way back to sleep. Afternoons she followed her mother's instructions about getting rid of clothes she wouldn't be needing anymore and packing away those she still wanted to leave at home. She spent one day selecting the books she'd take with her to Berkeley, though Marilyn, who had come home for the weekend, lectured her about how many books she'd be buying new and how little time she'd have to read anything but history, biology, and so forth. Another day she packed up her collection of army badges, her crayon drawings of sailing ships, the bow and target to her archery set, and her commando comic books and offered them to

Rosemary to give to Debby and Jack. Her sister didn't want them, so she drove the boxes down a country road to the dump.

Every morning when she went downstairs to breakfast she wondered, a little tensely, whether Joann might have changed her mind and telephoned while she had been in her cocoon. Mrs. Lewis usually came into the kitchen and handed her the paper just about the time she was taking her first bite of cereal covered with milk and fruit. Maureen turned immediately to the funnies, waiting to be told she was supposed to call Joann. But Mrs. Lewis wanted only to comment on the political news, one example after another where Truman had betrayed the New Deal in his campaign for president. When Maureen took her bowl to the sink to rinse, her mother began reminders of what she expected her to accomplish that day, and Maureen felt relieved to be so immersed in the small and necessary tasks. She told herself that Joann was busy getting ready for college too.

M A U R E E N

"Do you remember...I did try to talk with you, didn't I?" I ask. "It was a few days after you told me you wanted to be by yourself forever."

You shake your head, no.

I continue, "Sometimes I found myself picking over every scene, searching for the tiny pieces of selfishness or carelessness I could have bruised you with because I didn't know enough or wasn't sensitive enough to you. It did occur to me that you felt guilty about having an abortion and blamed me for pushing you into it. Then I wondered whether you had just used me all summer to get what you wanted, especially the next year after I heard that you didn't go away to school and that you had run away with Gil Henderson."

I shake my head—a gesture I use more often, the older I get, as all the mistakes and misfortunes of sixty years rise to consciousness and have to be sent back down. I select another thought: the last time I caught sight of you was four days before I was to leave for school. You were coming down the library stairs following a group of Camp Fire Girls, their white blouses soiled and their scarves askew. Your summer tan was already beginning to fade. There were tiny flaky patches along your arms where the last burn was peeling. You picked at the skin, concentrating on it as I climbed into my mother's car. She had a fresh copy of *The New Republic* on the seat beside her, and she started talking about it as soon as I got in. She was full of excitement about the possibility that Henry Wallace might come to California and that she could combine a visit with me at Berkeley with some meetings where he might speak. "Maybe you could come with me?" she asked. I could have answered maybe, or I could have answered he won't win anyway, or I could have reminded her I wasn't old enough to vote, and someone else would decide my fate for me anyway. But so what? That's what I say under my breath, so what, so what, so what, as I hold myself back from running to you and begging you to let me walk home with you.

"What made you call me, what made you come to Refugio after all these years?" Joann is asking. Over her shoulder I see a pair of waitresses come out to the patio, file among the tables, and light candles. I start to take my hand away from hers, but she has gripped it, and I am aware of its warmth.

"To find out how you were, I guess, to see if you'd tell me what I did that made you reject me. But the main reason was I guess I've always believed I abandoned you, somehow, that it was my fault we never saw each other again," I answer. "And I guess it was."

Then she tries to comfort me. "A part of me does believe what Miss Tynan says, that I've done remarkably well. Maybe if I tell you another story—do you remember that night I dived down into the lake? There was one time I lost my sense of direction, I had gone down so far, and it was so black when I opened my eyes. For some reason I wanted to stay, and then I started rising to the surface. I kept thinking what a rotten swimmer I was that I couldn't reach the tree or the weeds or whatever, and then just as I came up within a couple of feet of the surface, I had a strange vision of your face looking down at me. I couldn't make out the features but I decided to reach up and there I was out of the dark, and you said it was time to go home."

"I've missed you," I say.

She grins, "You'll have to try not to miss me anymore."

I recall a day with Joann at the beach at Silveira when we were young, when I thought it possible to discover the connections, the affinities, the bridges, the bonds, the links, the ribbons, the touches, the invisible touches of all the associations between the life we were experiencing and the life of all the world. And as I am remembering this day, we gather our purses, stand, set off—Joann slowing her pace a bit until my arthritic stiffness lets go of me—and at the top of the stairs leading down to the trail along the creek, she takes my hand again and I grasp hers. Onlookers be damned.

I have one memory of that afternoon of reunion ending right then, curtain drawn down, the drama over, but Joann tells me that we drove off in her car to the hills above Pecho Bay to watch the sunset and then down to the waterfront to eat fish at a place where she called the owner Pete. What did we talk about? The kids, her decision some time ago to leave the Catholic Church, her fear she might be like her father, what I was going to do when I was elected to city council, how bad Sheila's bed had been on my back, her plans to take a long hike on the Muir Trail the next summer, and, after I wished her well, she said—maybe a little reluctantly—that I could come too, if I got in shape and didn't mind long silences.

The first day they had spent together in the summer of 1948, right after graduation, they had gone swimming at the beach. Striking out through the white and foamy shallows together, each holding one knee high above the water, then the other, then jumping up and into the rush of small breaking waves, they were soon thigh deep. They laughed out loud at the cold as a higher wave splashed against their breasts and shoulders, but neither screamed. When they had passed the point where the lowest waves broke, they lowered themselves into the green and sandy water to breast stroke and dog paddle out to deep water where an occasional big roller formed. Their heads bobbed among the crests. The rush of the surf upon the shore and the cries and shrieks of distant waders came to them in bursts, each sound, each voice clear and separate.

"Listen," Joann called. "It's as if they were in another world."

On the shore a child cried, wailing, "Mommy, Mommy."

"No," Joann said. "Correction. They aren't in another world. They are in the real one."

Maureen responded eagerly, sensing an easy return to their childhood friendship—pirates, spies, magicians. "Maybe a mist has descended between us, and they're fading slowly away." An image pushed forward. "Do you suppose this is what it feels like to die? Suddenly everything's different; you're weightless, your body's just flashes of pale flesh shining through green, and the sounds of your friends calling you are hollow?" She was about to say something to Joann about butterflies, when a wavelet separated them and she had to stop to spit salt water from her mouth.

Joann put her face down and kicked, arms outstretched. For a moment she lay stretched out, her face in the water, adrift as a dead woman. She jackknifed abruptly, and Maureen followed her down, trying to make out her silhouette on the murky bottom. Suddenly she saw the contours of a face, the cheeks faintly touched by green, hands and arms and long strands of kelp waving gently around it, an apparition from an illustrated book of fairy tales.

When they surfaced again, the kelp was draped over Joann's shoulders and drifted and swirled about her. "What if you didn't die? What if you just disappear into the mist, and when you look back…" Pausing for a breath, she took a strand of kelp between her fingers and wrapped it loosely around her waist. "There's a translucent green surface holding you back, you can't get out." She leaned backward and flipped into another dive, pulling the kelp down behind twisting feet.

"Well?" Maureen demanded when she came up. "All right, so you can't get out, then what?"

Joann's bathing cap had come off, and she was shaking it with one hand and pushing her hair out of her face with the other. The kelp mingled with her hair, spread out upon the swell presently passing by. "You have to answer first. I was the one who said, What if?" Joann insisted.

"I'd adapt. Become an expert on the other side of the mist. Like playing games or reading a book. What if, yourself?"

"Struggle to get out. That's the only thing that would make it fun."

"Keep feeling around the same old mist and pushing at a barrier? You sure wouldn't. It'd be like an eternal game of solitaire," said Maureen.

"I like solitaire."

Slimy leaves of kelp brushed Maureen. She was annoyed, and kicked away, swimming fast toward the beach.

"Did I say something wrong?" Joann asked when they were sitting on towels in the car, their sweatshirts damp from their halter tops. She was trying to braid her wet hair, now sticky with salt and sand.

Maureen shook her head as she started the car. "I'm just thinking."

Joann remained silent, willing her uterus to contract and expel the thing whose web ensnared her. Strange, she thought, I surround that which captures me.

They were coming around Refugio Mountain before Maureen had the words just right for what she wanted to say. Even so, she faltered. "It can't be a struggle, against that barrier I mean. If you don't expect to get anywhere, scratching against the barrier can't be called a struggle. Better to hope to be rescued, somehow, or like I said, give up hope and adapt."

"I suppose so," replied Joann after a pause. "Now that I think of it, it's after you're rescued the struggle begins," she said.

T H E   E N D

ABOUT THE AUTHOR

CAROL ALMA MCPHEE has mothered three daughters, taught, and worked in local women's politics, and has published two books (with Ann FitzGerald) concerned with women's political history. She has a BA in English from the University of California, Berkeley, and an MA in English from California State Polytechnic University, San Luis Obispo. She lives in San Luis Obispo, California, the geographical model for the town of Refugio described in *Staying Under*.

RAINLIGHT
Alison McGhee

The ache we are left with after the death of a loved one is hard to resolve and even harder to relinquish when it is all we have left of them. Set in the Adirondack foothills, *Rainlight* glimpses the hearts and souls of characters whose lives were intricately entwined with Starr Williams, an Adirondacks woodcutter and the emotional compass for his family and friends. In alternating voices, Lucia, Tim, Crystal, and nine-year-old Mallie enrich us as they grow—alone and together—after a profound loss.

"McGhee's prose shimmers on the page." —*Julie Schumacher, author of* The Body Is Water

"Rainlight is a brilliant, subtle, moving book." —*Michael Dennis Browne, author of* Selected Poems 1965–1995

ISBN 1-57601-006-6, hardcover

CREEK WALK AND OTHER STORIES
Molly Giles

Molly Giles is uncannily observant of women's lives, both the small details and the larger emotions that guide them. In this highly acclaimed collection, Giles artfully weaves stories that are touching, sometimes alarming, and often funny, of women struggling to break the old patterns that have held them back and kept them silent.

"Molly Giles is a virtuoso of the short story...disturbing, compassionate, and vital." —*Amy Tan*

"Giles writes exquisitely voice-driven stories." —Publishers Weekly

"She is a master of the short story." —USA Today

"Arresting prose...powerful, honest storytelling." —Ms.

ISBN 1-57601-023-6, hardcover

FLYING HORSES, SECRET SOULS
Randeane Tetu

With humor and pathos, Randeane Tetu's latest collection of short stories pulls us deep into the imperceptible moments that underlie our everyday experiences and yet change our lives. Set in small New England towns, Tetu's wonderful ordinary folks—young and old—remind us that our childhood days of carousels and wonder can help us find our way in our adulthood.

"These spare, impressionistic, and finely crafted stories build a fascinating, sinuous

path to the final title story...an unforgettable lesson about the value and challenge of life itself." —*Wally Lamb, author of* She's Come Undone

ISBN 1-57601-020-1, trade paper

LATE SUMMER BREAK
Ann B. Knox

Award-winning author Ann Knox weaves poignant tales of parents, spouses, and lovers caught in shifting roles and circumstances. The compassionate women in these short stories understand that the pain accompanying family conflict is a source of growth and a part of being alive.
"These are simple, earth-grounded, elegantly written elegies to the passing of time and lives." —Booklist

ISBN 0-918949-64-5, trade paper
ISBN 0-918949-65-3, hardcover

MILKWEED
Mary Gardner

Confronted with the limited acceptable roles for women in the first half of the twentieth century, Susan Carson faces the difficult choice of either losing her own identity to society's expectations or living outside the norms. Replete with "powerful descriptions of a changing midwestern landscape." (Publishers Weekly)
"Susan Carson's true sisters are Willa Cather's tall-standing prairie heroines." —Washington Post Book World

ISBN 0-918949-45-9, trade paper
ISBN 0-918949-46-7, hardcover

MAUD'S HOUSE
Sherry Roberts

Welcome to Maud's famous house. As a brilliant child artist, Maud put her small Vermont hometown on the map with paintings that covered every inch of her house inside and out. Now pressured to paint a mural for her town, Maud searches for the inspiration that has eluded her for ten years.
"Ms. Roberts's talent is evident...her novel is lightly salted with folksy, good-humored insights and peppered with a spunky appreciation of life's whimsy." —New York Times Book Review

ISBN 0-918949-28-9, trade paper
ISBN 0-918949-32-7, hardcover

1. California's sparsely populated Central Coast of the 1940s symbolizes the isolation that produced the two main characters, Maureen and Joann. What are the major themes of *Staying Under*, and in what ways does the novel's setting reinforce those issues?

2. The story alternates between the morality of the 1940s and the openness of the 1990s. How are the issues facing young women today the same as those fifty years ago? In what ways are they different? Is it easier or more difficult to be a young woman now?

3. We watch Joann and Maureen's friendship grow and blossom, then abruptly dissolve. Do you feel Maureen's strength was an enabling factor for Joann? Joann always wanted to be braver than Maureen. How did that influence Joann's decision to end their friendship? They each took different directions with their adult lives; what were the similarities and differences?

4. *Staying Under* portrays the physical risks women may choose to take when abortion is illegal. How did these risks affect Joann's decision? How did her ultimate choice affect her self-perception?

5. Joann's father significantly affected both girls' growth and development. He did not believe in evil and was compelled to fight for good. How do you think his ideology affected them? Did his attitude influence Joann's decision to stay in Refugio?

6. When they discovered that Joann was pregnant, Maureen and Joann felt they could not tell their parents or teachers. They had no older or trusted friends to advise them nor any other place to turn to for information. Can you think of a difficult situation where you had trouble finding the assistance you needed? What did you do?

7. Maureen's daughters saw her as a "fix-it person," who would always make things work, even if she was not totally successful. They found it difficult to live up to her example. Maureen saw her willingness to help solve problems as being responsible. Describe your view of Maureen.

8. Joann played solitaire so she could "...think and not think. Because I keep thinking I might just win. But I never do." Is there a correlation between that kind of reasoning and the trap she created for herself by staying in the same town she grew up in? When her son died she felt her life was wasted, and she began to think about starting over. What do you think kept her in Refugio?

9. When the two friends finally reunite, their reminiscences remind them how important their friendship had been to each of them, how wrenching the breakup was. Since their individual perspectives were so different, do you feel that they understood each other? They grasped hands as they left the restaurant; what did this mean to them? What future do you see for their friendship?

PAPIER-MACHE PRESS

At Papier-Mache Press, it is our goal to identify and successfully present important social issues through enduring works of beauty, grace, and strength. Through our work we hope to encourage empathy and respect among diverse communities, creating a bridge of understanding between the mainstream audience and those who might not otherwise be heard.

We appreciate you, our customer, and strive to earn your continued support. We also value the role of the bookseller in achieving our goals. We are especially grateful to the many independent booksellers whose presence ensures a continuing diversity of opinion, information, and literature in our communities. We encourage you to support these bookstores with your patronage.

We publish many fine books about women's experiences. We also produce lovely posters and T-shirts that complement our anthologies. Please ask your local bookstore which Papier-Mache items they carry. To receive our complete catalog, send your request to Papier-Mache Press, 627 Walker Street, Watsonville, CA 95076, or call our toll-free number, 800-927-5913. For further information about Papier-Mache, visit our web site, http://www.ReadersNdex.com/papiermache.